MW00775299

MEETING ACROSS
THE RIVER

MEETING ACROSS THE RIVER

stories inspired by the
haunting BRUCE SPRINGSTEEN song

edited by JESSICA KAYE and RICHARD J. BREWER

BLOOMSBURY

Copyright © 2005 by Jessica Kaye and Richard J. Brewer

All rights reserved. No part of this book may be used or reproduced in any manner whatsoever without written permission from the publisher except in the case of brief quotations embodied in critical articles or reviews. For information address Bloomsbury Publishing, 175 Fifth Avenue, New York, NY 10010.

Published by Bloomsbury Publishing, New York and London
Distributed to the trade by Holtzbrinck Publishers

All papers used by Bloomsbury Publishing are natural, recyclable products made from wood grown in well-managed forests. The manufacturing processes conform to the environmental regulations of the country of origin.

"Meeting Across the River" by Bruce Springsteen. Copyright © 1975 Bruce Springsteen (ASCAP). Reprinted by permission.

"Meeting Across the River" © 2005 by Eric Garcia. "The Far Side of the River" © 2005 by William Kent Krueger. "Cherry Looks Back" © 2005 by Pam Houston. "Pirates of Yellowstone" © 2005 by C. J. Box. "The Real Thing" © 2005 by Gregg Hurwitz. "A Little Early in the Day" © 2005 by Michael John Richardson. "Crossing Over" © 2005 by Randy Michael Signor. "Keeping It Good" © 2005 by Richard J. Brewer. "One Fast Packard" © 2005 by Steve Hamilton. "Killing Time by the River Styx" © 2005 by Peter David. "Last Call" © 2005 by Eddie Muller. "The Other Side" © 2005 by Aimee Liu. "Claustrophobia" © 2005 by Philip Reed. "Payday" © 2005 by Barbara Seranella. "Mosquito Incense" © 2005 by Cara Black. "Bobby the Prop Buys In" © 2005 by David Corbett. "In the Midnight Hour" © 2005 by Paul Charles. "Lovers in the Cold" © 2005 by Wallace Stroby. "Trumpet Blues" © 2005 by Anthony Rudel. "Drink to Long Life" © 2005 by Jessica Kaye.

Library of Congress Cataloging-in-Publication Data

Meeting across the river : stories inspired by the haunting Bruce Springsteen song / edited by Jessica Kay and Richard Brewer.—1st U.S. ed.
p. cm.
ISBN-13: 978-1-58234-283-2 (pbk.)
ISBN-10: 1-58234-283-0 (pbk.)
1. Short stories, American. 2. United States—Social life and customs—Fiction.
I. Kaye, Jessica. II. Brewer, Richard (Richard J.) III. Springsteen, Bruce.

PS648.S5.M44 2005
813'.0108—dc22
2005041152

First U.S. Edition 2005

10 9 8 7 6 5 4 3 2 1

Typeset by Westchester Book Group
Printed in the United States of America by Quebecor World Fairfield

This anthology is dedicated,
with much love, to Clare and Bryce Mills,
who, like this collection of stories,
are a constant source of surprise and delight.

Contents

Meeting Across the River
BRUCE SPRINGSTEEN

Hey, Eddie, can you lend me a few bucks
And tonight can you get us a ride
Gotta make it through the tunnel
Got a meeting with a man on the other side

Hey Eddie, this guy, he's the real thing
So if you want to come along
You gotta promise you won't say anything
'Cause this guy don't dance
And the word's been passed this is our last chance

We gotta stay cool tonight, Eddie
'Cause man, we got ourselves out on that line
And if we blow this one
They ain't gonna be looking for just me this time

And all we gotta do is hold up our end
Here stuff this in your pocket
It'll look like you're carrying a friend
And remember, just don't smile
Change your shirt, 'cause tonight we got style

Well Cherry says she's gonna walk
'Cause she found out I took her radio and hocked it
But Eddie, man, she don't understand
That two grand's practically sitting here in my pocket

And tonight's gonna be everything that I said
And when I walk through that door
I'm just gonna throw that money on the bed
She'll see this time I wasn't just talking
Then I'm gonna go out walking

Hey, Eddie, can you catch us a ride?

MOST STORIES—THE great ones, anyway—are about character, a man or woman standing at one of life's many crossroads. The storyteller puts them there because they then must make a choice, and the choice they make will bare their soul. Who they *are* determines what will happen.

We meet the nameless narrator of Bruce Springsteen's "Meeting Across the River" at one of those crossroads, and in six short verses we're treated to an epic character story that Springsteen tells with the spare precision of haiku. Two lines into the lyric, and you already smell the guy's cheap cologne. He reveals himself in a monologue that unfolds like a whispered plea in a tenement doorway, a dark story told by a man who does not understand—will never understand—the smallness of his dreams. He has convinced himself that redemption is waiting somewhere out there, across a river, in a vague and distant place where bluff might be enough, or might get you killed. Either way, he has decided, it's worth the risk. But first:

> Hey, Eddie, can you lend me a few bucks
> And tonight can you get us a ride

And so the journey begins, a melancholy dance to piano, trumpet, bass, and voice that you just *know* is going to end badly. Why? Because you know this guy. No cash. No car. Flunky loser friend named Eddie. And, somehow, you just knew he'd have a pouting girl named Cherry, and that he'd have something to prove.

Of course, it's what's *not* in the lyric, rather than what is, that makes the song so intriguing—and so ripe for the artful elaborations contained in this anthology. For all Springsteen's precision in defining his characters, he left much more unsaid than said. His narrator has no past, save for an implied history of bad choices, including the one that got him on Cherry's bad side. He has no future, except for the one he thinks he can buy for the two grand he doesn't yet have but that's "practically sitting here in my pocket." His present is nothing more than a hopeful plea for help. All we really know is that his life somehow went wrong, and that, from this point forward, anything could happen.

The origins of the song are as mysterious and sketchy as the narrator.

Springsteen seldom plays it in concert, and he has made scant comment about what one critic has called his "most underrated song." Mike Appel, the songwriter's first producer and manager, claims he and Springsteen disagreed about whether the song even belonged on his breakthrough *Born to Run* album, which was released in 1975. In a 1992 book called *Down Thunder Road* (Simon & Schuster), Appel claimed Springsteen agreed to include it only after Appel argued vigorously to do so. Appel liked the song a lot, once comparing it to *Naked City*, a 1948 film noir classic set in New York City and directed by Jules Dassin.

Springsteen, it seems, was thinking cinematically as well during that phase of his career. When he was writing the title track, for example, Springsteen said he fixated on the phrase "born to run" because "it suggested a cinematic drama I thought would work with the music I was hearing in my head . . . This was a turning point, and it allowed me to open up my music to a far larger audience. *Born to Run* was a long time coming; it took me six months to write. But it proved to be the key to my songwriting for the rest of the record."

Another clue about Springsteen's intentions in writing "Meeting Across the River" is buried in the nearly forgotten history of the song's title. The handwritten lyric—on a piece of three-hole, lined notebook paper, reprinted in the Springsteen-penned book *Songs*, and now enshrined in the Asbury Park Rock 'n' Roll Museum—includes no title at all and offers no other insights, other than that a few insignificant words were changed by the time the song was recorded.

But according to a 1989 book called *Springsteen: The Man and His Music*, by the editors of a fan magazine called *Backstreets*, early pressings of the *Born to Run* album were issued with a postcard-sized placard that listed the original title of the song as "The Heist." That early pressing—known as the "script cover" because of the scripted font used for the type, as opposed to the block lettering on the released cover—was sent out in early 1975 to radio stations and a few in the music industry and has since become a to-die-for Springsteen collectible.

That bit of trivia raises a question: Why was the original title, "The Heist," changed to the less crime specific "Meeting Across the River"?

Maybe it was the last-minute decision of a record company marketing executive. Or maybe it was something else entirely. My guess is that Springsteen, as a writer, recognized that the original title undercut the power of the story. While "The Heist" conveyed the same feel of 1940s street cred as the music itself, it didn't accurately describe what the lyric suggested was taking place. As told, the story in "Meeting" doesn't involve a theft, or heist, so much as it involves some sort of unspecified deal-making between the narrator and his big-shot connection. Fencing? Numbers? Drugs? Impossible to say—and better because of it. Left vague, the story becomes a metaphor for every doomed small-timer with a sad little dream.

And a powerful story like that can go just about anywhere.

Meeting Across the River
ERIC GARCIA

THUNDER ROLLED ACROSS the sky and, as always, Jimmy Parker moved along.

The grime of the county jail hung on his clothes, and it would be weeks, maybe months, before he could get the stench of prison smokes off of his skin. Every time, it took a little bit longer to get rid of that odor. In a way, it was almost comforting. Some of the repeat offenders Jimmy knew told him they committed crimes once they were out just to get that smell back.

No one was waiting for him at the jail gates. Eddie was probably back at the house, fixing up the car. He knew Jimmy was getting out today. Cherry knew, too, but Jimmy was sure she wouldn't show. She never showed anymore, and he didn't blame her. Jimmy didn't want to see himself looking like he did, and didn't expect anyone else would want to either. Jimmy walked a few steps down the road, then popped his thumb and hitched a ride in a passing Mustang.

The driver was a young kid, barely old enough to drive. He twitched nervously in the seat as Jimmy shook out a cigarette and lit up. "I'm n-not supposed to let people smoke in the car."

"That your rule?" asked Jimmy. "Or your mama's?"

The boy looked back at the road. "My mom's." His cheeks quivered. "Fuck it, though, you can do what you want."

Jimmy hadn't planned on any different. The cigarettes they let him have in jail were crap, nothing but cheap tar and rolling paper, but they were his, and now that he was back in the real world, he wasn't taking orders from anyone, let alone some spoiled kid's mama.

As they drove, the thunder rolled again.

"Drop me off at St. Charles Place," Jimmy told the kid. The Mustang rolled through a stop sign and came to rest at a curb. Jimmy hopped out without another word to the boy, and wasn't surprised when the car sped away as soon as he shut the door.

The house on St. Charles was a rickety affair, little more than a red pile of beams and nails thrown together by Jimmy and Eddie's dad twenty years ago. Mr. Parker hadn't been much of a carpenter, and though the house always looked like it was on the verge of collapse, it had held up through decades of fire and rain. He had raised his two boys in that house, and when he died, Jimmy and Eddie took over the job of caretakers. They didn't love the house the way their dad had, but they respected it, and understood that the time and money it took to build something like this was something to be admired. Neither of them had ever done anything particularly important in their lives. It was all just a big circle, one day after the next, around and around with no real purpose. But Jimmy knew that was all about to change. One way or the other.

He found Eddie in the garage, just where he'd expected him to be. Half-buried underneath his hot rod, overalls smothered in grease.

Jimmy kicked his brother's foot. "You could have picked me up."

"That today?" Eddie didn't move from underneath the car. "I been real busy here."

"I called. From the jail."

"Like I said, I been real busy." With a grunt, he slid out from under the hot rod and sat up. His boyish face was smeared with grease, the round cheeks puffing out as he staggered to a knee. "Help me up."

Jimmy lifted his brother to his feet and the two embraced for a brief moment before letting go. "You talk to Cherry?" Eddie asked.

Jimmy shook his head. "I was thinking I'd go down there, maybe surprise her—"

"I don't think that's a real good idea."

"She still burned about the whole thing?"

Eddie shrugged as he grabbed a wrench and slid himself back under the car. "We didn't talk much when you were away. Just a hey or howdy if we passed each other down at the waterworks, but . . . yeah, she's still real burned about it."

Jimmy lit a second cigarette with the butt of his first and crushed the used one underfoot. He took a deep drag and exhaled slowly, letting the smoke curl up from the corner of his mouth. Taking his time. In jail, all he did was smoke. No visitors. Nothing to look forward to. So it came down to smoking. The longer it took, the better.

"So," Jimmy said, "I guess I'll go down there."

"Do what you want," said Eddie. "I'm not gettin' involved with this." A stream of oil poured from beneath the hot rod, and Eddie let loose with a torrent of curses. He slid out from beneath the car again, grease dripping from his chin and neck. "And don't goddamned smoke so close to the car, you'll get us both killed."

The thunder rolled, and Jimmy moved along.

Cherry and Jimmy met at the waterworks. There were only two utility companies in town, and if you didn't have the grooming or the schooling or the chops to make it as a clerk or bellboy at one of the big hotels, you worked at the electric company or the waterworks. Both places were owned by the same man, Mr. Darrow, which meant he could charge more and get away with it, but no one seemed to care. Sometimes it seemed to Jimmy like everything in town was owned by four, maybe five people tops. They were the ones with the big houses, the ones who could afford to stay in all the nice hotels on the boardwalk. The ones who owned property and didn't have to worry about how they were going to make the next payment.

Jimmy's dad had worked for the waterworks as long as Jimmy could remember. He was a ditch rider, one of the men who walked the canals and irrigation pipes of the countryside, clearing out obstructions so the water could get to its designated location. He killed rats and plugged pipes and bent gates and dug a few ditches of his own, and he never came back home without a sheen of sweat. "Ain't nothin' wrong with riding ditches," he told his boys, "but if you can do something else, you better goddamned do it."

Three days after his eighteenth birthday, Jimmy walked into the water-works and signed on up. They gave him the job that they give all new un-skilled and uneducated employees at the waterworks: filter cleaner. Deep inside the bowels of the plant, Jimmy spent his days suctioning sand and gravel onto regrading screens, picking out the bones, feces, and balls of wax that somehow ended up in the mix. Some days he'd use a trowel to scrape thick clumps of dirt from the edge of the filter bed. When the whole mess would calcify into solid stone, preventing the water from filtering through, he'd be sent down into the rock bed to jackhammer the sand back into sub-mission, and for days after, his arms and shoulders burned with pain. At the end of the week, they gave him two hundred dollars.

Cherry came from two towns over, and she worked the pumps and flowmeters, testing the water for alkalinity, acidity, potability, and whatever else the bosses told her to check. She walked the catwalks of the waterworks with a lunchbox full of test strips, stopping at every grade and checking the levels before turning around and starting the process all over again. Some-times she'd do three full circuits of the waterworks before lunch—squatting down, standing up, squatting down—and another three before quitting time—squatting down, standing up, squatting down—and for days after, her thighs burned with pain. At the end of the week, they gave her two hundred dollars.

They met on a Friday, two hours before quitting time. Jimmy had just come up from the bottom of the filter bed, his face and neck covered in granulated silt. He paused for a breather, leaning hard on his jackhammer, as Cherry rounded the corner, lunchbox in tow. She stopped short.

"Oh," she said. "I'll come back."

"You here to check the water?" asked Jimmy. He'd already noticed that her coveralls were snug in all the right places.

Cherry nodded. "My supervisor said the water from Gate Four is testing out at nine on pH. That ain't right."

Jimmy shook his head gravely, as if the proper pH balance of water meant more to him than his own life and livelihood. "No, ma'am. That ain't right at all."

They were laid out on the filter bed ten minutes later, Jimmy's workpants bunched around his ankles, Cherry's coveralls half-buried beneath a crumbling pile of gravel, her thong pulled to one side as he thrust into her. Sweat dripped from Jimmy's forehead onto Cherry's lips, and she licked it up, flicking her tongue out to catch some more. As Jimmy neared his climax, he pushed forward with his legs, his feet losing purchase as they kicked out against loose rock. He fell hard into Cherry as her naked back slammed down on a rough section of granite, tearing skin and drawing blood. She didn't notice. They came together, and when they stood up from the filter bed, weak-kneed and light-headed, their silhouettes remained on the ground, the rock and sand discolored from their sweat.

Jimmy and Cherry dated for nearly two years before Jimmy was hauled in on his first burglary charge. It was a bullshit B&E up in swanky Marvin Gardens—he wasn't even near the joint that night, but there were three half-blind witnesses and they all picked him out of a lineup. Jimmy's court-appointed attorney slept through half the trial and burped through the other half. The charge stuck. Jimmy was sentenced to three months in the county jail, and fought off the bailiff on the way out of the courtroom so he could kiss his best girl one last time. Inside the joint, he learned how to smoke. It beat pretty much anything else.

When they let him out that first time, Cherry was waiting at the gates with nothing beneath her overcoat except bare skin and a six-pack of Bud. They had sex for two days straight, then took a pause while Jimmy went out to score more cigarettes. He realized too late that he'd left his wallet on the nightstand, and when he asked the clerk to give him credit, the dumb little shit got all defensive on him. Started calling him names. Yelling at him, like the guards had done, every day and night for the past three months. Jimmy got hot, and mistakes were made.

Six months later, Jimmy was released from prison for the second time, and Cherry was there once again, waiting inside the car as Jimmy stepped out of the gates. She honked when she saw him, and he slid into the passenger seat. They kissed for five minutes, and then Cherry had to go to back to work. Jimmy stayed home and watched TV.

Over the next eight years, Jimmy spent nearly as much time in jail as he did out of it. He didn't look for trouble, but trouble dogged him every step of the way. Every time he thought things were about to turn around, he'd flip over the wrong card and land himself back inside. Sometimes he'd get lucky, and a slip of a fifty dollar bill to the right cop would get him out of jail, but mostly, he served his time. Two months, three months, whatever. Cherry didn't come to pick him up at the gates anymore, but he didn't expect her to. He took a cab or a bus or hitched a ride back into town, then waited for her to get home so they could work out their physical needs before drifting off to sleep.

Slowly, somehow, it started to get better. Jimmy would go long stretches of time—four, five months—without a run-in with the cops, and he and Cherry started to talk about marriage and kids and all those things you're supposed to do because everyone else around you has already done them. It was all going to happen, and everything was going to be perfect.

Then the thunder came, and Jimmy rolled snake eyes again.

"I know you're home. I already been down to the waterworks, and the boss told me you knocked off early and came on back here, so don't pretend you ain't home."

Jimmy pounded on the cracked wooden door of the house on Tennessee Avenue. They used to live there together, back in the days before Cherry threw him out, and Jimmy still thought of the place as their home. Cherry rented the house from a bloodsucking landlord for the princely sum of $385 a month. The property owner rarely made repairs, and raised the rent each time he added another dilapidated house to the already crowded block. The door was nearly broken, the cheap pine shot through with knots. If Jimmy closed one eye and squinted with the other, he could almost see through the holes in the wood, almost make out Cherry's body standing on the other side, arms crossed, chest heaving, trying to figure out whether or not to give up and let him inside.

"Come on," he shouted at the door, "it's cold out here."

No response, but Jimmy was doubly sure he could hear her mumbled epithets through the splintered wood. "For fuck's sake, Cherry, I'm freezing my ass off. Now cut the bullshit and open up so we can talk like normal people."

The door flew open and Cherry came with it, her hair wild and loose, teeth gnashing as the words spit from her mouth. "*Normal* people? *Normal* people? Normal people don't lie and steal and—and—and—"

"Hold up, you gotta give me a—"

"And leave. Normal people don't leave."

Jimmy grabbed her by the shoulders. He couldn't let her push him off the porch. "Baby, I told you, it was a parole violation. They took me right in."

"You stole my radio. You were gonna hock it." Jimmy's look of surprise pleased her. "That's right, Eddie told me what happened. Said you went down to Baltic Avenue trying to pawn off my stereo—the one I got for my sixteenth birthday, with the CD player and the turntable—asking two hundred dollars—"

"But that ain't—"

"And when the cops came in you froze up—"

"Yeah, baby, and that was that. I went straight to jail. I didn't even collect that two hundred dollars."

"Fine," said Cherry. "Then where's my radio?"

"I dunno. You gotta ask the cops about that. I bet the fat one took it. He was eyeing it the whole time, real hungrylike." Jimmy let his soft eyes fall to the floor; he knew he could hangdog Cherry into taking him back. It had worked before. It would work again.

In many ways, Cherry did want Jimmy back in her life. The house on Tennessee Avenue was cold without him, and it wasn't just the broken heater or the crumbling insulation; without Jimmy, the air felt thin. Sometimes, late at night, when she lay awake in bed and thought about him all alone in that jail cell, she almost couldn't breathe.

But every time she thought of how he left her, her resolve to get rid of him strengthened and held.

"It ain't worth it," Cherry said softly, running her fingers through Jimmy's coarse hair for what she knew might be the last time. "Lord knows I love you, and damned if you can't screw with the best of 'em, but I gotta say bye, Jimmy." She backed up a few steps, into the crumbling vestibule of the house on Tennessee Avenue.

"Cherry, wait a sec, I can make it all better—"

The rotten door closed, and she was gone.

They gave Jimmy his old job back at the waterworks, just like they always did every time he got sprung from the joint, and he spent his days jackhammering and sweating and missing the hell out of his girl. During his breaks, he sat by the edge of the regrading trough, smoking and waiting, hoping to catch a glimpse of Cherry strutting by with her lunchbox of test strips.

Three weeks in, the foreman showed up, dragging a ragged, sinewy hunk of flesh behind him. There was more tattoo ink visible on the man's body than there was skin. "This is Skeetch," the foreman told Jimmy, pushing the new kid out in front of him. "He'll do what you tell him to." Then he turned heel and disappeared, leaving Jimmy and Skeetch to stare at one another in uneasy silence. Somewhere, a pressure alarm began to blare, followed by distant voices shouting hurried instructions. Jimmy and Skeetch held their ground, even as the alarm died out and left them in silence once again.

Jimmy broke first. "You ever done this before?"

Skeetch shook his head. His stringy arms twitched, the muscles jumping beneath the taut skin. "You ever humped a dog?"

Jimmy shrugged. "Only the ones turned their dicks up at you."

Skeetch lunged first, throwing his ropelike arms around Jimmy's midsection and squeezing tight, Jimmy laughing and pounding Skeetch on the back. The embrace was as short as it was heartfelt, and soon the two were standing at arm's length, giving each other the once-over.

"You sonofabitch," Jimmy said, "you don't look half bad. Last I saw you, you was down on all fours, shouting cusses at the guards and bleeding from the ears."

Skeetch grinned and pulled on his lobes. "Cleared up. Doc says I'll keep somethin' like eighty, almost ninety percent of my hearing. Says I got a real hard skull."

Jimmy had met Skeetch on his third trip to the county jail, and the two had hit it off immediately. Both were repeat offenders. Both had been busted for burglary and resisting arrest. Both maintained their innocence while smirking enough to tell you they didn't really expect you to believe it. Day after day, they sat in the rec yard, smoking and telling stories of their exploits. Sometimes, other cons would gather around to listen like kids at story time. Skeetch hailed from the south side of town, the dangerous blocks down near Baltic and Mediterranean Avenues, and his low-rent street cred instantly gave him respectability among the other inmates. The tattoos covering his body were mostly jailhouse quality, ballpoint ink and unsterilized hat pins doing the job, and the faded blue scrawls only added to his rep.

They hadn't seen each other in years, but soon the two ex-cons were laughing it up and telling all the old stories again. Jimmy knew the foreman wouldn't be checking in on them anytime soon, so they knocked off for the day and headed out to a bar up on Oriental Avenue that catered to the down-and-out. The waitress saw Jimmy coming and cleared his usual table in the back. She set down a couple of six-packs and stayed far away.

Four beers in, Skeetch laid it on the line. "I got a thing," he said.

"Hell, you always got a thing."

"Nah, it ain't like that." Skeetch finished off his longneck and started on the next. "This one's big. Bigger than any of the rest. And there ain't no way it can go wrong."

The beer in Jimmy's belly pulled his lips into a wide grin. "I love it when you say that, Skeetch. Makes me think of good times."

But Skeetch was dead serious. "I'm tellin' you, I got this one figured out. Guy on the inside and everything."

"Yeah?" said Jimmy, still more amused than anything else. "What is it? Liquor store? Bank machine?"

Skeetch belched, his cheeks puffing with rancid air. "Railroad."

"Railroad," echoed Jimmy.

"Four of 'em, actually."

"Four railroads."

"At the same time."

Jimmy set his beer on the table. The room wasn't spinning, not yet, but he had a good mind to set it in motion. "You got any particular railroads in mind, or you just pluck four of 'em out of the air?"

"Oh, I got 'em in mind, all right." Nodding his noggin like a bobblehead doll with a busted spring, Skeetch held up the four filthy fingers on his right hand and counted off his future conquests: "Reading. Pennsylvania. B&O. And last but not least, the mighty, mighty Short Line."

Jimmy's whistle was low and long, a soft exhale of air as the possibilities settled over him. Skeetch grinned; he knew his pal was hooked. "You stick with me, Jimmy, and we're gonna break the motherfucking bank."

"See, the thing is," Skeetch continued, "each of them railroads is owned by the same guy, the same fella who owns the waterworks and the electric company and half of them nice houses and hotels all across town."

"Sonofabitch."

"That's right. He's got a whole mess of properties, all under his command. It's like he's got one of them . . . them things . . . What they call it when you own everything and no one else can come in to compete. You know . . ."

Jimmy said he didn't know, but vowed to look it up the next time he stole an encyclopedia.

"Anyway," said Skeetch, "since this guy bought up all the railroads, he's been routing 'em over to the same refueling station at the end of each run."

"How you know that?" asked Jimmy.

"I just know it." Skeetch scratched at his arm, where a new jailhouse tat of Jesus riding the prow of a battleship was just beginning to heal. The skin was still red, raw, and puffy. "Okay. Guy I know works with another guy who used to date the chick who runs the lube service over on Kentucky Avenue. And she used to work for a guy who went to middle school with the fella who's clocking the trains in and out every night."

"Sounds solid."

"As a fucking rock. Up around two A.M. every morning, those trains pull into a central station near the free parking lot and don't leave again till six. I figure that gives us four hours to do our thing."

Jimmy did some quick math in his head. "Sounds about right."

Skeetch laid it all out for Jimmy, beat by beat, as they sucked down their beers and watched the afternoon crowd of hard-core drunkards begin to clear out, making way for those who preferred to substitute alcohol for their evening meals. Jimmy wasn't thinking about the money so much as he was about Cherry, about how a big score with Skeetch would finally show Cherry that he's the kind of man chicks want to keep around. That a guy who can knock over a train—no, *four* trains—is a guy who should be allowed back into the house on Tennessee Avenue.

"You got a car?" asked Skeetch.

"My brother does."

"Can you get it?"

Jimmy had never driven Eddie's hot rod. He'd only ridden in it once, for a quick trip around the block. Eddie treated the damn thing like a baby. Even hired a few local kids to watch over it if he had to go out of town for the night. But Jimmy figured he could pay his brother off with a share of the take, make it worth Eddie's while. "Sure," he told Skeetch. "I can get it."

"Good. Then let's do this. Next Tuesday good for you?"

Jimmy didn't need to check a calendar. Every day was pretty much like the last. "Tuesday'll do just fine."

The next week passed quickly, Jimmy and Skeetch alternately laughing and keeping stone quiet as they jackhammered and filtered and pretty much kept to themselves. The foreman was happy that the new guy was working out, and left the two men to their jobs. When Jimmy and Skeetch weren't talking about the plans for the heist itself, they were talking about what they'd buy with their share of the loot.

"Gonna get me a dairy farm," Skeetch said one day. "Let the goddamned cows do all the work for once."

It made Jimmy think about Cherry, who had once expressed a similar desire. She'd grown up on a working farm, watched her dad till the land and the soil and eventually get shut down by big agribusiness. Strange how Skeetch wanted the same thing. Maybe Jimmy attracted the kinds of people who want dairy farms. He didn't know; what he did know was that above all else, he wanted Cherry back in his life.

"First things first," Jimmy told Skeetch, "I'm gonna buy Cherry a new radio. Just like the one I . . . lost."

"She still pissed?"

"Won't answer the phone," said Jimmy. "Got one of those caller ID boxes. Even when I try from a pay phone, she knows it's me, won't answer. But I figure if I show up with some twenty-inch woofers, she'll open that door right up."

Skeetch's lecherous grin showed off most of his missing teeth. "System like that? Hell, she'll be doin' some woofing of her own."

"Now, wait a sec—"

"You know what I'm saying? Hot gal like yours?"

Jimmy knew exactly what Skeetch was saying, and didn't like it a bit. A man like that, talking about a woman like Cherry. The cold feeling settling in his gut told him to grab the nearest hammer and start swinging for the fences, but some small part of him took control and suggested that he walk away before more mistakes were made. It wouldn't do any good slugging Skeetch with five pounds of iron, not now when they needed to stick together for the good of the deal. Without Skeetch, there was no railroad job. Without the railroad job, there was no take. And without the take, there'd be no Cherry. Jimmy turned his back to Skeetch, grabbed a jackhammer, and spent the rest of the day busting silt. Four hours later, he clocked out and walked home.

In the weeks since Jimmy'd been out of prison, he and Eddie hadn't spoken more than a hundred words to each other. Eddie spent most of his time at work or in the garage, fixing up the hot rod. When they did see each other—the occasional dinner, passing in the hall—they didn't have all that much to talk about.

Jimmy hadn't brought up the railroad job yet; he needed to couch it just right, to smooth Eddie out before asking to borrow his prized possession. But time was running out. On Sunday night, two days before the job, he found Eddie slumped in front of the television, watching a game show.

"Eddie? You up?"

"Yeah. You seen this thing?"

Jimmy looked at the television. Three contestants were taking their turns moving game tokens around a board, landing on squares and paying each other astronomical sums of money in exchange for small cards. Two thousand here, four thousand there. "Never."

"Big load of shit is what it is." Eddie clicked the remote, and a fishing show popped on the screen. He left it there.

"Eddie, I been meaning to give you some money, help out with the place."

Eddie didn't even look up. "That right?"

"That's right. I got a big score coming my way, and I want you to be a part of it. Twenty percent, right off the top."

Eddie didn't move from the couch. He'd heard it all before. On the screen, an angler landed a wiggling fish. "Now that's a big trout," mumbled Eddie.

"You hear what I said? Twenty percent."

"That's great, Jimmy."

The conversation hadn't gone exactly as Jimmy had planned it, but he figured there was no turning back. "Only thing is . . . I need to borrow the car."

The TV was off in a flash, and Eddie was on his feet, halfway between Jimmy and the garage door, blocking his brother's path. "The hell you do."

"One night—"

"I can't even believe you'd ask me—"

"That's all I need, one night—"

"A thing like that. A thing like that. Shit."

Jimmy saw it then, saw it in his brother's eyes: There was no way he was getting the hot rod. He could offer 20 percent, 50 percent, all of it, but nothing mattered. Eddie cared more about the car than he did about his own brother. Jimmy didn't much blame him.

"Forget it," said Jimmy. "I was just fucking around."

Eddie held Jimmy's gaze for a moment. "You know I'm not giving you the car."

"I know it."

"I'm not."

"Fuck!" Jimmy yelled. "I know!" He stomped past Eddie and down the hall, into the small den he was using as a room until Cherry let him back into the house on Tennessee Avenue.

Jimmy sat on the stained pull-out sofa mattress and fumed. If that was how Eddie wanted to play it, that was fine with Jimmy. He'd been in tight spots before. Always figured a way out. Eventually, it would come to him. If he just sat tight, it would come to him.

The farther Jimmy got from the house, the better he felt. The hot rod purred beneath him, its steering and acceleration perfectly responsive, reacting with precision to his every command. Like an extension of his body, it moved where and when he wanted it to, and by the time he pulled up in front of Skeetch's run-down apartment building, he almost understood Eddie's fanatical devotion to this molded hunk of aluminum.

"Sweet ride," Skeetch said as he slipped inside. His plastic watch scraped against the passenger seat as he reached into his back pocket for a pack of cigarettes.

"Christ, watch the leather. And no smoking."

"That your rule?" asked Skeetch. "Or your brother's?"

Jimmy's only answer was to pluck the cig from Skeetch's lips and toss it to the curb. It was bad enough that Jimmy had stolen Eddie's car after plying him with enough vodka to knock him out for the night. He didn't need to be stinking up the interior with the stench of cheap prison smokes. If he played this right, Jimmy could get the car back inside the garage before Eddie woke up, and his brother would never know it had budged even an inch.

They headed through the west side of town, passing by the old electric company on States Avenue, eventually making their way into slightly nicer digs up by St. James and New York Avenue. The rents were higher up here, the residents more refined and less eager to help out their fellow man. Over the last few weeks, Jimmy found himself walking up this way—and farther, into even ritzier sections of town, like Ventnor or North Carolina Avenue— admiring the houses and hotels, wondering if he'd get enough scratch out of the railroad deal to set him and Cherry up in one of the stately manors. He'd heard the big landowners and bosses complaining on local TV about some luxury tax they had to pay on all their property and expensive goods, but Jimmy didn't care about that. He'd be happy to fork over 10 percent, as long as it was 10 percent of a hell of a lot.

The free parking lot was on the edge of town, and as they approached, Jimmy could smell the diesel fuel permeating the air, hear the hiss of steaming air brakes. "You smell that?" he asked Skeetch.

"Damn right I do. That there's the smell of success."

Jimmy worked the hot rod through the shadows, the engine growling as the car slunk into the lot. The railroad junction was nothing more than a short, squat box of a building, coupled with a refueling station.

"Take this," said Skeetch, pressing a knife into Jimmy's palm.

"I thought you said you could get guns."

Skeetch shrugged and held up his own weapon, a snub-nosed revolver that glinted in the moonlight. "Gun. I said I could get *a* gun. Who cares, it ain't like we're gonna use 'em. The guy I know says the conductors drive their trains on in and kick back for the night at some bar. Now come on."

Jimmy and Skeetch climbed out of the hot rod and snuck through the parking lot, pressing themselves up against the side of the junction building. Skeetch poked his head up, peering through a window before giving Jimmy the thumbs-up. They ducked around a corner and kept tight against the building as they approached the refueling station.

Two trains were already in the dock, backed into the junction on their respective rail lines, and as Jimmy peered through the darkness, he could make out the names on both: the Pennsylvania and the Reading. Ten box-cars and one powerful engine each. But they were older than Jimmy had imagined, stained and worn, run-down from decades of continual use.

"They look like shit," he whispered to Skeetch.

"We ain't gonna drive 'em, we're just gonna rob 'em. Shit."

As they waited for the other two trains to arrive, Jimmy thought about Cherry, about their last conversation. He knew it wasn't about the radio, or the money. It was about drive. It was about ambition. Women liked that sort of thing in a man; he'd seen that once on a talk show when he'd knocked off early from work one day to hang on the couch. Well, if it was ambition that Cherry respected, it would be ambition that she would get.

They heard it first, a low rumble on the tracks, followed by the high-pitched whine of brakes screaming against their metal wheels a good mile or two away. By the time the B&O pulled into the junction, the Short Line was already in sight. Within ten minutes, both trains were hooked up to their refueling pumps, and the conductors had disappeared into the darkness, heading for some saloon in which to wait out the hours until daylight.

"This is it," Skeetch said, his hands tapping against his knees. He looked nervous, and that worried Jimmy. Skeetch was the one with the plan, the guy on the inside, the supposed know-how. But it was too late to turn around now. "Follow me."

Taking off at a jog, Skeetch and Jimmy hopped the chain-link fence separating the junction from the free parking lot and soon found themselves standing on the tracks. "We should split this up," Skeetch suggested. "You start with the Reading, I'll take the Short Line. Grab whatever you can and meet back here."

"What if someone sees me?"

"There ain't any someones," said Skeetch. "And anyway, that's why I gave you the knife." He took off running down the tracks, stumbling once on a crosstie before righting himself and disappearing into the shadows.

The rear boxcar of the Reading was painted a gunmetal gray, and even in the meager light of the refueling station, Jimmy could tell it had seen better days. The lock on the sliding door had broken off a long time ago, so Jimmy just grabbed the bottom and hoisted.

The rattle was loud enough to make Jimmy spin around and crouch down low; the noise echoed across the nearby free parking lot and bounced back to him. After a minute passed with no sign of guards or conductors, Jimmy jumped into the boxcar.

Wooden crates stacked around the sides of the car surrounded a lower tier of boxes, each identical in shape and size. Jimmy reached into his pocket and pulled out his trusty lighter, flicking it on to get a good look at what he was doing. He grabbed at the nearest box, his heart racing at the expectation of gold or diamonds or—

Irons.

The kind Cherry used to smooth out wrinkles in her dresses when she was going someplace fancy. The kind he burned himself on when he was just a kid, when his mom left one on the counter and Eddie had pushed him from behind.

Fair enough, Jimmy figured. These trains moved merchandise all over town; there were bound to be a few household appliances here and there. He hopped out of the boxcar and over to the next, taking care this time to raise the sliding door without causing a racket.

Again, the boxes were all of a similar shape and size, but this time they were bigger, and as Jimmy struggled to pop one open, he could hear the contents inside rattling around. Sounded small. Coins, maybe. Gold ingots, whatever those were. He forced open the lid, thrust his hand inside—

Thimbles.

Thousands of them, enough to satisfy the world's largest convention of sewers and quilters. Tiny pewter thimbles, ready to protect housewives' fingers all across the globe.

Jimmy said simply: "What the fuck?"

The next car down was filled with boots. The one after that—wheelbarrows.

As he prepared to check out the next one, Jimmy heard footsteps behind him. He whipped out the knife and spun.

It was Skeetch, his eyes wide and wild, his chest heaving with exertion. "You won't—fucking—believe what I found," he panted.

"Irons?" said Jimmy. "Thimbles?"

"Fucking Scottie dogs. That's right, a whole goddamned train full of 'em. Yippin' and yappin' in their cages just as soon as I open up the doors. And that's just the Short Line. I checked out the Pennsylvania, and holy shit, all it's got is top hats. Top hats, like from the forties and shit! Don't that beat all?"

Jimmy felt like one of those bounce houses at the state fair—slowly leaking, threatening to completely deflate at any moment. His limbs felt weak, his guts churned. "Let's get out of here," he said. "This doesn't feel right."

Skeetch grabbed Jimmy as he tried to pass by. "Not yet, we got one more."

"What's the point? It's just gonna have more weird shit in it. This town—this town is fucked, we both know it. Come on, let's blow—"

"We said we'd hit all four, we gotta hit all four. We still got the B&O. There's bound to be something there."

Despite the gnawing in the pit of his stomach, the feeling that the shadows were closing in all around him, Jimmy followed Skeetch away from the Reading and toward the B&O Railroad line. The train was larger than the others—older, too, if the peeling paint was any indication—and Skeetch wasted no time in hopping onto the frame of the last boxcar and hoisting Jimmy up after him.

"Door's locked," he grumbled. "Stand back."

Jimmy had no sooner taken a step back than Skeetch had out his gun, firing a shot into the padlock. Jimmy flinched as sparks flew, and grabbed onto

the edge of the boxcar to keep himself from falling off. The shot echoed
about the railyard, and Jimmy slapped Skeetch in the back of the head.

"Are you insane? They're gonna hear that and come running."

Skeetch raised an eyebrow. "Then we better do this fast, huh?"

The door slid open a foot or two before it squealed to a halt and refused
to budge any farther. Jimmy dropped to his knees and crawled inside as
Skeetch executed a perfect limbo. Both popped their lighters.

Metal boxes, stacked one atop another, floor to ceiling. Each one a short,
squat rectangle of lead with a stout cover, none of which were currently
locked.

"Register boxes," Skeetch drooled. "We found a goddamned train full of
cash register boxes."

Jimmy's eyes began to water with the beauty of it all. He ran to the nearest box and ripped the cover off, and there it was, ripe for the picking—

Money. Bills. All denominations. Everything in its proper place.

Crisp white dollar bills. Pink fivers. Yellow tens. Blue twenties. Green
fifties. Beige hundreds. And the most precious currency of all: perfect orange five-hundred-dollar bills. In one box alone, there had to be over five
thousand dollars in cash. And there were at least a hundred boxes in this car.
And a good ten cars on the entire train.

Just wait till Cherry got a load of the radio he was gonna buy her now.

Jimmy had already stuffed two bags full of cash when he heard the gun
cock behind him. He was halfway into the third bag before he realized that
the barrel was at his head.

The last thing Jimmy saw was Skeetch's new tattoo of Jesus on a battleship racing for him at full speed as his partner flipped the gun around and
whacked him hard in the temple. Piles of cash broke his fall, and he slipped
into an uneasy slumber.

When Jimmy got out of jail, no one was waiting for him at the gates. This
time, he didn't bother hitching a ride. He had nowhere in particular to go,
no one to talk to. It was just as easy to walk.

They'd finally given up on him down at the waterworks. Hired someone
else to take his place full-time. Said they couldn't deal with the constant
trips to prison. Other folks walked the life, rolled the dice, and they didn't
end up in jail every turn or two. So they sent him a pink slip and one week's
pay and suggested that he have a good life.

Eddie wouldn't let him in the house. Said he could come back home once
he brought back the hot rod, but they both knew that wasn't going to happen. The hot rod was gone, and with it, any chance that Jimmy and Eddie
Parker would have a normal brotherhood.

So he walked, taking his chances when the thunder rolled and skipping around town, always ending up back in the same place, just in time to do it all again. The house on Tennessee Avenue was gone. The landlord had built a few more homes, then razed the whole block and put up a hotel, sending prices in the neighborhood skyrocketing. It was happening all over town—hotels going up, houses coming down, and soon there wouldn't be any place left for bankrupt folks like Jimmy. He'd do better just to stay in jail as long as he could, then get sent right back again before the landowners bled him for more and more money.

When he'd woken up inside that B&O boxcar, his head throbbing from the pistol-whipping Skeetch had laid on him, Jimmy knew he'd been screwed. He didn't make it ten feet out of the railyard before the cops were on him. The hot rod was gone, skid marks on the pavement of the free parking lot. There was no way to escape.

Once he was booked, Jimmy tried to call Cherry, but there was no point—she'd never pick up a call coming from inside the joint. He even found a cop who was nice enough to let him use his cell phone, but Cherry still didn't answer. They brought him up on charges, and Jimmy didn't fight. The judge sent him away for eighteen months. He was out in six.

Halfway through his stint, he got a postcard. It was the first letter he'd received in jail since his second time around, and for a moment, he considered flushing it without even bothering to see who it was from. But the smell of the card got to him first: It was milk. Fresh and unpastuerized.

"Dear Jimmy," the card read, in Cherry's bubbly script. "I hope this finds you well. Skeetch and I have bought a lovely farm outside of town, and we're very happy. I hope you can be happy for us. We wake in the morning when the rooster crows and once the cows are milked and fed, it's time to till the land. It's what I always dreamed about, Jimmy, and it's something that Skeetch could provide for me. We were real good, you and me, but in the end, it's about a lot more than that, isn't it? You take care now. Cherry."

He didn't think about that card much anymore. There wasn't any point. Someday, Skeetch and Cherry and the hot rod would be back through town; he knew that much. There was no way to escape. Everyone circled round and round, endlessly, and if you could just stay in one place long enough, you'd see everybody else pass you by, running as if there was some end, some finish line. Someday, they'd be back, and Jimmy would deal with that thing then.

So Jimmy kept walking. Past Eddie's place on St. Charles, past the new hotel on Tennessee Avenue, past the free parking, Marvin Gardens, the old waterworks, and the rest of the chichi suburbs on Pacific and Pennsylvania Avenues. Jimmy kept moving because he had no choice.

Soon he was past the high-rise towers on Park Place and heading for a walk on the boardwalk. After that, he figured he'd start all over again. Maybe find someone else to loan him two hundred bucks. It wasn't up to him. It never was, and it never would be. Because when the thunder rolled across the sky, Jimmy Parker, as always, moved along.

The Far Side of the River
WILLIAM KENT KRUEGER

NEAR THE END of September, the red maples along the river bleed. Scarlet leaves drop and pool, and in a strong autumn wind they become almost liquid in the way they flow over the river bluffs and run down the gullies to the Mississippi. Although this is a beautiful thing to see, it always puts me in mind of death. I've lived in Minnesota all my life, and I know that what comes after the fall is a killing season, a season without conscience and without heart.

Stan Marco came back to St. Paul a week after the maples had started to turn. I wasn't especially surprised to see him walk into Steps Café. I'd been dreading it for a year.

My name is Eddie. I'm an alcoholic. The day Stan set foot again in Steps I'd been sober for thirty-one months. The last thing I needed was to see him and to see how everyone smiled the moment he appeared.

Stan was a guy women noticed. He'd been a model for a while, Calvin Klein magazine ads and a few television commercials. He'd had an agent, an apartment in New York City overlooking Central Park, and a beautiful girlfriend named Cherry. Cocaine and booze ended his modeling career. It wasn't just that he became unreliable. The high living took the perfection from his face, altered some aspect of him that the camera didn't overlook. You wouldn't have known it, though, the way women still fell all over themselves when they were around him.

The minute she saw Stan, Rita dropped her pad and pencil on the table where she was in the middle of taking an order and let out a scream that made me think we were being robbed. She ran to him and landed in his arms. He caught her as easily as if someone had tossed him a loaf of Jewish rye. Partly this was because Rita had substituted chain-smoking and caffeine for her alcohol addiction, and the combination made her thin and brittle as a breadstick. But also, Stan was buff. In the year he'd been gone, he'd got rid of the vague suggestion of a paunch the booze had put on him, and he'd added a lot of muscle. He looked good and he knew it. He swung Rita around, then gave her an exaggerated smooch.

"Bet it's been a while since a man kissed you like that," he said with a laugh.

"Honey," Rita told him, "no man's ever kissed me like that." And she smeared his mouth with some more of the bruise-colored lipstick she wore.

Stan made his way toward the kitchen, saying hello to the staff and the regulars. They all wanted a little piece of him and he was patient. But I knew he was making for me straight as he could. I figured he'd been thinking about this reunion as long as I had.

When he reached the kitchen doorway, he looked me over. "Eddie," he said.

"Stan," I said.

"Got time for a cigarette?"

"Sure. Out back." I called to the other cook, "The griddle's yours for a few minutes, okay, Mike?"

I headed through the door to the alley. It was late afternoon. The shadow of the old brick building that housed Steps spread across the potholed gravel and ate up the Dumpster on the other side. There were flies and the smell of rotting cantaloupe. Stan offered me a cigarette from his pack of Camel filters. I took one and lit it with the silver lighter I always carried. On one side of the lighter was engraved TO EDDIE. BETTER THAN A BROTHER. STAN.

"You look good," I told him.

"I always look good. What you mean is I'm still alive and that's a surprise. I'm the first to admit it. I'm alive because of you, Eddie." He said this sincerely, and then he grinned. Swear to God, I was looking at the old Stan, in the days when we were closer than brothers and either of us would have died for the other. Or killed.

"You can't stay," I said. "Sid Heller's going to know you're back."

"He already knows. I saw him first thing I blew into town."

"You went to see Sid?"

"He was part of the reason I came back." Stan waved off one of the Dumpster flies. "I settled up with old Sid. I'm like a son again."

"So you're here to stay?"

"You don't sound happy."

"Just surprised."

"I'll be gone before the first snow. I've got a thing I'm putting together. And I want to see Cherry. She still around?"

"She's around. I'm not sure she'll want to see you."

"I just want to talk to her."

"You hurt her pretty bad."

"I'm off the booze. I'm off the coke. I'm straight now, Eddie. Do you know where Cherry is?"

"I'll talk to her," I offered. "If she's willing to see you, I'll arrange it."

"I knew I could count on you. I always could."

Not always. And we both knew it.

Stan knew Heller because he used to caddie for Sid a long time ago. Stan was in high school then. Summer, and on weekends during school, he'd thumb a ride over to the Town and Country Club on the hills overlooking the Mississippi and he'd caddy for all the rich bastards. I was delivering crates of vegetables in a truck for Cruikshank's, humping to make a buck ten an hour, while Stan'd come back from the country club with fins and sawbucks in his pocket, tips from the golfers. Sid Heller liked his style and was always telling him if he ever wanted a shot at the big time, Sid'd set him up. It was years before Stan finally accepted the offer.

When Stan came back from New York City with Cherry, he was pretty much on the skids. He tried a few things. I even got him a job at Steps for a while. But the primary rule at Steps is that you have to be sober, and Stan never stayed sober very long. Cherry tried to help him; she loved him a lot, it was clear. And it was also clear—to me anyway—that all he was doing was dragging her down with him. She had a problem with coke, and I finally convinced her to go into treatment. It wasn't long after that that she left him. I know Stan blamed me, although he never said as much.

He finally used the Sid Heller connection to set up a deal across the river in Minneapolis. Fifteen grand was supposed to have come from it, ten for Sid, five for Stan. Stan kept saying if he could just get a good stake together, he'd take Cherry and they'd head somewhere warm, somewhere they could start over. He still didn't get it. That you don't just turn your back on the demons and that's it. You can't run fast enough. You've got to face them and beat them. And you've got to accept that they never go away for good. They're always there, lurking in the dark, waiting for you to get careless, waiting for you to forget.

Stan had wanted my help. He practically begged me. Just give him a ride across the river, that was all. Just stand by him while the deal went down. I thought I could do it, help my friend, but in the end, I backed out. The deal went south. Sid Heller wasn't the kind of guy who'd just let ten grand slip away. Stan knew he couldn't stick around the Twin Cities. He left, vanished without a word to anybody.

Now here he was, in decent threads, looking better than ever. And he was square with Heller.

"You got a place to stay?" I asked.

"A little dump on Concord, over a Chinese market. Everything smells like cooked cabbage and fish, but I won't be there long. Like I say, I'm only in town until I finish this thing I'm putting together and to see Cherry. If I'm lucky, I'll be gone within a week, maybe two." Stan finished his cigarette, crushed it out on the gravel. "I'll stop by tomorrow, okay?"

"Sure."

"You'll talk to Cherry?"

"I'll talk to her."

Stan looked at me, looked at me in the old way. "You didn't let me

down," he said. I knew he was talking about Heller. "You made me see myself. You saved me, Eddie. All I could think of while I was gone this time
was how my whole life, you've been saving me." He punched my shoulder
and he left.

A river divides more than just the land. When you've lived on the poor side
of a river, you know that. Stan and I grew up in South St. Paul, on the flats
not far from the stockyards. All around us were salvage lots full of rusting
cars and chemical storage tanks that sat in the dead grass like huge white
carbuncles. We were too far from the river to be able to see the Mississippi.
The only body of water visible was the one I saw from my bedroom window
upstairs, a small lake to the north called Pig's Eye. Sometimes Stan and I
would hitchhike to Cherokee Heights and stand on the High Bridge. From
there we could see across the river to the tall office buildings of downtown
St. Paul, the cathedral on the hill, and the river bluff where Summit Avenue
ran, lined with mansions. Sid Heller lived there. Stan would point to a place
and say, "There. That's where the flabby old shit lives." Stan didn't like
Heller, but the man had money, lots of it, and Stan liked money. Heller also
had a gorgeous young wife, and Stan liked her, too. He used to tell me how,
when he caddied for Heller and his wife, she'd wear tight shorts that showed
white cheek whenever she bent over, and she bent over a lot. Stan said she'd
propositioned him once. They were in the trees looking for her lost ball. She
bent to look in some bushes, glanced back, and caught Stan staring. She
smiled and told him she didn't think caddying was man's work and that
when he was ready to do man's work, he should come and see her.

So far as I knew, he never took her up on the offer. As soon as he graduated from high school, he split for New York City and I didn't see him again
for seven years. During that time, I got married, started a family, took on a
mortgage, and went to work at the stockyards. I developed a habit of stopping off for a few drinks on my way home. Then I extended the habit to
drinking in the morning before I went to work. I lost my job. I lost the
house. Eventually, I lost my wife and my children to a preacher who took his
flock with him back to Oklahoma. But I was lucky. After I'd lost everything,
I found AA.

When I'd finished my shift at Steps, I drove to the Heights and sat a while
looking at the river. It was near sunset. The red maples had fire on their
branches. The river was yellow, reflecting the sky. The mansions along Summit Avenue were hard to see, lost in the deep evening shade of elms. I
thought about drinking. Whenever I had a tough thing facing me, I thought
about drinking. I knew I wouldn't turn to the bottle, but it was always a
thought. Finally, I headed home.

I was renting the upper part of a duplex, a nice old place off Annapolis. When I walked in, the lights were off. The glow of sunset came through the windows on the west side, and I saw Cherry asleep on the sofa. Photographs lay spread out on the coffee table. They were black-and-white shots of towboats pushing barges and towboats docked. In New York City, when Stan had met her at a stylish gallery that was showing her work, her subjects had been exclusively the derelicts, the junkies, the winos, the city's lost and forgotten people. Now she captured bridges and barges and riverbanks. Her work hung in Steps, among other places, and she was beginning to sell. That afternoon when he'd come to see me, Stan hadn't even noticed her work hanging there.

On her skin and clothes, I could smell the chemicals she used in developing. She wore her hair long. I brushed aside a few blond strands fallen across her cheek. She didn't stir. For a while I just sat there, amazed by her beauty and astonished at how lucky I was.

"She doesn't want to see you, Stan."

"Did you tell her I'd changed? I'm clean?"

"I told her. You hurt her too bad. She doesn't want that again."

We stood in the alley behind Steps. It was a much colder day than the one before. Stan wore only a light tan sport coat, but a good one, good looking on him, anyway. Underneath he had on a black turtleneck. His shoes were new, black and shiny. From the look, you'd think he was dressed for an ad shoot. He wore a strong cologne that he said he'd put on to cover the smell of cooked cabbage and fish from his room above the Asian market. The wind out of the northwest was chill, the kind that reminded you somewhere behind it was a hard winter. Stan turned up the collar on his coat and puffed on a Camel filter.

"If I could just talk to her," he said.

I shook my head.

"Look, Eddie, one way or another, I'm going to find out where she lives," he said. "I'll go see her."

"You drop in on her out of the blue, it's the worst thing you could do. I'll talk to her again, Stan. In the meantime, you said you had something to put together. Why don't you concentrate on that?"

"I already have. I think I'm set."

"Yeah? What's happening?"

He brightened a little. That was good. Getting his mind off Cherry.

"I didn't tell you how I squared it with Sid Heller."

"How?"

"Paid him the ten grand and some interest." He stuck the cigarette in the corner of his mouth, freeing his hands so that he could rub them together. "Aren't you cold?"

"Doesn't bother me."

He threw the cigarette down and crushed it in the gravel. "When I left here, all I had was the money I got from hocking Cherry's radio. I hitched down to Tucson, figured at least there I wouldn't freeze. But the whole way, I was thinking about everything. About you and how you helped Cherry get clean. I figured you had the right idea. Me, I was trying to beat the booze and the coke alone, and I couldn't do it alone. In Tucson, I hooked up with AA."

"I'm glad, Stan." And I meant it.

He turned his back to the wind. "The guy who pretty much ran the AA thing there, this guy Howard, took me under his wing. He owned a big motel and he hired me to do maintenance and stuff. Gave me a little room. Howard was a prick a lot of the time, loved to remind me of what he was doing for me. But, hey, it was basically okay. He had a wife, Maria. He used to order her around like she was a servant or something. He'd snap. She'd hop. Not what you'd call a pretty woman, but she was careful in how she looked. Very neat. You had the feeling she was always wearing clean underwear. You know what I really liked about her most? She smelled like this flower. Gardenia. I'd be cleaning the pool and she'd walk by and even over the chlorine I caught the scent of gardenia.

"It took a long time for anything to happen between us. I was trying hard to be grateful to Howard, and Maria had never been unfaithful before, or so she claimed. Then one day she asks me into one of the vacant rooms, says she's got an air conditioner going bad. I get inside and she closes the door. Room's nice. Cool and dark. She doesn't say a word, just turns on the television and starts a VCR she's hooked up. And suddenly, I'm looking at a couple of people going at it. Like a stag film, Eddie. And then I realize I know the room. It's at the motel. I look at Maria. She tells me Howard has some of the rooms fixed so he can film what goes on. 'He watches,' she tells me, 'and he touches himself. Sometimes he goes to whores. He says he's tired of me.' She's crying now, all angry and sad. 'I would not let him touch me now anyway,' she says. Then she looks at me with these soft brown eyes and she says, 'Do you want to touch me?' She seemed so alone and so sad in that dark room that I did want to touch her. I wanted someone to want that, at least, and I was the only one there."

"What about the money, Stan?"

"I'm getting to that. When I decided to come back here and clear things up with Sid and get back together with Cherry, I took a few videotapes Maria gave me and I went to see Howard. I told him I wanted fifteen grand or I was going to let Tucson know how he entertained himself. He forked over the dough without an argument."

"What's that got to do with what you're putting together here?"

"When I dropped by Sid Heller's place to give him the money, his wife was there. Old Sid's really getting on in years, but his wife's still quite a piece of work. Swear to God, Eddie, she gave me the same kind of look she used to at the country club. Only now I'm ready to do man's work. Sid had a golf date today, wanted me to come along. I turned him down. While he was golfing, I paid a visit to Mrs. Heller."

"Christ, Stan, you fucked Sid Heller's wife?"

"Not yet. Tomorrow night. Sid's got a standing poker game starts at midnight, usually lasts till dawn. Mrs. Heller has invited me over for a nightcap." He took a small tape recorder from the pocket of his sport coat. "I figure I'll catch all the action on tape, and then we'll discuss what old Sid might do if he has the opportunity to listen to all her little squeals of delight."

"You're going to blackmail her?"

"I figure she's good for ten grand easy."

I was getting chilly, but that probably wasn't what was causing the goose-bumps. "This is Sid Heller's wife, Stan. To stay Sid Heller's wife, this woman's got to have the soul of a black widow. You think she's just going to roll over while you squeeze ten grand out of her?"

"Ten grand is nothing compared to what she'd lose if Sid got hold of that tape. And don't forget, Eddie. She gets a roll in the hay with me. That's something might be worth ten grand in itself."

"It's crazy, Stan. You really think you can build a life with Cherry on something like that?"

He put his collar down and straightened his coat. "You never had any vision, Eddie. You never looked any higher than those river flats. I've been on Sid Heller's side of the river, and I'll be there again. And Cherry'll be there with me. Just help me talk to her. That's all I'm asking. Will you do that?"

He looked so cold. He looked like something exotic and out of place there where the snow would soon be flying. "I'll do my best," I said.

"Thanks, Eddie." He touched my shoulder. "Thanks a lot."

I took the afternoon off. I stopped home and asked Cherry if she wanted to go for a ride down by the river. She said sure and grabbed her camera. I hit Concord Avenue and headed south. After a couple of miles, I turned onto a road that no longer had a name. We crossed two sets of tracks, and then the road was blocked by a gated fence. The sign on the gate read CHEMEX CHEMICAL. PRIVATE PROPERTY. NO TRESPASSING. I parked the car, and we got out. Cherry looked at the white storage tanks beyond the fence, but she didn't seem inclined to want to photograph them. I started to climb the gate.

"What are you doing?" she asked.

"There's something I want to show you."

"You're trespassing."

"Nobody cares. Believe me."

She handed me her camera, then climbed the gate with me. We dropped to the other side and walked the now nameless road. Most of the trees on the river flats were cottonwoods, but at the end of the road was a stand of red maples. Among the maple trees stood a house, empty now, abandoned for years. The glass had long ago become the victim of vandals' rocks and pellet guns. Nails bled rust onto weathered boards. The porch had caved in under the weight of a late, wet snow two years before.

"This is it, isn't it?" Cherry said.

Yeah. This was it.

Home.

It was always ancient, even in my earliest recollections. We moved there after my old man died. I was ten years old. My father, as I remembered him, was a man who liked to laugh. He liked to drink, too. He'd been killed coming home one night after his shift at the meat packing plant. He stopped at Sobrieski's Bar on the way and had too many boilermakers. Afterward, he missed a sharp turn on Concord and wrapped his car around a tree. He'd bought the big Buick because he believed it was the best-made car in America. Turned out, the American Buick was no match for Canadian Club and a sturdy Dutch elm. He had a little life insurance, enough to keep us going until my mother got a job. She moved us all to the house on the flats because the rent was cheap. At one time, there'd been other houses, but by the time we moved in, only one besides ours still remained. It was on the other side of the road, isolated by more maples. Stan's house.

Stan's old man had worked the stockyards until something happened to his back. After that, he just stayed home and drank. He wasn't like my father, who got loose and happy after he had a few under his belt. Stan's old man got mean. I remember a lot of quiet nights that were broken by a pounding on our front door. There Stan would be with his mother, one or both of them bruised or bloodied from a drunken beating. His mother would sleep on the couch. Stan shared my bed. When he talked about his father, he'd tell me how lucky I was that my old man was dead.

Cherry had grown up in Westchester, New York. She stood among the red maples, looking at that ghost of a house, and she said softly, "My God, Eddie."

She said it like she figured it must've been hell. But it wasn't. It was hard, sure, but it wasn't hell. Mom worked the late shift at a bakery that made the cakes and doughnuts for a big grocery store chain. She'd head off a little before five in the afternoon and come home around two-thirty in the morning.

I took care of my two sisters, and saw to Stan and his mother whenever they needed a place to stay. It might have been worse if I'd been lonely. But I had Stan, and he had me.

"Where's Stan's house?" Cherry asked.

The underbrush had grown pretty thick. The foundation of Stan's house would have been hard to find if you didn't know where to look. When Cherry stepped within a few feet of the old cellar pit, I grabbed her. She stared at the burned remains, heavy blackened beams that lay nearly buried under creeping vines and blood-red leaves that had fallen from the maples.

"What happened?" she asked.

"His old man burned it down. He was a mean, drunk son of a bitch. He burned it down and then he disappeared."

"Abandoned Stan and his mother," Cherry said, for she knew that part of the story.

"That's right," I said.

It was not really a lie. Because he had abandoned his family long before the night Stan killed him.

I hadn't been asleep very long that night when Stan came knocking at the door. For a while, I'd just been lying in bed listening to the wind. For hours, it had been coming and going, a rasping in the dry maples followed by a long sigh. It made me think of an old man struggling to breathe.

I snapped awake at the knocking and right away I could hear Stan's mother sobbing on the front porch. It was such a regular occurrence that I didn't hurry as I went down to unlock the door, but I saw right away it was worse than usual. Stan's mother was tall and very thin, a little bit of flesh over a lot of bone. Her voice was always shrill, even when she wasn't crying. I got a basin of warm water and a cloth and I cleaned her face carefully. Her eyes were black like the eyes of the coons that rummaged through our garbage cans, and her nose was pushed at a funny angle. I knew it was broken, broken bad. I didn't have a way to get her to anybody, so I gave her aspirin and told her to lie down on the sofa until my mother came home from work. I covered her with an old quilt. She went to sleep pretty quick.

Stan had deep brooding bruises on his ribs. He said the old man had whacked him with a two-by-four. He said the old man was out of his mind. He said he wished the bastard were dead. I took him up to my room, but he was too jazzed to lie down. He paced back and forth, fuming. I tried to talk to him for a while, but I'd been through this before with him and finally my eyes got too heavy. Before I knew it, I was asleep.

Stan woke me up. Even in the dark of my bedroom, I could see how pale he was, like he was ready to pass out.

"You okay?" I asked.

"I'm going to the electric chair, Eddie," he said. "They're going to fry me for sure."

I sat up. "What are you talking about?"

"I killed him. I killed the son of a bitch."

"Who?"

"My old man."

"No."

"Oh yeah, I killed him."

"How?"

"Railroad spike." Stan was always picking up old rusty spikes when we goofed around on the tracks. He kept them in a drawer in his room. "I put a spike through that son of a bitch's heart."

"Oh, shit." I heard a car coming up the road and saw the wash of headlights against the maples. "My mom's home. You stay right here, Stan. Just stay here."

I went downstairs. Stan's mother was in a deep slumber, which was not unusual. She generally dealt with the trauma of the beatings by sleeping long and hard. My mother was alarmed at the damage to her face. She shook the woman awake and insisted they go to an emergency room. She asked me about Stan. I told her he was upstairs and he was okay. She didn't tell me to take care of things while she dealt with Stan's mother. She knew I would.

After they'd gone, I checked on my sisters. Both of them were sleeping fine. I went to my room. Stan sat on the floor in the corner, all folded up. "I'm going to have a look," I told him.

"I'm going, too."

I got dressed and we went outside. Through the trees I could see the lights of South St. Paul, spread out along the bluffs above Concord Avenue a half mile to the west. There were only two lights on the river flats—one from the porch on our house and one that shone through the kitchen window at Stan's place. The wind was up again. Dry leaves crawled like crabs around our feet as we crept through the dark toward that kitchen light. I opened the back door. The old hinges cried out our presence.

"Where is he?" I whispered.

"Living room. On the couch."

The kitchen was a mess. Chairs tumbled over, broken glass on the cracked and curled old linoleum. I'd seen this kind of damage before. Stan had lived with it for years. The living room was dark. I almost stumbled over a broken lamp. I was barely breathing as I approached the couch.

"He's not there," I whispered. I was scared bad, and I finally understood how awful it must have been for Stan in that house with that monster of a man who was his father.

Stan switched on a light, and we both saw what the darkness had hidden. Blood. Blood everywhere. And Stan's father sprawled on the floor near the front door. He lay with his right arm outstretched, as if he'd been trying to make it outside when he died. The old railroad spike lay near the couch, colored by a deeper red than the rust alone. It looked as though Stan's father had pulled the damn thing out and in doing so, had opened a gusher of a wound. It was a pretty gruesome sight, but it honestly didn't bother me that much. My own father, when he was alive, had taken me to the slaughterhouse on several occasions, and I'd seen a lot of blood and smelled the smell. Stan, on the other hand, looked ready to faint or puke.

"Jesus God," he moaned. "They'll kill me for this, Eddie."

"It was self-defense."

He shook his head miserably. "He was asleep when I stuck him. I murdered him in cold blood."

"Maybe we can get rid of him."

"How?"

"I don't know. Bury him?"

"Look at this blood, Eddie. They'll know."

"Not if we burn everything."

Stan looked at me.

"You like this place?" I asked.

"I hate this place."

"Then let's burn it."

Stan looked at his old man. "Him, too?"

"No," I said. "People don't burn up completely and I think they can tell how he died."

Together, we carried his old man way out into the trees. We dug a hole deep in the black soil of the river flat. We dropped him in and covered him with dirt and with a heavy blanket of autumn leaves. Then we went back to the house. Stan brought up a big can of turpentine from the basement. He spread it all over the living room, especially on the bloody, ratty couch. I held the matches. "Is there anything you want to take with you?"

Stan shook his head. "Not a blessed thing." He grabbed the book of matches from me and he lit the fire himself. We headed out the back door as the flames spread, hungry to have what Stan had prepared for them.

There are events that divide our lives forever, split us as surely as the river splits the land. One moment we are on one side, and the next we've moved across and stand in a place we can not go back from, ever. That was the way it was for me that night. And although I wasn't exactly certain where it was

I'd come to, I knew one thing for sure. Stan was there with me. We were there together, and we always would be.

As Cherry and I walked back to the car, I stopped on the road between the storage tanks. "There's something I have to tell you."

Cherry waited, smiling. Finally she said. "Yes?"

"I love you."

She stared at me, then she laughed. "That's it? We came all the way out here so you could tell me something I already know? Eddie, you're a very strange man." She kissed me, then kept walking toward the car.

You can tell guys who've been through hell and have come back from it. It's like the devil walked on their faces, but there's something quiet in their eyes. Al Burrows was like that. He'd been my sponsor from the beginning.

We sat in a coffee shop not far from the stockyards where Al worked. He swept up or something. I didn't really know. He had on a green ball cap and a green jacket. His hands quivered a little as he tore a packet of sugar and poured it into his coffee. He didn't say much, mostly just listened. When I stopped talking he put his cup down and said, "What were you hoping I'd tell you? That saying nothing ain't the same as a lie?"

"Stan and her, it wouldn't be good."

"That's for you to decide?"

"I'm scared, Al."

"Sure you are."

"She's the best thing that ever happened to me. If I lost her, I don't know. Going back to the booze would be tempting."

"Don't put that on her, Eddie. The truth for all of us is that when things are hard, going back to the booze is tempting." He reached across the table and lightly touched my hand. "You know what I think? I think you already know what you're going to do."

He picked up his coffee again, took a sip, then put a napkin delicately to his lips.

The photos were already on the table drying when I got home—the old house, gray among the maples, whose leaves, in the black-and-white print, were a charcoal hue; the cellar pit, where vines crawled over the blackened beams like snakes; the storage tanks through the trees, white and somehow menacing.

Cherry stepped in from her dark room. "What do you think?"

"Nice."

"Nice?" She took off her rubber gloves. "Nice?" She came over to me and stood with her small hands on her hips. "You're looking at art. Art is not nice. Art is liberating, illuminating, breathtaking. Never nice." She leaned to me and kissed me to show she was only joking. The smell of her developing chemicals was strong and, on her, wonderful. "How was your afternoon?"

"Nice," I said.

She slapped the side of my head gently. "Oh, you."

I went into the kitchen and pulled some bottled water from the refrigerator. "Guess who dropped by the café this morning."

"Who?" she called from the other room.

"Stan."

She hesitated in responding. A half-beat too long. "Oh? How was he? Drunk?"

I lingered in the kitchen, making sounds as if I were busy with something. "He claims he's clean and sober."

"Did he have my radio?"

"Not on him."

She was quiet then. I stepped back into the living room. Cherry was standing very still, staring out the window at a line of geese heading south for the winter.

"You all right?"

It was after midnight. I'd been watching her for a while from the bed. She stood at the window, a dark shape against the fuzzy light from a street lamp on the corner.

"Thinking," she said. "That's all."

"About Stan?"

I followed the tiny red glow from the end of her cigarette as it moved in a slow, predictable arc from where her arms were crossed over her breasts, to her mouth, and back. I thought I could see the smoke.

"I don't want to talk to him, Eddie. I don't want to see him at all."

"I told him that."

"Good," she said. "Good."

Stan was already at Steps Café when I arrived for work the next morning. He was sitting in a booth, having a cup of coffee and talking with Rita. As soon as she saw me, Rita moved on to another booth and pretended to be interested in taking the orders of the two women there. Stan looked at me, and I knew Rita had wised him up.

"Were you ever going to tell her, Eddie?"

I sat in the booth, across the table from him. I smelled the cologne he wore to mask the smell of cooked cabbage and fish. "I did, Stan. Last night. She doesn't want to see you."

"Last night." Stan tapped out a Camel filter and lit up. "So you lied to me yesterday when you said you'd talked to her, but you're not lying now. Is that what you want me to believe?"

"Believe it or don't. It's the truth."

Stan shot out a big cloud of smoke and considered me. "What is it you want out of life, Eddie?"

"A place of my own, kind of like this, maybe. A family. A clean conscience."

"That's it?"

"That about covers it."

"That's what you're going to offer Cherry? Damn, Eddie, you still haven't learned to look any higher than those river flats."

Stan scraped the tip of the cigarette along the edge of the ashtray, clearing the ember. "You love her?"

"Yeah, I do."

"And what? You expect me to just to walk away?" He shook his head. "You're some piece of work, Eddie." He crushed the cigarette out, crushed it good. "Damn. Jesus." He clasped his hands tightly and leaned toward me. "All right. I'm out of the picture. I owe you my life. Now we're even. But one last favor."

"What?"

"Give me a ride across the river tonight. I still have a date with Sid Heller's wife."

"I can't do that, Stan."

"Why not?"

"Because you intend to blackmail that woman. That would be tough for me when I take moral inventory on myself. Step Four."

He stared as if he didn't quite know what to make of me, then he stood up. "You know why Cherry won't see me. She's afraid, Eddie. I'm an addiction. The only way she can stay clean is to stay away from me. She knows that."

He walked out the door. For a moment as he blotted out the bright morning sunlight, he became a black silhouette, something that reminded me of the beams in the cellar pit, the remains of what we'd both tried to burn a lot of years before.

Cherry was gone when I got home that afternoon. Her camera wasn't there either, and I figured she was out somewhere, shooting. I started making spaghetti sauce for dinner. All day long, I'd thought I should be happy, but I wasn't. When Stan walked out the door, it was one of those moments where I found myself suddenly in a different place in my life, but this time Stan had not come with me. That was okay, I told myself. Cherry would be there. As afternoon melted into evening, and I turned the fire off under the simmering sauce and stood at the window looking down at the empty space in the alley lot where Cherry always parked, I began to be afraid that wherever it was I'd come to, I was there alone.

She returned home just after dark, carrying her camera.

"I was worried," I said.

"I lost track of time."

"Shooting the river?"

"A new roll, but nothing inspired me."

She held the camera in her hands, turning it over and over, looking at it instead of at me.

"You should have called."

"From now on I will."

I'd set the table Italian, a red-checkered cloth, in the center a wax-encrusted Chianti bottle with a candle plugged in its mouth. I lit the candle and turned off the lights. A breeze ghosted through the window and disturbed the flame. Cherry seemed to shiver in the light. I walked to her, and she stepped into my arms, smelling of cooked cabbage and fish.

Later I said, "I have to go out for awhile."

"Where?"

"Some business across the river." I kissed her. "I'll be back."

I parked in front of the Asian market on Concord. Upstairs, Stan opened the door when I knocked.

"Eddie," he said, as if he were surprised. But I knew he wasn't.

"I came to give you that ride."

"I arranged for a taxi."

"Cancel it."

He shrugged and made the call.

"How am I getting back?"

"You're not coming back."

He lit a cigarette and nodded. No big deal.

"We talked is all," he said. "Nothing happened."

"I know. But not because you didn't want it to." I checked my watch. "Time to go."

It was late, no traffic. I drove over the High Bridge. Below us, the river was a long strip of night without any stars.

"I had you figured wrong, Eddie. I had you figured for a loser, all that talk about wanting simple things. Turns out that's what Cherry wants, too."

The air was chilly and had a wet, dusty smell to it. A cold rain was on the way.

I pulled up in front of the big stone fortress on Summit Avenue that was Sid Heller's home. Stan opened the door, then turned back.

"Friends?"

I looked at the hand he offered me, and I didn't take it.

"We were friends once, but that was a long time ago, on the far side of too many things. So long, Stan."

"Whatever you say, Eddie."

He got out. The first big splats of rain hit my windshield as Stan Marco turned his collar up and headed to the house.

We walk along the river in all seasons, but the most beautiful and the saddest is fall. We take turns pushing the stroller that holds our daughter, a blond beauty we've named Hope. Whenever we walk along the Heights we stop and look across the Mississippi where Summit Avenue crowns the bluff and the great homes hide among the trees. We both know the house.

The initial police report indicated that Mrs. Sid Heller had killed an intruder. The investigation that followed confirmed her story. I could have stepped forward and questioned things, but what would have been the point? Stan was dead, and the truth was he'd put himself in front of the gun barrel.

When the red maples turn, and the branches drip scarlet leaves like drops of blood, I am always put in mind of death. But it's easy for me to remember that I am one of the lucky ones, that in the long, cold season ahead, I have plenty to keep me warm.

Cherry Looks Back
PAM HOUSTON

I GUESS I haven't ever had what you would call the greatest taste in men. I mean when you are the only girl born to a woman who said rosaries every single day of six full-term pregnancies only to deliver boy after boy after boy. When you are the flesh and blood result of what little her body had left to give for gestation period number seven. When you are born eight weeks premature and even tiny by those standards and they give you a name to make up for your size: Catherine Elizabeth Mastrofini Brunetti, as if the heft of name alone might keep you breathing inside your little Plexiglas incubator, as if once they let you out, the name itself might tether you to the earth. When you have just barely learned to breathe on your own and your father forever and irrevocably shortens that tongue twister of a name to Cherry—not Cathy or Lizzie or Beth or Kate—you have to know exactly what he had on his mind when he did it, and the minds of every man after, and so on, and so on, until you are ugly or dead.

I was the tiniest prize on the boardwalk and in junior high I'd watch those boys catch the gold ring, aim the water gun, pop the balloon, lift me high up onto their shoulders and win me a stuffed toy twice my size. We'd head out to the end of the pier every Friday night in little gangs and listen to Backstreets play "Jungleland" and "Rosalita," drink Rolling Rock longnecks, and if we had enough cash left over we'd split a cheesesteak hoagie six ways. My sister-in-law down in Point Pleasant said that band was still together, though they had to change their name to B-Streets because of recent developments in the pop music world. Thirty years is a long time to play the same covers all night, but thirty years is a long time to do a great many things, among them dream of the one right man who is going to come along and take you the hell out of north Jersey once and for fucking all.

By the time I was fourteen I'd heard so many variations on the cherry joke it seemed important to get it over with, so I did. Under Morey's pier down in Seaside Heights with a guy named Ricky who was sixteen and drove a gold Chevy Malibu with a decal that said SHE'S ONLY ROCK AND ROLL stretched out over the back window. He bought me a giant vanilla Kohr Brothers frozen custard, *to fatten you up*, he said, *like a turkey*, and took me on the Zipper right afterwards, which made me so sick I would have gone anywhere with him just to get away from the lights and the noise. He brought something he called weed for us to smoke, but I don't think it was much more than sage and oregano in a Ziploc. The sand was cold against

my bare ass and I was mostly focused on trying not to puke and I had heard
there would be pain, but I don't remember there being any.

I had a radio in my bedroom in those days, just a little silver AM/FM that
used to belong to my grandpa. During the day I would listen to the local
rock-and-roll station, but at night, especially when it was cloudy and I
touched the antenna up against the crack that ran through the Sheetrock
near the window above my bed, I could pick up stations from all over: Fort
Wayne, Indiana; Norman, Oklahoma; and some USO station that never
said where it was coming from but was talking to soldiers stationed all over
the world. I heard Top 40 country, which they never play around here, and
livestock and grain prices, and weather reports with kinds of weather we
don't even have. On Kasey Casem's Top 40, people would call in requests
from everywhere you can think of: *This one goes out from Barney in Fargo
to his sweetest heart Jenny in Charleston*. I had a globe in my room and I
would always look to see how far the messages had to carry; I'd locate the
islands that were lying in the path of the typhoons.

In high school I was a cheerleader—yeah I know, big surprise—and I went
to my junior prom with a linebacker named Danny Fattore who wore a
white suit with lavender piping and brought me my first wrist corsage. My
mama liked him because he was Catholic and Italian, but he could hardly fit
himself into the backseat of his Datsun when we'd go parking, and all that
flesh and muscle on top of me made me feel even smaller than I was.

That summer, down the shore, I met a guy named Dave Murray, and I
would crawl out my bedroom window when my parents were asleep and
we'd climb up into the lifeguard chairs and he would play guitar and we'd
wait for the sun to rise over the Atlantic. When I went back to Jersey City
and he went back to Morristown he sent me letters with weird cartoons
drawn all over them and my mother took one look at them and called him
the Antichrist, but my father said her real problem with Dave Murray was
that he came from the other side of the tracks, which is to say, the *right* side.

Dave Murray showed up at our house one grey December morning in his
daddy's brand-new Seville with "Thunder Road" blasting out the speakers.
He had called from a 7-Eleven a few miles away and told me he had a wallet
full of his dad's credit cards and he was headed for California, and I knew I
was supposed to waltz down the front porch just like the girl in the song,
and I might have, too, if my mama hadn't been standing in the kitchen, ser-
rated knife stuck point first, just a millimeter into the soft flesh on the un-
derside of her wrist, screaming suicide threats in Italian at me while my
father kept on making breakfast as if nothing at all was happening. "Thunder Road" ended and "Tenth Avenue Freeze-Out" began and I guess Dave
Murray got tired of waiting because he ran into our brownstone, straight up
to the third floor, with a wrench in his hand and started making a hell of a

noise in the bathroom. My father waved his spatula at me in a way that said, "Go see," and I arrived at the top of the stairs just in time to see Dave Murray hoist the upstairs toilet in his skinny but wiry arms and send it sailing through the bathroom window. I rushed over in time to see the impact, a porcelain bomb sending slivers in every direction, luckily no cats or grandkids in the yard.

"This is your last chance," Dave Murray said to me, and I could see that he had cut his left hand, quite deeply, and I reached out to touch it, and he was gone, back down the stairs before my father even got the stove turned off under the brown-and-serve sausages.

Later, my father walked around and around the exploded toilet in our little piece of shit patch of a yard while my mama looked out the kitchen window twisting a dish towel tighter and tighter in her hands and whispering prayers of thanks that I hadn't gotten into that Seville with Dave Murray, that I would finish my last year of high school, that I would stay in the neighborhood and find a nice Italian boy to date, that I wouldn't be in the Seville, seventeen days later in Santa Monica, California, when the police finally caught up to Dave Murray and put him in whatever version of juvie rich kids go to, that as it turned out he was right about that day being my last chance and that I had found a way not to take it.

I met Lennie at the Maryland Chicken the night after graduation. I worked there part time since my senior year until the grease got into my hair and my clothes and even my dreams and I had to quit. I asked him what he wanted to eat and he took one look at me and fell to his knees, reached into his jacket pocket and pulled out a package of Tastykake Butterscotch Krimpets and offered them up like a sacrifice. Lennie had a late-model Trans Am and on our third date he brought me real eighteen-karat-gold earrings. He took me to the 5-7-9 shop at the mall and let me pick out anything I wanted and I picked a white tank top with a band of fur around the V-neck and sparkles, size three, and he wanted to know why they had size three at the 5-7-9 shop and I told him that in pants I wore a two.

Lennie had a bunch of money most of the time, except sometimes when he had absolutely nothing, and I'm not so dumb I didn't figure out that he was doing something illegal to get it, but in our neighborhood sometimes it is a fine line between what is above the law and what runs underneath it.

My mother kept waiting for Lennie to propose, even though I told her it wasn't going to happen. I spent the longest lunch of my whole life at the Red Lobster with her trying to tell me—without being explicit—that if I got down onto the floor after sex and put myself into a kind of a shoulder stand for fifteen to twenty minutes I'd increase my odds of getting knocked up. To this day she doesn't know I've been on the pill for those same thirty years Backstreets has been singing "Jungleland."

Lennie and I moved in together on my eighteenth birthday. I took a bunch of clothes and makeup, a blender that my mother got as a Christmas gift but didn't ever use, my album collection, my globe, and my grandpa's radio. Lennie was gone most nights, into the city on what he always called "official business" with a big grin on his face, which I noticed sometimes was a little strained around the edges. Lennie's friend Eddie always said that Lennie was just smart enough to get himself into really big trouble, and I guessed that was true because he could talk himself into anywhere, without stopping to think if it was a place he wanted to be or not.

Eddie was a sweetheart, and looked up to Lennie, mostly because he couldn't seem to get himself laid, and Lennie had no problem in that department. Lennie was always ordering Eddie around, treating him like a kid who couldn't think or dress or figure anything out for himself. One night Lennie was headed off on some top secret project and as he left the apartment he told Eddie not to move a muscle and Eddie and I looked at each other and rolled our eyes and decided if Lennie was going to be such a prick we'd have a little fun with it, so I opened a bottle of red and we tried to see how much of it I could get into Eddie's mouth without him moving a muscle. And later, when we had mostly given up on the game and we were both a little drunk, Eddie said, "I wonder how many muscles I would have to move to kiss you," and I said, "I don't know, why don't you find out," and he came over to where I was sitting and gave me the longest sweetest kiss I've ever gotten, sweeter still because it was the only kiss I can ever recall that wasn't on the way to something else—Lennie would kill us both if it went any farther—so that one kiss had to be everything, and it must have been to have lasted this long in my mind.

It was two months to the day before Lennie took a bullet in the brain that he pawned my grandpa's radio. Whatever he'd gotten himself into had gone south and fast, because one week we were eating prime rib every night down at Delucca's and the next week he was gone to the city five nights out of six, slinking in just before daylight and fighting off killers in his dreams. He even asked me if I could go to my parents for a loan—that's when I should have known how bad it was. Lennie would have gone to jail before he threw himself on anybody's mercy. I should have known right then it was the money or his life. When I came back from my parents' house with $250, he laughed at me, but he took it. The next day I noticed the Trans Am wasn't parked in any of the usual places. The next day it was the TV and the microwave. The next day he took my grandpa's radio down to Dudley's Pawn.

He promised he'd buy it back for me by the end of the week, and when that didn't happen, I moved what was left of my belongings back into my childhood room—I guess you can't pawn a globe, even in Jersey City. Whatever he was up to every night even scared Eddie off, and nobody wanted to

please Lennie more than Eddie, not even me. At the funeral Eddie said he
was supposed to go with him that night, and when I said he should thank
his lucky stars, Eddie said, "Cherry, you don't get it, if I'd a been there I
coulda saved him." Took a bullet for him is what he really would have done,
because if there had been anybody there to outtalk or outrun, we both knew
that Lennie would have done it.

When Eddie got his next paycheck from the plant he went down to Dud-
ley's and bought me back my radio, but it was a long time until I felt like
turning it on. He and I started having dinner every Wednesday night and
damned if it isn't almost thirty years now we've been keeping that date. First
couple years after Lennie died Eddie and I kept trying to find a way to fall in
love with each other, but there was too much of Lennie in the middle. Eddie
used to say he hung around a lot more often once he was dead, that getting
dead always seemed to be what Lennie was trying to accomplish, and now
that he had he was all loaded up with free time.

I dated some in my twenties, a gaggle of small-time crooks that Eddie
dubbed "the impersonators," quite a bit less in my thirties, and here in my
forties not at all. I guess even size two doesn't keep you from turning invisible when your time comes. These days I wish I was a little bigger just for
practical reasons: seeing over heads in the movie theaters, keeping warm
during the winter months, looking a bit tougher when I have to walk home
from the bus stop all by myself. My mama passed on a few years back and
my father opened a restaurant with the insurance money. Cherry's Place he
calls it, wouldn't you know. Pizza, pasta, stromboli, a little veal. Some
Wednesdays Eddie and I go in there for dinner, but sometimes we try someplace new. Eddie says it's good to venture outside of the neighborhood once
in a while, and all I can say is amen to that.

Pirates of Yellowstone
C. J. BOX

IT WAS COLD in Yellowstone Park in early June, and dirty tongues of snow glowed light blue in the timber from the moonlight. The tires of the van hissed by on the road.

"Look," Vladdy said to Eddie, gesturing out the window at the ghostly forms emerging in the meadow. "Elks."

"I see 'em every night," the driver said. "They like to eat the willows. And you don't say 'elks.' You say 'elk.' Like in 'a herd of elk.' "

"My pardon," Vladdy said, self-conscious.

The driver of the van was going from Mammoth Hot Springs in the northern part of the park to Cody, Wyoming, out the east entrance. He had told them he had to pick up some people at the Cody airport early in the morning and deliver them to a dude ranch. The driver was one of those middle-aged Americans who dressed and acted like it was 1968, Vladdy thought.

The driver thought he was cool, giving a ride to Vladdy and Eddie, who obviously looked cold and out of place and carried a thick metal briefcase and nothing else. The driver had long curly hair on the side of his head with a huge mustache that was turning gray. He had agreed to give them a ride after they waved him down on the side of the road. The driver lit up a marijuana cigarette and offered it to them as he drove. Eddie accepted. Vladdy declined. He wanted to keep his head clear for what was going to happen when they crossed the huge park and came out through the tunnels and crossed the river. Vladdy had not done business in America yet, and he knew that Americans could be tough and ruthless in business. It was one of the qualities that had attracted Vladdy in the first place.

"Don't get too high," Vladdy told Eddie in Czech.

"I won't," Eddie said back, "I'm just a little scared, if that's all right with you. This helps."

"I wish you wouldn't wear that hat," Vladdy said. "You don't look professional."

"I look like Marshall Mathers, I think. Slim Shady," Eddie said, touching the stocking cap that was pulled over his eyebrows. He sounded a little hurt.

"Hey, dudes," the driver said over his shoulder to his passengers in the backseat, "speak American or I'm dropping you off on the side of the road. Deal?"

"Of course," Vladdy said, "we have deal."

"You going to tell me what's in the briefcase?" The driver asked, smiling to show that he wasn't making a threat.

"No, I think not," Vladdy said.

Vladimir and Eduard were branded "Vladdy" and "Eddie" by the man in the human resources office for Yellowstone in Gardiner, Montana, when they showed up to apply for work three weeks before and were told that there were no job openings. Vladdy had explained that there must have been some kind of mix-up, some kind of misunderstanding, because they had been assured by the agent in Prague that both of them had been accepted to work for the official park concessionaire for the whole summer and into the fall. Vladdy showed the paperwork that allowed them to work on a visa for six months.

Yellowstone, like a microcosm of America, was a place of wonders, and it sought eastern Europeans to work making beds, washing dishes, and cleaning out the muck from the trail horses, jobs that American workers didn't want or need. Many Czechs Vladdy and Eddie knew had come here, and some had stayed. It was good work in a fantastic place, "a setting from a dream of nature," as Vladdy put it. But the man at human resources said he was sorry, that they were overstaffed, and that there was nothing he could do until somebody quit and a slot opened up. Even if that happened, the nonhiring man said, there were people on the list in front of them.

Vladdy had explained in his almost-perfect English, he thought, that he and Eddie didn't have the money to go back. In fact, he told the man, they didn't even have the money for a room to wait in. What they had was on their backs—cracked black leather jackets, ill-fitting clothes, street shoes. Eddie wore the stocking cap because he liked Eminem, but Vladdy preferred his slicked-back hair look. They looked nothing like the other young people their age they saw in the office and on the streets.

"Keep in touch," the hiring man had told Vladdy. "Check back every few days."

"I can't even buy cigarettes," Vladdy had pleaded.

The man felt sorry for them and gave them a twenty-dollar bill out of his own wallet.

"I told you we should have gone to Detroit," Eddie said to Vladdy in Czech.

Vladdy pressed his forehead against the cold glass of the van window as they drove. The metal briefcase was on the floor, between his legs.

He had not yet seen the whole park since he had been here, and it was

something he very much wanted to do. He had read about the place since he
was young, and watched documentaries on it on television. He knew there
were three kinds of thermal activity: geysers, mud pots, and fumaroles. He
knew there were over ten thousand places where the molten core of the
earth broke through the thin crust. He knew that the park was the home of
bison, elk, mountain sheep, and many fishes. People from all over the world
came here to see it, smell it, feel it. Vladdy was still outside of it, though,
looking in, like Yellowstone Park was still on a television show and not right
in front of him. He wouldn't allow himself to become a part of this place
yet. That would come later.

Eddie was talking to the driver, talking too much, Vladdy thought. Eddie's English was very poor. It was embarrassing. Eddie was telling the
driver about Prague, about the beautiful women there. The driver said he always wanted to go to Prague. Eddie tried to describe the buildings, but was
doing a bad job of it.

"I don't care about buildings," the driver said. "Tell me about the
women."

The girl, Cherry, would be angry with him at first, Vladdy knew that. While
she was at work at the motel that day, Vladdy had sold her good stereo and
DVD unit to a man in a pawn shop full of rifles for $115, less $90 for a .22
pistol with a broken handgrip. But when she found out why he had done it,
he was sure she would come around. The whole thing was kind of her idea
in the first place, after all.

Vladdy and Eddie had spent that first unhappy day after meeting the nonhiring man in a place called K-Bar Pizza in Gardiner, Montana. They sat at
a round table and were so close to the human resources building that when
the door to the K-Bar opened they could see it out there. Vladdy had
placed the twenty-dollar bill on the table and ordered two tap beers, which
they both agreed were awful. Then they ordered a Budweiser, which was
nothing like the Czechoslovakian Budweiser, and they laughed about that.
Cherry was their waitress. She told Vladdy she was from Kansas, some
place like that. He could tell she was uncomfortable with herself, with her
appearance, because she was a little fat and had a crooked face. She told
Vladdy she was divorced, with a kid, and she worked at the K-Bar to sup-
plement her income. She also had a job at a motel, servicing rooms. He
could tell she was flattered by his attention, by his leather jacket, his hair,
his smile, his accent. Sometimes women reacted this way to him, and he appreciated it. He didn't know if his looks would work in America, and he
still didn't know. But they worked in Gardiner, Montana. Vladdy knew he

had found a friend when she let them keep ordering even though the twenty dollars was spent, and she didn't discourage them from staying until her shift was over.

Cherry led them down the steep, cracked sidewalks and down an alley to an old building backed up to the edge of a canyon. Vladdy looked around as he followed. He didn't understand Gardiner. In every direction he looked, he could only see space. Mountains, bare hillsides, an empty valley going north, under the biggest sky he had ever seen. Yet Gardiner was packed together. Houses almost touched houses, windows opened up to other windows. It was like a tiny island in an ocean of . . . nothing. Vladdy decided he would find out about this.

She made them stand in the hallway while she went in to check to make sure her little boy was in bed, then she let them sleep in the front room of her two-bedroom apartment. That first night, Vladdy waited until Eddie was snoring and then he padded across the linoleum floor in his bare feet and opened Cherry's bedroom door. She was pretending she was asleep, and he said nothing, just stood there in his underwear.

"What do you want?" Cherry asked him sleepily.

"I want to pleasure you," he whispered.

"Don't turn on the light," she said. "I don't want you to look at me."

Afterward, in the dark, Vladdy could hear the furious river below them in the canyon. It sounded so raw, like an angry young river trying to figure out what it wanted to be when it grew up.

While Eddie and Vladdy checked back with the nonhiring man every morning, Vladdy tried to help out around the house since he had no money for rent. He tried to fix the dripping faucet but couldn't find any tools in the apartment besides an old pair of pliers and something cheap designed to slice potatoes. He mopped the floors, though, and washed her windows. He fixed her leaking toilet with the pliers. While he did this, Eddie sat on the couch and watched television, MTV mostly. Cherry's kid, Tony, sat with Eddie and watched and wouldn't even change out of his pajamas and get dressed unless Vladdy told him to do so.

Vladdy was taking the garbage out to the Dumpster when he first saw Cherry's neighbor, a man whose name he later learned was Bob. Vladdy thought it was funny, and very American, to have a one-syllable name like "Bob." It made him laugh inside.

Bob pulled up to the building in a dark, massive four-wheel-drive car. The car was mud splashed, scratched, and dented, even though it didn't look very old. It was a huge car, and Vladdy recognized it as a Suburban. Vladdy watched as Bob came out of the car. Bob had a hard, impatient look on his face. He wore dirty blue jeans, a sweatshirt, a fleece vest, and a baseball cap, like everyone else did in Gardiner.

Bob stepped away from the back of the Suburban, slammed both doors, and locked it with a remote. That's when Vladdy first saw the metal briefcase. It was the briefcase Bob was retrieving from the back of the Suburban.

And with that, Bob went into the building.

That night, after Eddie and Tony had gone out to bring back fried chicken from the deli at the grocery store for dinner, Vladdy asked Cherry about her neighbor, Bob. He described the metal briefcase.

"I'd stay away from him, if I was you," Cherry said. "I've got my suspicions about that Bob."

Vladdy was confused.

"I hear things at the K-Bar," Cherry said. "I seen him in there a couple of times by himself. He's not the friendliest guy I've ever met."

"He's not like me," Vladdy said, reaching across the table and brushing a strand of her hair out of her eyes.

Cherry sat back in the chair and studied Vladdy. "No, he's not like you," she said.

After pleasuring Cherry, Vladdy waited until she was asleep before he crept through the dark front room where Eddie was sleeping. Vladdy found a flashlight in a drawer in the kitchen and slipped outside into the hallway. He went down the stairs in his underwear, went outside, and approached the back of the Suburban.

Turning on the flashlight, he saw rumpled clothing, rolls of maps, hiking boots, and electrical equipment with dials and gauges. He noticed a square of open carpet where the metal briefcase sat when Bob wasn't carrying it around. He wondered if Bob wasn't some kind of engineer, or a scientist of some kind. He wondered where it was that Bob went every day to do his work, and what he kept in the metal briefcase that couldn't be left with the rest of his things.

Vladdy had taken classes in geology and geography and chemistry. He had done well in them, and he wondered if maybe Bob needed some help, needed an assistant. At least until a job opened up in the park.

Cherry surprised them by bringing two bottles of Jack Daniel's home after her shift at the K-Bar, and they had whiskey on ice while they ate Lean Cuisine dinners. They kept drinking afterward at the table. Vladdy suspected that Cherry had stolen the bottles from behind the bar, but said nothing because he was enjoying himself and he wanted to ask her about Bob. Eddie was getting pretty drunk, and was telling funny stories in Czech that Cherry and Tony didn't understand. But the way he told them made everyone laugh. Tony said he wanted a drink, too, and Eddie started to pour him one until Vladdy told Eddie not to do it. Eddie took his own drink to the couch, sulking, the evening ruined for him, he said.

"Cherry," Vladdy said, "I feel bad inside that I cannot pay rent."

Cherry waved him off. "You pay the rent in other ways," she laughed. "My floor and windows have never been cleaner. Not to mention your other . . . services."

Vladdy looked over his shoulder to make sure Tony hadn't heard his mother.

"I am serious," Vladdy said, trying to make her look him in the eyes. "I'm a serious man. Because I don't have a job yet, I want to work. I wonder maybe if your neighbor Bob needs an apprentice in his work. Somebody who would get mud on himself if Bob doesn't want to."

Cherry shook her head and smiled, and took a long time to answer. She searched Vladdy's face for something that Vladdy hoped his face had. When she finally spoke, her voice was low, for a change. She leaned her head forward, toward Vladdy.

"I told you I'd heard some things about Bob at the K-Bar," she said softly. "I heard that Bob is a bio pirate. He's a criminal."

"What is this bio pirate?"

He could smell her whiskey breath, but he bent closer. "In Yellowstone, in some of the hot pots and geysers, there are rare microorganisms that can only be found here. Our government is studying some of them legitimately, trying to find out if they could be a cure for cancer, or maybe a bioweapon, or whatever. It's illegal to take them out of the park. But the rumor is there are some people stealing the microbes and selling them. You know, bio pirates."

Vladdy sat back for a moment to think. Her eyes burned into his as they never had before. It was the whiskey, sure, but it was something else.

"The metal briefcase," Vladdy whispered. "That's where he keep the microbes."

Cherry nodded enthusiastically. "Who knows what they're worth? Or better yet, who knows what someone would pay us to give them back and not say anything about it?"

Vladdy felt a double-edged chill, of both excitement and fear. This Cherry, he thought, she didn't just come up with this. She had been thinking about it for a while.

"Next time he's at the K-Bar, I'll call you," she said. "He doesn't bring his briefcase with him there. He keeps it next door, in his apartment, when he goes out at night. That's where it will be when I call you."

"Hey," Tony called from the couch, "what are you two whispering about over there?"

"They talk *fornication*," Eddie said with a slur, making Tony laugh. As far as Vladdy knew, it was Eddie's first American sentence.

Vladdy was wiping the counter clean with Listerine—he loved Listerine, and thought it was the best disinfectant in the entire world—when the telephone rang. A bolt shot up his spine. He looked around. Eddie and Tony were watching television.

It was Cherry. "He's here at the K-Bar, and he ordered a pitcher just for himself. He's settling in for a while."

"Settling in?" Vladdy asked, not understanding.

"Jesus," she said. "I mean he'll be here for a while. Which means his briefcase is in his apartment. Come on, Vladdy."

"I understand," Vladdy said.

"Get over there," Cherry said. "I love you."

Vladdy had thought about this, the fact that he didn't love Cherry. He liked her, he appreciated her kindness, he felt obligated to her, but he didn't love her at all. So he used a phrase he had heard in the grocery store.

"You bet," he said.

Hanging up, he asked Eddie to take Tony to the grocery store and get him some ice cream. Eddie winked at Vladdy as they left, because Vladdy had told Eddie about the bio pirates.

The metal briefcase wasn't hard to find, and the search was much easier than shinnying along a two-inch ridge of brick outside the window in his shiny street shoes with the mad river roaring somewhere in the dark beneath him. He was happy that Bob's outside window slid open easily, and he stepped through the open window into Bob's kitchen sink, cracking a dirty plate with his heel.

It made some sense that the metal case was in the refrigerator, on a large shelf of its own, and he pulled it out by the handle, which was cold.

Back in Cherry's apartment, he realized he was still shivering, and it wasn't from the temperature outside. But he opened the briefcase on the kitchen table. Yes, there were glass vials filled with murky water. Cherry was right. And in the inside of the top of the briefcase was a taped business card. There was Bob's name and a cell phone number on the business card.

Vladdy poured the last of the Jack Daniel's that Cherry had stolen into a water glass, and drank most of it. He waited until the burn developed in his throat before he dialed.

"What?" Bob answered. Vladdy pictured Bob sitting at a table in the K-Bar. He wondered if Cherry was watching.

"I have an important briefcase, full of water samples," Vladdy said, trying to keep his voice deep and level. "I found it in your flat."

"Who in the hell are *you*? How did you get my number?"

Vladdy remembered a line from an American movie he saw at home. "I am your worst nightmare," he said. It felt good to say it.

"Where are you from that you talk like that?" Bob asked. "How in the hell did you get into my apartment?"

Vladdy didn't answer. He didn't know what to say.

"Damn it," Bob said, "what do you want?"

Vladdy breathed deeply, tried to stay calm. "I want two thousand dollars for your metal briefcase, and I won't say a word about it to anyone."

"Two thousand?" Bob said, in a dismissive way that instantly made Vladdy wish he had asked for ten thousand, or twenty thousand. "I don't have that much cash on me. I'll have to get it in Cody tomorrow, at my bank."

"Yes, that would be fine," Vladdy said.

Silence. Thinking. Vladdy could hear something in the background, probably the television above the bar.

"Okay," Bob said. "Meet me tomorrow night at eleven P.M. on the turnout after the tunnels on the Buffalo Bill Dam. East entrance, on the way to Cody. Don't bring anybody with you, and don't tell anyone about this conversation. If you do, I'll know."

Vladdy felt an icy hand reach down his throat and grip his bowels. This was real, after all. This was American business, and he was committed. *Stay tough*, he told himself.

"I have a partner," Vladdy said. "He comes with me."

More silence. Then a sigh. "Him only," the man said. "No one else."

"Okay."

"I'll be in a dark Suburban, parked in the turnout."

"Okay." Vladdy knew the vehicle, of course, but he couldn't give that away.

"If you show up with more than your partner, or if there are any other vehicles on the road, this deal is over. And I mean over in the worst possible sense. You understand?"

Vladdy paused, and the telephone nearly slipped out of his sweaty hand like a bar of soap.

"Okay," Vladdy said. When he hung up the telephone it rattled so hard in the cradle from his hand that it took him two tries.

Vladdy and Eddie sat in silence on the couch and listened as Bob crashed around in his apartment next door. Had Vladdy left any clues next door, he wondered? Eddie looked scared and had the broken .22 pistol on his lap. After an hour, the crashing stopped. Vladdy and Eddie watched Cherry's door, praying that Bob wouldn't realize they were there and smash through it.

"I think we're okay," Vladdy said, finally. "He doesn't know who took it."

Vladdy kept his cheek pressed against the cold window as they left Yellowstone Park. He closed his eyes temporarily as the van rumbled through the east entrance, then opened them and noted the sign that read ENTERING SHOSHONE NATIONAL FOREST.

Eddie was still talking, still smoking. He had long ago worked his way into the front so he sat next to the driver. A second marijuana cigarette had been passed back and forth. The driver was talking about democracy versus socialism, and was for the latter. Vladdy thought the driver was an idiot, an idiot who pined for a forgotten political system that had never, ever, worked, and a system that Vladdy despised. But Vladdy said nothing, because Eddie wouldn't stop talking, wouldn't quit agreeing with the driver.

They went through three tunnels lit by orange ambient light, and Vladdy stared through the glass. The Shoshone River serpentined below them, reflecting the moonlight. They crossed it on a bridge.

"Let us off here," Vladdy said, as they cleared the last tunnel and the reservoir sparkled beneath the moon and starlight to the right as far as he could see.

The driver slowed, then turned around in his seat. "Are you sure?" he asked. "There's nothing out here except for the dam. It's another half hour to Cody and not much in between."

"This is our place," Vladdy said. "Thank you for the drive."

The van braked, and stopped.

"Are you sure?" the driver asked.

"Pay him, Eddie," Vladdy said, sliding across the seat toward the door with the metal briefcase. He listened vaguely as the driver insisted he needed no payment and as Eddie tried to stuff a twenty in the driver's pocket. Which he did, eventually, and the van pulled away en route to Cody, which was a cream-colored smudge in the distance, like an inverted half-moon against the dark eastern sky.

"What now?" Eddie asked, and Vladdy and Eddie walked along the dark shoulder of the road, crunching gravel beneath their shoes.

"Now?" Vladdy said in English, "I don't know. You've got the gun in your pants, right? You may need to use it as a threat. You've got it, right?"

Eddie did a hitch in his step, as he dug through his coat.

"I got it, Vladdy," Eddie said, "but it is small."

*　　*　　*

Vladdy's teeth began to chatter as they approached the pullout and he saw the Suburban. The vehicle was parked on the far side of the lot, backed up against the railing of the dam. The car was dark.

"Are you scared?" Eddie asked. He was still high.

"Just cold," Vladdy lied.

Vladdy's legs felt weak, and he concentrated on walking forward toward the big car.

Vladdy said, "Don't smile at him. Look tough."

"*Tough*," Eddie repeated.

Vladdy said to Eddie, "I told you to look professional but you look like Eminem."

"Slim Shady is my *man*," Eddie whined.

At twenty yards, the headlights blinded them. Vladdy put his arm up to shield his eyes. Then the headlights went out and he heard a car door open and slam shut. He couldn't see anything now, but heard fast-moving footfalls coming across the gravel.

Vladdy's eyes readjusted to the darkness in time to see Bob raise a pistol and shoot Eddie point-blank in the forehead, right through his stocking cap. Eddie dropped straight down as if his legs had been kicked out from under him, and he landed in a heap.

"Some fuckin' nightmare," Bob said, pointing the pistol at Vladdy. "Where are you boys *from*?"

Instinctively, Vladdy fell back. As he did so, he raised the metal briefcase and felt a shock through his hand and arm as a bullet smashed into it. On the ground, Vladdy heard a cry and realized that it had come from inside of him. He thrashed and rolled away, and Bob cursed and fired another booming shot into the dirt near Vladdy's ear.

Vladdy leaped forward and swung the briefcase as hard as he could, and by pure chance it hit hard into Bob's kneecaps. Bob grunted and pitched forward, nearly onto Vladdy. In the dark, Vladdy had no idea where Bob's gun was, but he scrambled to his feet and clubbed at Bob with the briefcase.

Bob said, "Stop!" but all Vladdy could see was the muzzle flash on Eddie's face a moment before.

"Stop! I've got the—" Vladdy smashed the briefcase down as hard as he could and stopped the sentence. Bob lay still.

Breathing hard, Vladdy dropped the briefcase and fell on top of Bob. He tore through Bob's clothing and found the gun that shot Eddie. Bob moaned, and Vladdy shot him in the eye with it.

With tears streaming down his face, Vladdy buckled Eddie's and Bob's belts together and rolled them off of the dam. He heard the bodies thump into some rocks and then splash into the reservoir. He threw the pistol as far as he could and it went into the water with a *ploop*. The briefcase followed.

He found a vinyl bag on the front seat of the Suburban that bulged with two thousand dollars in cash. It puzzled Vladdy for a moment, but then it made sense. Bob had flashed his lights to see who had taken his briefcase. When he saw two out-of-place guys like Vladdy and Eddie—*especially* Eddie—Bob made his choice not to pay.

Vladdy drove back through Yellowstone Park in the Suburban, thinking of Eddie, thinking of what he had done. He would buy some new clothes, new shoes, one of those fleece vests. Get a baseball cap, maybe.

He parked on a pullout on the northern shore of Yellowstone Lake and watched the sun come up. Steam rose from hot spots along the bank, and a V of Canada geese made a long graceful descent onto the surface of the water.

He felt a part of it, now.

A setting from a dream of nature, he thought.

The Real Thing
GREGG HURWITZ

ABBUD'S HEAD HAD been blown apart by sniper fire, his scalp lying beside the bone like a bad rug or a misplaced halo. Ebi Al-Mansouri stood frozen in place, bits of window glass embedded in his bearded face, his heart hammering so loudly it seemed to jar his vision. Bullets split the fifth-story flat, raining in from all sides. CNN squawked from the miraculously still-intact TV in the corner, providing horrifying helo footage of the ambush in progress: "terrorist cell identified on this block of Hell's Kitchen, rumored to have biological weapons of mass—" A fresh volley of bullets chiseled chunks of plaster from the ceiling.

Ghassan was leaning propped against the wall, hands pressed to his gut, which had gone black and shiny. A crimson bubble swelled at his lips with his breath. There were bodies everywhere, blood and gray matter swathing the white walls in swoops and flicks.

Ghassan looked at Ebi. "Go," he croaked. With the word, the bubble at his lips popped. "Take the package." He fell over.

Ebi leapt over his fallen cell member, his foot striking one of the dropped AK-47s and sending it into a lazy, scraping rotation on the hardwood floor. He dove behind the couch, not yet aware that the onslaught had halted.

At the window, Habid returned fire from a one-knee crouch. A single crack, then a sniper bullet struck his skull with a dull thud. He slumped forward, head and arm draped out the window, his weapon dangling uselessly from his neck.

Ebi raised his head and took in the carnage. Dust danced in the shafts of artificial light, settling over the sticky corpses. An almost peaceful tableau. He crawled forward, plucked the softball-sized package from its foam nesting in a metal briefcase, and flattened against the floor. The ice-blue light of the timer, inset on the steel exterior, was in countdown. Just under twenty-three minutes until it would burst open with terrific force, sending out a deadly mist of aerosol-infectious Ebola-smallpox. A nasty little hybrid—the killer effect of Ebola combined with the communicability of smallpox. Once a pathogen like that got loose in the world, there would be no closing Pandora's box. The package hummed and vibrated in Ebi's sweaty hands.

There was no way to stop the countdown. Abbud, the engineer, had made sure of that.

The TV now sat on end on the floor; one of the stand's legs had splintered out from under it. Words spat from the screen, edged with fuzz. Ebi's cheek was mashed against the floor; from his terrified sprawl, the picture appeared perfectly upright.

"—so-called total containment vessel summoned to the scene from Fort Dix, New Jersey, is stranded in the flooding at the west mouth of the Lincoln Tunnel. The tunnel has been closed since last Monday, when a suicide bomber blew out an embankment—"

Ebi's face remained blank as the shot cut away to a six-foot metal globe lashed with thick metal chains to the bed of a massive truck. The vehicle was stranded in a wash of murky liquid at the Weehawken side of the tunnel. The total containment vessel, with its 1.5-inch high-strength, high-impact steel, was designed for the express purpose of sustaining a massive explosion in its belly without leaking a puff of air.

America's last hope for preventing a deadly epidemic was spinning its wheels in the sludge of a neighboring state.

Gathered around the TCV was a phalanx of emergency response vehicles, their lights flashing meekly into the thickening dusk. FBI agents gathered around the sawhorses, pacing, shouting orders into radios and barking into cell phones. A gathering of some of America's most valuable terrorist fighters.

The building shook as the front door smashed open and legions of invading boots tramped up the stairs. The ice-blue timer near Ebi's nose was now at twenty-two minutes.

He rolled to the door, which had been picked apart by gunfire, and into the hall. The footsteps were louder now; it seemed any second a torrent of agents would round the corner and riddle him with bullets. He popped to his feet and sprinted down the hall, gripping the package tightly so the sleek ball wouldn't slip from his grasp. In e-mail correspondence, they'd referred to the package only by its ironically understated code name—Cherry Bomb—but someone had cracked their formula nonetheless.

The hall's terminating window looked out on the rusty fire escape of the neighboring building. The drop stretched sixty feet to concrete. Ebi stuffed the package in the pocket of his jacket, praying it wouldn't fall out. His hands trembled as he slid the pane open and placed one sneaker on the ledge. Agents spilled into the hall behind him, shouting and shuffling, then a cop looked up from the alley below, shouted, and grabbed his gun.

Ebi was airborne before he realized he'd jumped. He felt a bullet strike him under the arm and he shrieked, spun around midair, and crashed into the fire escape across the alley. Bullets were pinging off the metal around him. He pulled himself up and through the door, running down another hallway, no time to check his wound.

Another window, another jump, another fire escape, this time with no one in the alley below. As he dashed down the corridor, a woman returning home with groceries yelped and flattened herself against her door, keys jangling unturned in the lock. Ebi half fell, half ran down the stairs, taking them three, four at a time. He stumbled through the lobby and out onto the street, chest lurching. A mass of flashing lights illuminated the neighboring block.

He turned the opposite direction, limping now, and ran toward Ninth Avenue. A stream of blood tickled his ribs, soaking his new jeans at the waistline. He reached back inside his jacket as if grabbing a gun from a shoulder holster and pressed his palm against his slick flesh. A hole in his lateral muscle, just beneath his armpit. Exit wound a few inches to the back. Not fatal, but he was losing blood fast. A passing bicycle messenger took note of his blood-drenched shirt and veered sharply out of his way. Ebi wished he could change his shirt, but with eighteen minutes on the timer, he'd just have to remember to stay cool, don't grimace, don't smile, just keep your head down and walk. Lessons he'd learned all too well as an Arab man in America.

A hot dog vendor had his radio cranked high. A group of drunk college kids in blazers and ties were gathered around the cart, hot dogs forgotten in their hands. Listening to the newscast.

"—report some progress draining the flooding at the Lincoln Tunnel, but little chance the biological warfare response equipment will make it through anytime soon. In retrospect, the GW bridge or Holland Tunnel would have been better—"

One of them looked up, knocked his buddy with the back of his hand, and pointed at Ebi.

"—Arab guy with the blood."

"—probably one of the ragheads who—"

One of them raised a cell phone to his head.

Ebi started jogging away, though his side had thawed from numbness and was beginning to ache. A bunch of people had gathered around an electronics store window, where twenty or so TVs were blaring diverse news coverage of the event. An attractive blond anchor spoke from the loudest TV.

"—one cell member, believed to be injured, is at large."

Three burly guys took note of Ebi limping by. Heads swiveled to the screens, then back to him. One of them wore a stretched T-shirt with an American flag, scruffy hair protruding from beneath a Yankees cap.

"There's the motherfucker!" he yelled.

Ebi bolted, almost knocking over a thin-necked girl zoning out on her Walkman. He turned down an alley with a maze of dripping pipes overhead. The three men were in pursuit, shouting at him; he could hear their shoes splashing through puddles.

"Fucking sand nigger!"

"We're gonna beat your brown ass."

Big as his pursuers were, the throbbing in Ebi's side slowed him to almost their pace. And then they were gaining, the drumroll beat of their footsteps quickening behind him.

The alley dead-ended in a chain-link fence. He had only a few moments to register blind panic at the prospect of being torn apart in an unlit alley before he struck the fence hard, almost falling into it. He summoned strength from somewhere deep inside himself and climbed, yelling a wavering animal cry at the screeching pain in his side. One of the men leaped and grabbed his shoe and Ebi shrieked and yanked. His foot pulled free of the shoe. He rolled over the fence top and fell the ten feet to the ground, landing on all fours, palms and knees striking asphalt. The package rolled free of his pocket, striking the fence and rebounding toward him. He scooped it up with trembling hands. No cracks. Fifteen minutes, twenty-three seconds and counting.

The men were cursing at him, their faces lit with rage and hatred. One of them was climbing the fence, which bowed under his weight. Another spit at Ebi, the gob just missing his cheek.

He thought to himself calmly: Get up, Ebi. Keep running. The stakes are too high for you to give up. You'll get it done, *Inshallah*.

He rose and limped a few yards down the alley, his wet sock slapping ground. A back kitchen door was open and he ducked through, colliding with a sous-chef who sent a tossed salad airborne. He moved through the restaurant, now grunting against the pain. Utensils clinked to plates; white faces pivoted. He made it out onto the sidewalk again. Sirens were screaming, but he couldn't tell if they were approaching. He glanced at a street sign to get his bearings—Thirty-eighth.

He staggered forward, moving toward Ninth, leaving drops of blood on the concrete. He'd given up any hope of maintaining low visibility; people parted before him. Most stared, all blind hate and disgust. Some had likely heard the news broadcast; some had not—it probably wouldn't change most of their reactions to a bleeding Arab. He was deep in enemy territory; he did his best to keep to the side of the street.

He thought about his childhood, moving from Saudi Arabia to Manhattan at the age of five. The schoolyard beatings, the tauntings in bars, the rousting by cops when he crossed into the wrong neighborhood. His father, an intensely patriotic and appreciative man, kept a copy of the U.S. Constitution on the refrigerator door; Ebi had read a line from it every time he got a soda or a snack. This is the greatest country in the world, his father would tell him. You have no idea of this country's greatness. He'd listen respectfully, usually hiding a bruise beneath his T-shirt or the latest hate note in his school bag.

As a young man, he'd returned to Saudi Arabia, and from there, he'd found himself winding his way deeper and deeper into religious study, his journey ending at the Farmada training camp outside of Jelalabad. It had been hard winning their trust, convincing them he really was true. He'd done so at gunpoint—on firing ranges and obstacle courses, never letting them smell his fear. Once, he'd stood in the middle of a TV transmission of Bush and fired at the screen to a roar of spontaneous applause.

Jelalabad had been a trial and a pleasure, knowing the great events the future stored for him. Knowing how necessary he was for a great cause. He remembered his time there as a blur of images and sensations—rice with dates and raisins, brilliant gold and red sunsets, dust so thick he could feel it coating his lungs. One day the wind had whipped so hard it had caused a brownout; he'd huddled in a cave reeking of chappali kebab, knowing that someday it would all be worth it.

By the time Ebi reached Ninth Avenue, he was lightheaded and knew he was close to fainting. He couldn't run much farther. A glance at the package showed he had just under ten minutes now before the plague was unleashed.

As his breathing grew panicked, his thoughts stayed calm. You gotta make it, Ebi. You gotta catch yourself a ride.

A cab had been left at the curb, its driver a few steps away buying a knish. Ebi slid behind the wheel and pulled out. The driver dropped his food and gave chase on foot, but Ebi screeched across the street, crashed through the sawhorses blocking off the Lincoln Tunnel, and shot into the darkness.

The package's vibrating quickened in his pocket. Overhead, great air ducts swept gusts to two states. The tunnel's emptiness was hypnotic—nothing but the hum of the wheels, the lights flying past, abandoned construction equipment in the slow lane. His head felt even lighter and he cursed himself to stay conscious. Not much longer; his mission was almost complete.

His blood had almost soaked through the side of his jacket. He removed the package and set it on the passenger seat. The timer was now at five minutes. He started the Salah prayer, softly.

His vision spotted, then cleared. Up ahead, police lights flashed off a pool of waist-deep water that claimed the whole west entrance to the tunnel. At least twenty FBI agents, six NYPD units—half a joint task force standing around helplessly, watching a truck's tires spin listlessly in the mud and water.

Ebi slowed down, his sweat-drenched hands slipping on the wheel and causing the cab to skip the raised curb and smash into the wall of the tunnel. The package rolled from the passenger seat onto the floor. He reached for it, but was having trouble seeing—he realized through a cacophony of thoughts that he'd struck his forehead on the dash and was bleeding into his eyes. His fingers grasped the deadly steel ball.

He kicked open his door, pulled himself out, and found himself facing nearly fifty gun barrels across the twenty-foot stretch of water. He held the package up over his head with both hands as he waded into the enormous pool, his cries drowned out by myriad shouted commands. He emerged from the water, screaming to be heard. Two agents rushed him, one striking him in the face with the butt of his gun. Ebi went to a knee, then rose, then Harry Williams appeared from nowhere like an angel, his FBI task force windbreaker fluttering; he was yelling, "Goddamnit. Back off! Back the hell off him."

Ebi rose and staggered toward the total containment vessel, still moored to the stranded truck, shouting to the attending Explosive Ordnance Detail tech, "Open the hatch!" The timer was inside of two minutes.

The tech climbed up on the truck's bed and swung open the door in the side of the massive steel globe. Ebi limped over and tossed the package inside. It bounced twice, rattling and echoing, and the tech slammed the hatch shut and secured it. Ebi leaned over, hands on his knees. The men waited, breathing together, staring with wide eyes at the big metal ball.

A loud crack as the package detonated. The TCV rocked on its moorings, snapping one of its anchoring chains. It settled back into place. Intact.

A massive collective sigh. A chorus of celebratory cries.

Harry walked over to Ebi and helped straighten him up. "Jesus Christ. Two years counterintelligence and you're alive." The two men embraced, Harry murmuring, "You made it, you made it, you made it."

Ebi nodded, his breath starting to hitch in his throat. "*Mashallah*," he managed.

Harry hugged him tighter. The cops and other agents were standing around, watching with shy smiles and budding comprehension.

Harry released him, but Ebi clung to him even tighter, knowing he would fall if he let go. Harry shouldered his weight, ducking under his good arm, and started walking him to the waiting ambulance.

"It's good to have you back, friend," he said.

A Little Early in the Day
MICHAEL JOHN RICHARDSON

I'VE OWNED THIS bar for a little over twenty years now, and I can tell you that most of the people who walk through my doors can be placed into four basic categories, the first bein' the Party People. They get to the bar round ten at night, lookin' to have a good time and maybe find someone they can take home with them.

The second are the Social Drinkers. They usually get to a bar shortly after work, right around six-thirty or seven. Most have had a pretty crappy day behind a desk, or under their boss's thumb, and they're lookin' to wind down with a coupla friends before fightin' the traffic home.

Next are the Sad Sacks. They shuffle in about three to five in the afternoon, lookin' to get seriously plastered. These people are usually the one-time drunks. People who've had somethin' really shitty happen to them in the last day or two. They're lookin' for comfort at the bottom of a bottle and a kind face behind the bar. They just want to forget, even if it's only for a little while.

Then there's your Hard Core Drunks. They come in all shapes and sizes and usually will hit a bar about noon. These I call my regulars. They keep the bar runnin'. Most aren't any trouble. They drink until they pass out or puke, then I put them in a cab and send them on their merry way.

Of course, there are always exceptions to the rules, the ones that refuse to be pigeonholed. And some days, dependin' on who stumbles in, it just ain't worth openin' my doors at all.

Like today, I opened the bar at ten. I was tryin' to get a little ahead of some of the work I had to do, you know, before the regulars show up. A kid I know was my first customer, and while I was workin' on replacin' the filter on one of the taps, he was workin' on his third Bud. It was still before ten-thirty and we were the only ones in the place.

It was Mike DeCurso. Sometimes we call him Mikey, sometimes Da Cursed One. Of course, not to him or his father's face. Anyway, he drained the last out of his bottle, then slapped it and a fiver on the bar. "Set 'em up, Joe." Mike thought he was a comedian but he's the type that the world laughs at, not with.

So, I shot him a look that said to shut the fuck up and this little punk started bustin' my balls.

"What's wrong, Joey? I thought all you ol' timers were Sinatra fans? I thought that everybody loved Frank."

I placed a bottle down on the counter in front of him, nice and easy. "I never much cared for the Rat Pack. Just a bunch of Hollywood sissies playin' at bein' gangsters."

"You gotta be kiddin' me. They was the coolest thing goin'." Mikey tipped back the bottle and drained half of it in one go. "You know, they say Sinatra was connected."

I shook my head and punched up $3.75 on the register. "They got nothin', Mikey. They couldn't prove a thing."

"That's cuz Sinatra was slick, man. With that Lawford guy in his group, he had the Kennedys in his hip pocket."

"Till they shot John."

"That goes without sayin'." Mikey finished his beer and slammed the bottle down hard on the bar top. "Hit me again."

I gotta tell you, this little snot was startin' to piss me off. I just had my bar resurfaced less than a month ago and here he was, dingin' the shit out of it. "You fuckin' do that again and I'll smack you upside your head."

He looked at me like I was speakin' friggin' Greek.

"I got a bat under here, understand?"

Some guys just don't listen. "Come on, Mikey, why don't you just give it up and go to work? Better yet, go home and get some sleep. It's a little early in the day to get yourself shit-faced."

"I'm of age."

"Barely." I snatched the empty from in front of him and shook it in warnin'. Some beer shot out the end and landed on his jacket. He didn't even notice. And it was real leather, too. "Your mom ain't gonna be none too friendly with me if you go out and do somethin' stupid after I let you get drunk."

"I ain't gonna do nothin' stupid."

I eyeballed him and he didn't look too frosted, so I put a fresh bottle and a glass in front of him. "This'd better last you a good ten minutes or I'm tossin' you out on your ear. The only reason I'm servin' you in the first place is because your old man and I went way back."

Mikey shook his head and started to nurse his brew. When he went back to watchin' the highlights from last night's Met's game, I figured that was the last of it and went back to workin' on the beer tap.

"Why is it, Joe, that every guy I know has a Y on the end of his name?"

"What the hell you talkin' about, Mikey?"

"You know, Bobby . . . Pauly . . . Jimmy . . ."

"It's a throwback to the old days when everybody still had a nickname. It just, I don't know, flowed."

Mikey's eyebrows furrowed.

This kid was as thick as a brick and twice as stupid. "You know, Freddy, the Freak, Eddy, the Eel . . ." I had just managed to get the fulcrum back on the tap when Mikey decided to blow. He kicked his bar stool halfway across my freshly waxed floor, smashed his glass against the pool table, and knocked a fuckin' bowl of pretzels into my sink. I had a coupla clean pitchers soakin' in there!

He was screamin' like a whore with her tits caught in a vice. "Goddamn him, Joe!"

"Okay, that's it. I'm cuttin' you off and callin' a cab."

"How the hell could he take that fat fuck Eddie instead of me, Joey? How?"

"I don't know, Mike. Maybe . . ."

"Maybe nothin'. He had to know that I'd watch his back. Hell, Eddie don't even own a gun. What was he gonna to do, talk 'em to death?"

"Eddie was a good guy."

"Eddie was a friggin' coward. You know how they found him? Face down in the gutter, shot in the back. The only way that happens is if you're runnin' away!"

I couldn't believe what I was hearin'. "Hey, coulda been an ambush. If they came up behind them, they woulda never had a chance."

Mike slammed his fists down on the bar. "I shoulda been with them. Three's always better than two! I coulda helped . . ."

My hand was edgin' toward my Louisville Slugger while I was tryin' to keep him calm. "Mike, you gotta know, Frank was only lookin' out for you."

"Bullshit!"

"Mike, it was for your own good. You oughta show Frank a little more respect."

"Nah, he was a selfish bastard who didn't want to cut me in on the deal. Fuck him!" Mikey slammed his empty bottle down so hard that it shattered in his hand, several pieces of brown glass cuttin' him good. "Fuck!"

"All right, that's it. You're headed for . . ." Then I finally saw the blood. "Jeez, Mikey, will you look at what the fuck you did? We gotta put somethin' on that before it gets infected."

"Screw it. I'll be fine."

I grabbed a cheap bottle of bourbon. "Get your ass over here and put your hand over the sink."

"Just give me a towel or somethin'."

"You're bleedin'."

"No shit," he said. "I'm okay."

If my eyes were a blowtorch, this little shit woulda been cut in two. I told him, "Let me put it to you another way. I got an inspection comin' up in two days and your blood on my bar is definitely a fineable offense. So get your punk ass over here or get the hell outta my bar . . ."

Mikey thought about it, then slowly made his way round the end of the bar and joined me at the sink.

I uncorked the liquor and grabbed his wrist. "You ready?"

When I poured, Mikey tried to jerk his hand back, but I had hold, and anyone will tell you that when I get my hands on somethin', it don't go nowhere unless I let it. "Don't be no pussy."

"It fuckin' stings."

"No shit." I pulled a couple of pieces of glass from his hand, grabbed a cigarette out of his pack, tore it apart and stuffed the tobacco into two of the larger gashes.

"What the hell's that for?"

"It'll keep the wound clean and help stop the bleedin' 'til we can get you to a hospital."

"Really?"

"Hell, you don't think God intended us to smoke this shit, do you?"

Then all of a sudden, Mikey started to cry.

"What the hell's wrong now?"

Mikey wiped his eyes with his good hand. "Why the fuck didn't he take me with him, Joe? Why?"

What could I say? I took Mikey's face in my hands, like the way my grandpa used to. It left a short smear of blood on his cheek but who the fuck cares? "You know he was in here with Eddie last night before they crossed the tunnel into Manhattan? Eddie asked him the same question."

"What'd he say?"

I couldn't stand it, this little shit had me on the edge of cryin' myself. I told him, "He said that after all the shit your mother gave him when he pawned you guys' radio, he didn't wanna face her if somethin' happened to you."

"So you tellin' me he was a fuckin' wimp."

"No, I'm tellin' you he was tryin' real hard not to lose the most valuable thing he had. He was tryin' real hard to be your father."

I got Mikey out from behind the bar, picked up his jacket, and laid it across his shoulders. "Come on, let's go."

Mikey stopped just inside the door. "Go where?"

Damn, the boy was thick. "We gotta get to the doctor's and get you stitched up." I turned out the lights and locked up.

On the street, I looked him straight in the eyes and tried to smile. "Now, I ain't bein' no wuss neither but I'd hate to think what Cherri'd do to me if I let her only son bleed to death in my bar. 'Specially after just losin' her ol' man."

And you know what the little shit told me as we were walkin' to the doctor's? He said his mother woulda had my nuts in a wringer. You know, some days it just ain't worth doin' nothin' nice for nobody.

Crossing Over
RANDY MICHAEL SIGNOR

TWENTY-EIGHT YEARS DOES things so I wasn't sure the pumped dude across the yard by the free weights was who I thought it was, dude standing there sizing up the equipment, flexing his biceps, so I could see that little ripple all the way over where I was, leaning on a wall south of the ball court.

But then he shot a glance my way, not looking at me or nothing, just one of those quick turnaround looks, see who was watching what, and I knew: It was Joe.

Seeing him kickstarted the strangest shit. Kind of dude made you question things you thought you'd settled.

I was on the downhill part of a twenty-year hit, but hoped to get out in another five or six; this pop another career move gone haywire with the speed of a nightclub fire.

It was my second big fall. Fronted some bearer bonds that turned out I didn't own. A setup from the get-go, run so slick I never gave it a thought and woke up one morning with a cell mate and an empty calendar.

The other one had been twenty-eight years back, for murder. Some story there. It was the night I learned you fuck up in the wrong place at the wrong time, you're owned from then on. In my case, I was owned out of the gate. I got twenty-five to life and got out after a clean sixteen.

I read and worked out, the usual time killers. Saw every episode of *Starsky and Hutch* and knew all the questions you could ask on *Jeopardy!* Picked up a nifty tatt on my arm and a nice bone-white scar that ran down my face, left side, from eyebrow to chin. Little disagreement about who owned what; I got the scar and the thing, whatever it was, can't remember now.

Joe brought back memories. For me, and I bet I did for him.

We'd started out together and here we were again.

And seeing him, seeing his Roman nose, his hair somehow still full and dark, his total ease, my chest tightened, like a sponge getting the water squeezed out of it. My eyes dropped to my crossed feet, had this nice lean going, the exact perfect angle. Arms crossed, too.

At one time he could've asked me anything. We were still babies when we met, our mamas good friends. We did everything together. Kids on the shore, chasing chicks and getting into these hundred mile an hour country-lane road races, run for pink slip, if we could find someone that stupid. Between the two of us, on any given weekend, we could come up with a driveable car, one of ours bound to be running, put together from the week before. No trip too short couldn't be made shorter, every Stop sign a green flag, see how much tire you could leave behind, how much gorgeous roaring noise you could make. We worked hard to be fast and we drove the shit out of things.

No one would race us 'cause it was common knowledge we'd do whatever it took to win and no one wanted to be on the same road with us.

We wandered into a little freelance down-beach loan sharking, drove over a couple townships and pulled some strong-arm stuff, roughed up a couple gamblers leaving after-hours joints, just low-profile shit, knives and baseball bats, not cowboy enough to get the big guys' attention.

But I guess in this world you always get the big guys' attention.

We were sitting in a car—Joe's, I think; Southside Johnny and the Jukes were on the radio—and this other car, a black Caddy, pulled up side us, the window rolled down and in there were two guys the size of something kept in a zoo, dark suits, hats, faces round like bowling balls. And nothing anywhere close to a smile.

Voice rolled out the window, said, "You guys are out of business, as of this minute."

No hello, no asking who we were.

Joe looked at me, like I had something bright to add, then at the guy behind the wheel, and said, "You the cross-river employment agency?"

The two guys gave each other a look, a practiced version of indignation, like they weren't supposed to believe what they'd heard. The one riding shotgun, he shook his head, maybe smiled or laughed, hard to say.

The guy behind the wheel said to his partner, "Why is it always like this?" Then he returned his attention to us. "If it helps you punks any, think of us as the last thing you'll see on the planet. Any part of that unclear?"

Joe met the guy's eyes, I counted the passing seconds, then Joe nodded, said, "Sure, message delivered. But you can take one back, too, tell Little Suits Tony that we are willing to field job offers."

Said it just like that, "field job offers," like this was the Sears Roebuck and he'd applied for a job selling wool-blend suits.

"You aren't getting the underlying message here," said the driver. "We'll have this talk again. Except it'll be one a them nonverbal talks." The Caddy pulled away.

Joe never listened to no one, not me, not his girl, no one. He had his own take on things and it always centered around him being just a little smarter than the other guy. Or at least crazier, which was often better. Sometimes worse.

Joe said he believed us coming to the attention of Little Suits Tony was good, how it could lead to something.

I'd wanted to point out what it led to, those two zoo specimens.

I had my doubts but Joe was Joe and the only voice he listened to regularly was his own. Not a bad thing in life, to believe in yourself, except maybe in his case it was.

I wondered if he'd changed.

I wondered if I had.

I wondered how this was going to go, how much I would remember and how much Joe would remember, and how much we'd silently agree to forget.

Joe took his turn, did three sets of bench presses, looked like maybe he was doing 200, 225, fifteen reps each, very respectable, dude his age.

Some of the brothers were watching him, and off aways the Aryan Brotherhood guys watched, too. This could be someone's idea of a lab experiment, couple social studies grad students up in the warden's office, watching us with binoculars, listening to the sounds picked up by their hidden microphones. Their biggest concern what to call the dissertation: "The Introduction of Fresh Bait into a Small Pool Where Two Rival Societies Struggle for Prominence."

Joe acted like he didn't have either group's attention. After the bench presses he moved to the leg press machine, loaded it with about four hundred pounds and then positioned himself on the incline.

Big brother named Tyrell—shaved head, goatee, muscles like an action hero—walked toward the weight area, his focus clearly on Joe; and the Aryan Brotherhood's führer—lug named George—broke away from his bunch and walked that way, too. Both groups shifted toward their leaders, toward the machines.

I pondered that just about everyone in both crews had a shaved head, same facial hair, same overcranked look. Evidently there was a dress code, or perhaps they were just slaves to fashion. I was momentarily impressed; these guys had stage presence. But even from where I was, the vibe didn't register. Looked like it was an early rehearsal.

Joe's legs pumped the weights up and down, his eyes apparently locked on some point in the sky, his hands gripping the support handles hard, his knuckles, even from where I stood, white. Man did some serious work, all wrapped up in it.

Tyrell got there, stood three feet away, near Joe's head, seemed to look straight down at him. George positioned himself off Tyrell's left shoulder, maybe six feet.

No one said anything. Joe pumped the weight, his breath ragged, in and out, big woofs of air.

He finished the first set, dropped his legs to the side of the machine but continued to lie there, eyes still focused on something up in the sky. I looked up, saw up there about thirty thousand feet a slice of white like a scar, bunch of citizens going somewhere.

The three of them there quiet and unmoved, it could have been a painting in some museum, *Lifting Weights in the Yard*. Or, no, *Watching the Weight Lifter*. That was better.

Joe started his second set, same concentration, same mechanical movements, same woofing noises. He had a good sweat going, shined like a wet rock on the beach.

The brother leaned toward him some, maybe said something, because Joe's head shifted, just the tiniest bit. His legs continued to fold and unfold as he worked the weights.

Nazi leaned in a little, too, said his own piece. Brother turned his head a fraction of an inch, hunched his shoulders. Both groups contracted like wildflowers closing up for the night.

Joe finished the second set. Figured to be one more. Everyone did three, way it's done.

About then the rest of the yard quieted as cons stopped to watch whatever was going to happen happen. A kind of crackling light glanced off things, the weights, eyeglasses, earrings, rocks on the ground, anything that could reflect light, and you could almost hear it.

I think that was when I knew something, remembered something about what I'd felt.

I came off the wall and ambled over to the weights. Since no one else was moving, you could hear my steps as I crunched closer.

I came in at an angle and both groups had to turn, see who was joining the party.

Even Joe looked. No one would have known he'd ever seen me before, just some other dude pissing in the dirt, his face said.

But I knew different. I stopped, about the same four or five feet from Joe as the others.

"Tea time?" I asked of no one in particular.

Tyrell smirked, George frowned, Joe pretended none of us were there, now about a quarter the way into his third set.

"I can't resist a crowd." I grinned at the world. "We're all here just to have fun, am I right?" I spread cheer everywhere.

I got these looks, not good looks, but maybe not all that bad either. On the confused side. Then it kicked in, a slow dawning what I wanted, hardass chin muscles crimped, eyes drifted away as mine drilled in.

"This is personal. That trumps politics. Call a truce and get lost," I said. "Anything else, take a number."

It was important they stare at me in a significant way for a manly period of time before one nodded or scowled or waved a finger, some paramilitary gesture, and they shuffled on to some other amusement.

"I think it was the part about taking a number—none a them zeroes wanted to chance being second," Joe said, himself waiting a good long while after the tough guys had gone. "You're the guy."

"I am that and more," I said. "Been twenty-eight years or almost."

"And here I thought it seemed just last week."

Quick glance around, things almost looked normal.

"Good to know time passed like that for you," I said. "Me, I had a slightly different angle."

"Yeah," he said. "I heard about that."

"Figured that."

One of his nails needed his attention. He worked it over.

"I know what happened," he said. He gave me a glance, just the hint of something. He knew I'd see it.

"I'd think so," I said. "Newspapers, TV. Hard to miss. I was on so much I almost got my SAG card."

"Mama was right," he said, "humor is never the answer."

"I always said you'd thank me someday."

"Hope you didn't tell too many people," he said. "You'll get a reputation."

"Oh, hell, Joe, I've got a reputation." The yard needed looking at. I did a quick 360. It's what you did out here, you kept track of things.

"You asked me to go," I said, things scoped. "You wanted me to stuff a toy gun in my pocket and take my car and go with you and face up to Little Suits Tony. A cap pistol, Joe."

"Starter pistol. It was a starter pistol."

"No, it was a cap pistol. There was a buckaroo on the plastic grip."

"Oh, yeah, I remember the buckaroo," he said, smiling. "I forgot about that."

"Sometimes, Joe, people forget their manners. Damn right I went and got a piece. I'm still pretty pleased that wasn't no cap gun I pulled out of my pants. You still have your health, I see."

"Good genes and even better luck."

I stared into his eyes, saw more than I cared to see.

"As soon as I saw that cap pistol, Joe, I knew exactly how it would end."

"I knew you had something to tell me," he said. It wasn't a smile and it wasn't pity and it wasn't resignation. His eyes and his mouth made a perfect bargain: I had a clear shot at his soul, a one-time deal.

"That wasn't no job interview, Joe. Little Suits didn't want to hire you. He wanted to get rid of you. You thought you were a rising star but all Little Suits saw was another Jersey pain in the ass he had to deal with. You thought it was an audition, Joe. It wasn't. It was an execution, you fucking idiot."

Joe studied the yard or counted to ten or worked on his grammar. Something.

"We all have dreams, Eddie," he said eventually. "I thought it was possible Little Suits had a job for us."

He went back to thinking. He made a little smile.

"We pulled some stuff, Eddie. I thought, I dunno, maybe that rated something. I thought we showed promise."

"Yeah, I think that's what got Little Suits's attention," I said. "A little too good for our own good."

The smile had gone, replaced, now, by a kind of loosening, a kind of exhaling. His head seemed to nod.

"You knew I'd bring a real gun, didn't you," I said. "I was your insurance but you didn't want to ask me; you needed me to think of it for me to truly do it. You wanted me to save you. And I did, didn't I? I surprised everybody and killed those guys and then took the heavy fall and no one ever heard your name, it never came up."

"That wasn't so hard, now was it?"

Anyone else, they'd said that, it wouldn't figure. Locked up a quarter century counts for something. Hard, from the outside, just wasn't a word you'd want to use.

He had a certain look about him. You could see his face fill with memories, see images ripple through his thoughts. I sensed things shift and settle. I paused. It was a timing thing.

"Easier than I thought it would be."

"Good," he said. I got the big smile then, twenty-eight years stored up in my memories, and even all those nightmares couldn't prepare me for what it did, that smile.

I kissed him.

It shut him up more than it should and it sure quieted the yard although my eyes never left Joe's so it was just this impression I had, of sudden heavy silence, of sounds receding into a kind of hum that seemed to grow, now, did certainly grow until it roared and shut out all other awareness.

"Yeah, I knew that, too, Eddie," he said quietly. "I counted on it."

Keeping It Good
RICHARD J. BREWER

THE CIGARETTE BUTT sailed through the air. It landed in the river with a short hiss before it died and was carried off by the current. Of course, it wasn't really a river. In actuality, it was an irrigation ditch, fed by the reservoir three miles outside of town. But it was a body of water that flowed through the town of Visalia, California, and the locals had called it "the River" for as long as anyone could remember.

Roy sat on the fender of his car and debated whether or not to light another cig. He was supposed to meet Benny at eleven P.M., but the traffic from Los Angeles had been almost nonexistent and he had made the two hundred–mile trip in record time. It would be at least three hours before Benny would arrive. There was no sense in trying to reach him. If you could believe it, Benny didn't have a cell phone and he was coming to the meeting directly after his job at one of the local dairies.

It seems Visalia was a big place for cows. As far as Roy could see that was about all it had going for it. On the drive in he had seen a hot dog stand, a car wash, and a Wal-Mart with a McDonald's attached to it. "Man," Roy thought, "that must have brought some excitement to this shit hole. 'Golly, Ma, there's a McDonald's right there in the Wal-Mart.'" The thought made Roy chuckle and then he shook his head. Who the fuck would want to move to a place like this? Roy looked at his watch and checked himself in the reflection in the windshield of his car for the tenth time. The new shirt looked good on him. The silk felt cool against his skin and the jacket hanging in the car matched it nicely. If nothing else it was a sure bet that he was the best-looking thing this hick town had seen in quite some time, probably ever.

Speaking of the jacket, he was starting to think he should get it and put it on. The sky had been gray and overcast since he'd come over the ridge and into the Central Valley, but now the clouds were lowering themselves to the ground and becoming a thick gray fog that limited Roy's visibility to five, maybe six feet.

"Shit," said Roy as he pulled on the light suit jacket. He looked around at the thickening blanket of fog. "What the fuck is this fog all about."

"It's called the Tule fog," said a voice from behind him. "Comes in at night off the Tule River. Some days it gets so thick, you can't see the house across the street."

Roy turned to find himself staring into a familiar face. It took him a moment to get his bearings, for although the face was familiar, the body most definitely wasn't. The woman standing in front of him was incredibly pregnant.

"Cherry?"

"Roy."

They didn't hug, even though they had known each other most of their lives. Their relationship wasn't the kind that had ever warranted hugs. Still, Roy gave a little smile as he stared at the woman he used to know. "Holy shit," he said. "What the hell happened to you?"

"I got pregnant, you dope." Cherry put her purse down and turned to the side, giving him a profile view of her bulging figure.

"Benny know?"

Cherry nodded her head at the question. "He kinda figured it out after the third month."

"How long?"

Cherry touched her large belly. "Six months. Due in April."

"No shit? You and the Benster havin' a baby. I can't leave you two alone for a minute."

"You left us alone for almost five years, Roy."

"Yeah well, I meant to write . . . meant to call." Roy reached in his pocket and pulled out his pack of Marlboros and shook out a cigarette.

"Hey!" said Cherry, indicating her swollen belly. "Pregnant woman here!"

"Jeez, what's with you?"

"I've worked hard for this baby. So sue me for wanting it to turn out right." She picked up her purse, slipped it back over her shoulder, and looked up at him. "Benjamin and I have tried a couple of times over the past three years to have a baby, this is the first one that looks like it's going to stick. I gave up coffee, cigarettes, chocolate and I take long walks every day. So I don't want to take any chances of something messing it up. That includes secondhand smoke. Is that okay with you?"

"It?"

"What?"

"You said 'it.' You don't know what your packin' in there?"

"No."

"I thought they had tests for that sort of thing. Tell ya if it's a boy, girl . . . whatever."

"They do. We decided that we don't want to know. Let it be a surprise. They keep telling us it's healthy and that's all we care about."

Roy looked at her and then, with a shake of his head, stuck the cigarette back in the pack and the pack back in his pocket. He studied her for a moment. "Gotta say, it's pretty weird seeing you like this."

A hint of smile crossed her face. "Gotta say, it's pretty weird being like this. But it's good. Ya know? It's really good."

Roy leaned back against his car and crossed his arms. "So how'd ya know I was going to be here?"

Cherry shifted her weight. "I heard Ben talking on the phone the other day. I could tell it was you on the other end of the line."

"You guys weren't so easy to find. But, now that I know where ya live . . ."

"I hope you'll forget it."

"What do ya mean?"

"Roy, we got a good thing going here. Ben and I have put the old life behind us. I don't want anything messing us up."

"Hell, baby, there ain't no plans for anything to happen here." He looked around. "Not that there's really anything that could happen here. Unless you're into cattle rustling or something like that."

"Roy . . ."

"You got nothing to worry about. What I got going is back in the city. Me and Benny, we go meet these guys . . . do a little business . . . and that's it. I'll have him back in no time."

"He's got to work tomorrow."

"So he calls in sick one day. It's gonna be worth it. He gets two grand just for showing up. Job or no job, he walks away with two grand. How long does it take him to make two grand at the milk factory?"

"That's not the point . . ."

"The fuck it's not. That's always the point." His eyes, suddenly hard, locked with hers. "Money . . . is . . . always . . . the point. And don't you pretend it isn't." He pointed a finger at her. "You know what I'm talkin' about here. You forget. I know you, Cherry. Money means something to you, always has, and if things go right tonight there will be plenty of it coming down the way. Enough to buy this kid of yours its own fuckin' Toys 'R' Us if ya want."

"And what if it doesn't go right? What then, Roy? Ben goes back inside? Or worse, he goes dead, like Eddie." Roy's eyes darkened dangerously at the mention of Eddie, but she moved closer to him anyway, trying to reason with him. "I'm telling you, Roy, we've got it good here. We've had five years to get something started . . . something real. And we have. We've got friends, a nice place to live. Sure, we're not rich, but, Roy, we were never rich before. It didn't matter how much we made, whatever money came in was gone the next day. We drank it, or smoked it, or just blew it. But Ben and I are here now. We're here, and we're building something."

Roy looked down at her, searching her face. Finally he said, "What the fuck happened to you?"

"What do you mean?"

"This isn't you. And it sure as hell isn't Benny." He shook his head in disbelief. "You can't tell me that you two have suddenly turned into fuckin'

Ward and June Cleaver. I'm offering you guys a chance to get back into
things. Make some serious cash. And you're telling me you want to stay here
in *Leave It to Beaver* land? Bullshit. I'm not buying it. Where's Benny? Have
him tell me this."

"Roy, you know Ben. He's never been that strong, especially when it
comes to you. Ever since you were kids, he'd do whatever you wanted him to
do. Right or wrong, it didn't matter. But things are different now. We've
both been clean for over five years. We go to meetings every day. We watch
out for each other. And you want us to get back into . . . into . . . what?"

Roy pushed himself off the car and moved toward Cherry. "You don't get
it. I'm helping you guys out here. I'm hooking up with real players now. This
isn't like the old days. Although as I remember you enjoyed those days yourself. You weren't so bothered about what we did or where the money came
from. You went along with everything just as easily as Benny. As long as you
got a taste you were perfectly happy. So don't go getting all high and mighty
on me. I'm not one of these cow town hillbillies you've got fooled. Benny—"

"His name is Ben!"

"Ben, Benny . . . I don't give a shit what you want to call him. The bottom
line is that he is coming along with me tonight . . . and any other night I
need him."

"Or what?" she asked. "Huh, Roy? Or what?"

"Or maybe some of your Mayberry friends find out their sweet little
neighbors have a sweet little past. Hell, even here they know a person
doesn't go to prison for jaywalking. Does Benny's boss know that the guy he
hired is an ex-con? An ex-con who spent four years in prison because he
robbed a 7-Eleven so he could buy drugs? Think that would go down well in
the lunchroom?"

Cherry started to protest, but Roy cut her off.

"And what about you? What about little 'Cherry Red'? How do you think
they would look at you if they found out about the years you spent working
the streets? Bet that would keep you out of the quilting circle. But you never
know, it might be good for you. Maybe you could reopen for business right
here. I'll bet you could make a lot of dough, even like you are now. I know
guys who would pay big money to be with a pregnant gal."

"You bastard. You disgusting basta—"

"Yeah, right . . . sticks and stones, baby. Look, I'm here to do business
with 'Ben' not with you. So why don't you get in the car and I'll run you
home. Then I'll come back here and wait for my old pal Benny. You listen to
me, Cherry Red . . . once this is over and done, you are going to be thanking
me for finding you and getting my ass up here."

He turned his back on her and began walking toward the car. Cherry watched him as he moved away from her. Finally, she slipped the purse from her shoulder and walked quickly after him.

Later that night, she stood in the shower, letting the warm water run over her. She was tired and her legs were killing her but the shower was helping and she knew that by the time she got out she would feel a world of better. As she stood there she stroked her belly and was rewarded with a strong kick from the little person growing inside her. It wasn't time yet, but it wouldn't be long. "Boy or girl?" she thought. "What are you going to be?" It was while she pondered this question that she heard the front door open and close.

"Ben?" she yelled, turning off the water.

"Yeah," came the reply.

Stepping out of the shower, she grabbed a towel. As she began drying herself off Benjamin poked his head into the bathroom. He was cute in a scruffy kind of way. His hair was a little too long, a little too stringy, and his attempt at a beard was truly pathetic, but he was her guy and every time she saw him she was aware that she couldn't love him more.

"You're late," she said, and saw him frown.

"I was supposed to meet someone after work," he said.

"And?"

"And he never showed."

"Someone from the group?"

There was a slight hesitation before he answered, and then it was with a simple, "Yeah."

"I hope he's okay."

"I'm sure he's fine. I'll try to get ahold of him tomorrow and see what happened. I'm sure it's nothing."

Benjamin came over to her and put his arms around her. Leaning down, he kissed the top of her head. She took his hand and placed it against her stomach, willing the baby to give a little kick. She was rewarded with one that would have made any soccer mom proud. Benjamin gave a start at the unexpected movement but when she looked at him he was grinning down at her with a mixture of joy and wonder.

"Come on," she said. "I'll make us something to eat."

On her way out of the bathroom she grabbed a nightgown and pulled it over her head. She thought of the maternity dress she had worn that night. It was one of her favorites but she doubted she would ever be able to get the blood out of it. It hadn't been as easy as she thought it would be. The brick in her purse had certainly done the job but the first blow to the back of Roy's skull had only dropped him to his knees. It had taken two more swings before she was done and then she'd had to sit in the car for some time to get her wind back.

The next step was even worse. It had taken all her strength to pull Roy's body to the back of the car and put it in the trunk. Next, she had driven the car up the hill and down the old service road that wove its way behind the reservoir to the place where she had parked her car. Then she had driven Roy's Caddy to the edge of the embankment and, with the motor running, she had jammed the engine into drive and watched as the car ran itself over the edge and into the water. Her fear that the place she had picked wouldn't be deep enough had proven unfounded. The car sank quickly below the surface. With any luck it would be years before it was discovered. By then there wouldn't be much of Roy to identify.

Her thoughts were interrupted by Ben talking to her.

"Sorry, honey," she said, not having heard him.

"I said, what did you do this evening?"

"Oh, you know, the usual. Watched a little TV. Took a walk. The Johnsons down the street got a new Chevy pickup. You better make sure to get over there tomorrow and do some oohing and aahing." They both shared a smile over that and, as Cherry scrambled some eggs, she let herself enjoy the moment. This was good, she thought. This town, this man, this baby, it was all so good. And, she told herself, that was the way it was going to stay.

One Fast Packard
STEVE HAMILTON

"WHADDYA SAY, FRIEND? You gonna be under that thing all day?"

I tried to ignore the man. I'd heard him pull his car into the garage, heard him get out and walk around the place like he owned it. From where I was I could see the man's black leather shoes and the shiny stripe down his pant leg, could hear him whistling along to the radio, ruining a fine rendition of "Am I Blue?" by Ethel Waters. That was enough.

"You're not taking a nap down there, are ya?"

I didn't say a word. I kept working on the gearbox. It was a hard enough job without this mug pacing all over the joint, knocking into everything, and chattering at me like a monkey. With the floorboards out, I was eventually treated to a good look at the man as he stuck his face in the vehicle and peered down at me. Even from that angle, I could see he was a large man, with a face that had clearly seen more than a few rounds in the ring. When I rolled out to get a better look, he didn't look any smaller, his shoulders almost splitting open the arms of his coat.

"Listen, pal," I said. "I'm working down here. If you need some service, you go out into the office and talk to the manager."

"Take it easy, friend. I already talked to your boss, and as soon as I dropped my boss's name, he told me to roll this baby right in."

I looked over at the "baby" he was referring to. It was a big 745 Custom Town Car, with a pure black exterior, all business, the shining goddess of speed on the radiator cap the only adornment. This was twelve smooth feet of Packard, one of the most expensive cars on the road.

"My boss is having a little meeting up in the Hudson's Tea Room," the man said. The big department store was just a few blocks down on Woodward. A few more blocks east was the Packard plant itself, where this car and every other Packard in the world was made. I figured that made my garage kind of special.

"He picks up the phone in the back and I can't hear a word he's saying," the man said. "So he asked me bring her by to get it fixed."

I looked inside the car. This model had the enclosed passenger's compartment, with the expensive cloth seat and the little phone he could pick up to give instructions to the driver up front, who got the less-expensive leather seat and the canvas cover. I took another look at the man, standing there busting out of his suit. This was the man who got paid to drive this car, and

God only knows what else. I figured it was in my best interest to be a little more accommodating.

"Probably just a bad connection," I said. "I suppose I can take a look at it."

"That's more like it, friend. You go right ahead."

I climbed into the front cab and took apart the speaker. While I was working, the man kept walking around, picking up tools and putting them down again. It was August, the hottest month yet in that long summer of 1931. Even with both fans going full blast, it still had to be ninety degrees in the garage. I was in my work overalls, with my shirtsleeves rolled up. I couldn't imagine how hot he must have been in that suit.

"Ask the man who owns one," he said. That was the Packard slogan. He was reading it off the advertisement poster. "You know what it should say instead?"

"What's that?" I said. I kept my head down and concentrated on what I was doing.

"Ask the man who can afford one," he said. "Whaddya think?"

"Sounds about right," I said. Fix the thing and send him on his way, I thought. The sooner the better.

"What do these things go for nowadays, about four grand?"

"Thereabouts," I said. "This one was a lot more, I'm sure."

"You ever been to the tea room?" he said.

"Excuse me?"

"The Hudson's Tea Room. You ever been there? I can't imagine my boss sitting up there drinking tea."

"I haven't been there," I said. "But I don't think you have to drink tea there. I think you can get anything you want."

"Why do they call it a tea room then?"

"I don't know."

"Whatever they call it, my boss says it's a good place to have a nice quiet conversation with somebody. Funny you gotta go to the biggest department store in the world to have a quiet conversation these days."

I knew J. L. Hudson's was the tallest department store in the world, now that they'd just opened up the tower, but I was pretty sure the Macy's in New York was still bigger. I wasn't about to correct him.

And I sure as heck didn't want to know who his boss was. That was the last thing I needed to know.

"What's this you were working on here?" he said. He looked into the back window of the Packard I was just underneath. "Some kind of ambulance?"

It's huge and white, I said to myself, with a flashing light on top. It even has big letters on each side that happen to spell AMBULANCE.

"Sure is," I said.

"What's wrong with it?" He kept looking in the back window.

"It's shifting a little rough," I said. "You want an ambulance to run well, I'm sure you'd agree."

Stop talking to him, I thought. I finally had the speaker apart and could see where one of the wires had gotten disconnected. Simple to fix.

"I bet this thing can go," he said. "I bet this is one fast Packard."

"Same as your car," I said. "A hundred and six horsepower."

"These are pretty small windows," he said. "On such a big car."

I didn't know what to say to that one. Or why he would even notice such a thing. I put the wire back in place and twisted it. Good as new.

"I think we're all set here," I said.

"Already? That was quick."

"It was a loose wire, just like I thought."

"Here, let me try it." He opened up the back door, but he didn't get inside. He leaned in and carefully took the little phone off the hook. He could barely reach the thing. A man as big as him, with his boss up in the tea room several blocks away, and yet here he was being extra careful to stay out of the passenger's compartment.

"You be the driver," he said. He pressed the little button. The speaker buzzed once and then his voice came through, sounding an octave higher than the real thing. "Take me to the tea room," he said. "I feel like having a little tea this afternoon."

"There's no charge," I said. "It only took me a minute, after all."

The man gave me a long look. "You don't want any money, friend?"

"No need," I said. "Glad to help."

He took a wad of bills out and pulled off a twenty. He put it in my shirt pocket, right below my name.

"Eddie," he said. "Don't you like money, Eddie?"

"Of course I do. Who doesn't?"

"You're handy with cars, aren't you?"

"It's my job."

"I bet you can drive them well, too. A man who knows cars as well as you do . . ."

"I'm as good a driver as most people. Nothing special." I wanted him to leave. I wanted him to be long gone.

"Now you're being modest, Eddie. I think you're the kind of man who can be depended upon. Maybe I'll stop by and see you again some time. Name's Louis, by the way. Just call me Lou."

As he drove off in that big black Packard, I went back under the ambulance, hoping that I'd never see Lou again, as long as I lived.

But in my gut I knew he'd be back.

*   *   *

When I walked out of the garage a few minutes after five o'clock, Lou was there, leaning against the brick building. He had taken his coat off. He wore black suspenders over his white shirt, and he had undone the top three buttons.

"Still a scorcher, eh, Eddie?"

I tried not to show my surprise. Or my fear.

"You got that one right."

"You must be kinda thirsty after working all day. Let me buy you a drink."

"Nah, that's all right," I said. "I appreciate it."

"Nonsense," he said. He put one huge hand on my right shoulder. "Let me buy you just one."

The way I figured it, I didn't have much of a choice. Not with that hand on my shoulder. So I went along with him. We walked down Woodward a few blocks, away from Hudson's. He took a right onto Grand River and led me past the butcher shop and then the men's shoe store. Behind that store there was another building that looked like a warehouse. He knocked three times on the door—three long knocks spread out like he was sending the letter O in Morse code.

Another big man opened the door and gave us both a once-over. He nodded his head and we walked in. The place had a wooden bar and a few tables and not much else. There were maybe thirty men in the room, mostly local working men with their lunch pails sitting under their chairs. There were four fans in the room, one in each corner.

"You like whiskey, Eddie? Good whiskey?"

"Of course," I said. What else was I gonna say?

The man serving the drinks did a quick double take on Lou. I was surprised he didn't give himself a case of whiplash. Lou put one hand up. That was all it took for the bartender to start breathing again. Apparently a visit from Lou wasn't always a happy occasion.

"Two," he said to the bartender. That was it. The bartender filled up two double shot glasses and slid them our way.

"Give this a try," Lou said. "Here's to you."

I took a sip, waiting for it to hit my tongue like a hot iron. But it was smooth. Real smooth.

"How's it treating you, Eddie? This stuff is top-notch, wouldn't you say?"

"It's fine whiskey," I said.

"Let's have a seat over here," he said. He showed me to a table in the far corner. A couple of the men looked up at him as he walked across the room, but most just kept their noses in their glasses.

"So let me ask you something," he said as he sat down. "That ambulance you were working on today . . . Is it still in the garage?"

"They'll pick it up tomorrow," I said. "Tomorrow morning. Early." I could feel a line of sweat starting to run down my back.

"That's interesting," he said. "Because I'm wondering what would happen if we wanted to take it for a little ride tonight. You know, just to make sure that gear box is all fixed now."

I didn't know what to say. I took another drink.

"Reason I ask," Lou said, "is that I think we could do a little business tonight. One quick trip to Windsor and back."

"In an ambulance?"

"A nice fast Packard ambulance," he said. "With you driving. Whaddya think?"

What I was thinking was that I was in some kind of big trouble. That I had no idea how I was gonna get myself out of it.

"Why would you want me driving?" I said. "I told you before, I'm nothing special as a driver. Why don't you get a real pro?"

"I'd rather not bring another man into the game, if you know what I mean. You're the one who can get the ambulance out of the garage for a little while."

"Oh, I don't think so," I said. "Someone will notice it's gone."

"Not if we leave after midnight," he said. "We'll be back by three o'clock, easy."

"I don't know." I had to come up with something quick—some ironclad reason why it wouldn't work.

"Naturally, I'd make sure you were well taken care of for the trouble."

"Lou, really . . ." Think, man, think.

"If you were to buy your own Packard, say, what would a nice down payment be? Maybe two thousand dollars?"

I stopped thinking.

Lou smiled at me.

"I'll meet you at the garage at midnight," he said. "Wear a nice white shirt. And a white hat, if you got one."

I still didn't get it. Why an ambulance? Moving whiskey from Ontario to Michigan was almost as easy as going out for a bottle of milk these days. It was practically a statewide pastime. Men would smuggle bottles across the border in watermelons, hot water bottles, hollowed-out loaves of bread. Women would hang the bottles from strings under their long dresses. It was a long, open border, and the federal agents hardly had a sporting chance.

"I'll tell you why," Lou said to me. "Smuggling a couple of bottles is child's play, but if you're carrying a big load, you need something that never gets stopped. What could be better than an ambulance?"

We were already on our way to Windsor, me behind the wheel of that big Packard ambulance, and Lou on the passenger's side with his window wide open. He had a shoulder harness over his shirt now, a silver revolver riding just over his left pocket. He had brought another gun for me, had told me to put it in my pocket. When he had seen the look on my face, he thought better of it and kept it for himself.

"Which way are we going?" I said. "Across the bridge?"

"I think we should try out that new tunnel, Eddie. I got a good feeling about it."

"The new tunnel?"

"Yeah, sure. You been down in the tunnel yet?"

"No, Lou. I haven't." Truth was, the tunnel made me a little nervous. I had been reading about it in the paper, this engineering marvel, a long tunnel dug right underneath the Detroit River. It took over two years to dig. But just the thought of it, going down there with all that water on top of you. I just didn't like the whole idea. Not one bit.

"I think the tunnel might work in our favor, you know what I'm saying? Once you get that light going, it'll be flashing all over the place, bouncing off those walls. Everyone will be sure to get out of our way."

"I don't know, Lou . . ."

"This thing has a siren, too?"

"Of course."

"Even better. We'll sound twice as loud in that tunnel. We'll be louder than the Fourth of July."

"But what are they gonna think when they see an American ambulance coming over from Windsor? Why would we be over there in the first place?"

"They won't have time to think about that, Eddie. They'll be too busy getting out of the way."

"It's not gonna look right, Lou. Someone will notice. Ambulances just don't cross the border."

"People don't think, Eddie. You gotta remember that. People don't think."

I kept driving. We made our way down Woodward to Michigan Avenue, then down Randolph toward the river, the streets mostly quiet after the long hot summer day. The few cars on the road made way for us, even without our light and siren on. I was hoping Lou was right. I was hoping nobody would be thinking too much tonight. We got in the line for the tunnel, right behind a Ford Model A.

"How much does that car go for?" Lou said. "Five hundred dollars?"

"Something like that."

"Tomorrow you'll be able to buy four of them if you want."

I swallowed hard. Two thousand dollars. That's why I was doing this. Two thousand dollars was more than I made in a year. Easy money for one night's work, right? Now that we were on the road, I wasn't so sure anymore. But there was no turning back.

The line started moving and soon we were in the tunnel. There were lights running along each wall—that and the headlights from all the cars made the tunnel a lot brighter than I had expected. Still, all that water right above us. A whole river's worth. I tried hard not to think about it.

When we got close to the Canadian side, Lou told me to turn on the flashing light and the siren.

"Why do we need that?" I said. "We're running empty now."

"Fine, you explain to the customs agent why we're bringing this ambulance over then."

I hadn't thought of that part.

"Just give it a try," he said. "If they stop you, tell them you just got a call. Somebody in Windsor needs to go to the hospital in Detroit."

"Why wouldn't they go to a hospital in Windsor?" I said. "In a Canadian ambulance?"

"I don't know, Eddie. Because the Canadian hospital doesn't have the right kind of medicine. Don't worry about it. Just blow that horn."

I flipped on the siren and the flashing light. The Model A in front of us moved over as close as he could to the wall, giving us just enough room to pass.

"See what I mean, Eddie? An ambulance spooks everybody."

I hit the gas and passed each car in my lane. Even the cars coming in the opposite direction slowed down to let us through safely.

"Thank you, citizens!" Lou said, laughing. "Thank you and good night!"

When we came out the other side, one of the Canadian customs agents ran out of his little booth and waved us over. I thought he was going to stop us, but instead he lifted one of the closed gates and motioned us through.

"It's too easy," Lou said as we sailed through. "I bet we could drive this thing right through Hoover's living room."

"So where are we going now?" I said. I pulled out my pocket watch and checked the time. It was almost one in the morning.

"It's not far," he said. "They'll be waiting for us at Bruce Avenue Park."

We kept going south from the tunnel. I remembered learning in grade school that this was the only part of America where you actually went south to get to Canada. When we got to the park, I saw a big truck with wooden panels, parked right under a street lamp.

"We're gonna do this right out in the open?" I said.

"Who's gonna stop us?" Lou said. "It's not illegal here anymore, remember?"

Oh yeah, I thought. All bets were off now, with Ontario having repealed their own version of Prohibition. They were building docks all up and down the Detroit River, and the flow of liquor into Michigan was heavier than ever. Which made me wonder why Lou had this idea in the first place. If there was already so much booze coming into Detroit, why go to all this trouble to bring in a little more?

I got my answer as soon as I pulled the ambulance up to the truck. Without exchanging a word with Lou, the two men hopped out of the truck and lowered the back gate. There in the bed of the truck was more whiskey than I had ever seen in one place in my entire life.

"That's not gonna fit in here," I said. But they were already loading up the ambulance, carefully stacking the crates in the back, using up every inch of room. These guys obviously knew how to pack a vehicle with whiskey.

Lou stood by, watching them. He wasn't helping them, so I figured I didn't have to, either. Twenty minutes later, the bed of the truck was empty. The ambulance had crates stacked all the way from floor to ceiling. The men had slipped white sheets over the crates, so you couldn't see them through the windows.

"You got a couple extra bottles?" Lou said.

"Naturally," one of the men said, the only word either of them would speak. He gave Lou two bottles, tipped his hat to both, then got back into his truck with his partner.

"Here you go." Lou handed me one of the bottles. "A little bonus."

I took one look at the label. Old Log Cabin, the best of the best, forty dollars a bottle. It also happened to be the exclusive import of a man named Al Capone. That's the exact moment I realized just how deep I was in this. Not one bottle of Old Log Cabin entered the country without Capone's knowledge, whether or not the feds could make an airtight case of it. Now all of a sudden I was working for him.

"Let's get rolling," Lou said.

The ambulance was riding awfully low with the big load in back, but I got behind the wheel and started it up. There was nothing else to do now. Just get back to Detroit, take my money, and try to forget all about it.

With every turn of the wheel, I could hear the bottles rattling in the back. This is crazy, I thought. We'll never get through. But I kept driving, back up the streets of Windsor to the tunnel. Lou didn't have to tell me to flip on the light and siren this time. We hit the gates and the same man came out to open a lane for us. Once again the cars all pulled over to let us through. One mile of tunnel, one more gate on the American side, and then we'd be home free.

Lou was rubbing his big hands together now. He looked jumpy and agitated, which didn't help my nerves any.

"You got a girl, Eddie?"

"What's that?" It was hard to hear him over the noise of the siren.

"I say you got a girl?"

"No," I said. "Not really."

He nodded his head at that, like he was expecting that answer out of me. "I got a girl named Cherry," he said. "She likes to tell me I'm nothing but a big ape in a suit, taking orders from real men."

She didn't sound like much of a keeper to me, but I was keeping my mouth shut.

"She says I do all the heavy work and get nothing but peanuts. Says I should ask the man for a raise. Can you imagine?"

I shook my head.

"She doesn't know anything, Eddie. She doesn't know how the world works."

Drive, I thought. Drive and get home.

"I can't wait to see the look on her face when I bring home those diamonds and pearls. Here ya go, Cherry. Try these on for size."

Drive, drive, drive.

"Better yet," he said. "You know what I'm gonna do? I'm gonna take a big wad of cash and just throw it on the bed. 'You want money, Cherry? Here it is.' Then I'll just walk out."

I could see the cars ahead slowing down.

"Yeah, that's what I'm gonna do. Throw that money on the bed and just take a walk."

This was it. The end of the line. The cars ahead of us were stopped now. I wished I had a button on the dash to make the siren even louder.

"Keep going," Lou said. "Don't slow down."

"There's no room," I said, slowing down. There were two lanes coming out of the tunnel, and they were both jammed solid. "I can't get around."

"What's the holdup?" he said. "Why is everybody stopped?"

The car immediately ahead of me tried to move over into the other lane, but there was nowhere for him to go. I could see the driver raising his hands in exasperation. Finally, the lane on the right cleared enough for the car to move over, but when we pulled around him, there were still seven more cars in our way.

"Why don't they do something up there?" Lou said. He rolled down his window and started yelling toward the booths. "Move those cars out of the way! Emergency coming through!"

It felt like we were stuck there for hours on end, totally exposed to the other drivers and the federal agents and whoever else happened to be watching us. No doubt they were all wondering why an American ambulance was coming through from Canada with its siren on, and why all they could see in the back windows was something covered with a white sheet. It would all end right here. I'd be taken away in handcuffs and put away in the big house for the rest of my life.

But then finally, inch by inch, the cars started to clear out of the right lane and the cars in our lane started to move over. At last only one car was in front of us. When he pulled through the booth, I could see nothing ahead of us but an open street and freedom and money and a long drink. I was just about to hit the gas pedal when—

No! Who's that? A man stepping out of the booth, right in our way!

It was a federal agent. I could see his pinched-in little face, his eyes staring right at us from beneath the brim of his hat, looking us up and down. He held up his hand to stop us.

"Oh, you gotta be kidding me, friend," Lou said. He reached to pull the revolver out of his shoulder harness. "Let's see you stop *this.*"

"Don't shoot him!" I punched the gas and sent the ambulance right at him. I was hoping I'd be moving just fast enough to convince him to get out of the way, but not so fast that I ran him over.

He didn't move. He kept standing there with one hand up.

"Get out of the way!" I yelled. "You idiot, get out of the way!"

I tried to hit the brakes. The bottles clattered behind us as we pushed our way through the booth, missing the agent as he finally dove out of our way. I think we cleared the man by all of a quarter inch. When we were clear I hit the gas again, and we were off running. As I looked in the side-view mirror, I could see the agent scrambling to his feet.

I sped down Randolph Street, lights still flashing and siren still screaming. Lou was looking at me, his gun still in his hand. The warm smell of whiskey filled the cab.

"You should've let me ice him," he said, breathing hard. "However many bottles are broken, it's coming out of your share."

I could have laughed like a maniac right then, but I was too busy driving. I knew that agent would be on the phone. It was only a matter of time before they came after us.

"Where are we going?" I said.

"Just drive."

"I want to know where we're going," I said. "Give me the address."

"Take it easy, Eddie. It's a garage over by the stadium."

I took a hard left on Michigan Avenue, causing another crash of bottles behind us.

"If you break any more of those," he said, "I swear to God . . ."

I wasn't listening anymore. I opened it up on Michigan, barreling through each intersection without even slowing down to look. With my own siren on, I couldn't tell if there were any police behind us. I kept looking at the side-view mirror, but the street behind us was empty.

"Where is it?" I said. "Give me an address."

"Take a right on Trumbull," he said, just as we passed it. "No, it was right back there!"

I started to hit the brakes, but thought better of it. "We'll go around," I said. The huge gray form of Tiger Stadium loomed above us. I took the next right and started to circle around it, just as I caught sight of the lights behind us.

"They found us," he said. "We're gonna have to outrun them now."

"We can't," I said. I flipped the lights and siren off. "We're too heavy. Where's the garage?"

I took another right turn, and then another on Trumbull. I saw a police car flash by ahead of us, heading west on Michigan Avenue.

"Up here," he said. "On the left."

I killed the headlights just as we came into the alley.

"Right up here," he said. "To the right."

With the headlights off, I could barely see where I was going now. It was a narrow alley, with buildings on either side of us, and then up ahead I saw the open door. As I swung to the right, I could hear the sickening scrape of metal against brick. I adjusted too hard to the left and caught the front quarter panel as we finally slid into the garage. Then I hit the brakes one second too late. As the front bumper hit something solid, I could hear the grill being pushed in. That was followed by one more final rattling of the bottles, and the sound of one last bottle breaking.

Then silence.

I listened for the police cars. I heard sirens in the distance. They were getting farther and farther away. I let my breath out.

It was completely dark in the garage. I had no idea how much damage the Packard had suffered. For now, I didn't want to know.

"We made it, Eddie."

"Now what?"

"Now we wait a few minutes, make sure the cops are gone."

"What about the garage door? Shouldn't we close it?"

"We will. Just rest a while. They can't see us from the street."

"Is somebody going to meet us here?"

"Here? No, we gotta go to Chicago."

"What? You didn't tell me this."

"Stay cool, Eddie. We don't have to take the ambulance. There's a truck right next to us. All we have to do is switch the load and go."

"I'm not going all the way out to Chicago, Lou."

"That's the deal, Eddie."

"I'm not going."

"Then you won't get your two grand."

I put my head against the steering wheel. Easy money. That's what I thought it would be. Easy money.

"I can't wait to see Cherry's face," Lou said. "Teach her to laugh at me. It'll never work, she says. You can't go around your boss like that."

I picked my head up. "What did you say?"

"That's the scam, Eddie. Why do you think we're getting paid so well?"

"What are you talking about, Lou? Who's getting this whiskey? It's Old Log Cabin, isn't it?"

"The boss's private brand," he said. "The best of the best."

"Are you telling me . . ."

"Fifty cases, Eddie. Fifty cases of Old Log Cabin delivered right to Moran."

Moran. I couldn't believe what I was hearing. George "Bugs" Moran. I thought of those seven bodies they found in Chicago, all men working for Moran, gunned down by men working for Capone. The St. Valentine's Day Massacre, they called it. That was two years ago, when everything started getting serious.

"You're crazy," I said. "You're out of your mind."

"That's what Cherry said."

"You told her about this?"

"Sure, why not? She told me I'd never make it back."

He told her. He told Cherry his plan.

I knew I had to get out of there. Never mind the whiskey. Never mind the money. Never mind my job, which I knew I wouldn't have anymore. This is what happens when you make a deal with the devil.

There was only one thing left I could save.

"I'm going out to close that door," I said.

"I'll do it," Lou said. "It's tricky."

"No, I got it," I said. I opened up the door before he could say anything else.

It was still dark. My eyes hadn't adjusted to it. I fumbled my way along the side of the ambulance to the back to the garage, out into the open air.

The lights came on just as I turned the corner in the alley. I turned and saw the men standing there in the garage, standing against the wall. They had been waiting patiently for us to arrive.

I couldn't see Lou's face. I couldn't tell if he saw the men before they opened up on him, if he knew in that one last moment what Cherry had done to him.

The night hadn't cooled off any. It was a hot night in the summer of 1931, and all I could do was run.

Killing Time by the River Styx
PETER DAVID

EDDIE PUT A bullet in my brain. A goddamn bullet. Do you *believe* this shit?

You hang with a guy since you were kids. You think you know him. And time passes in an eyeblink, which it has this nasty habit of doing (you're not really all that aware of it until you look behind yourself and kind of goggle in surprise and say, Damn, where did all *that* go?) And the next thing you know, you're horizontal and they're sticking a tag on your toe.

But you don't think you're gonna wind up that way because of someone like Eddie. I mean, I'd read these stats about how all these murders go down between people who are family and friends, but you still never expect it somehow.

And over a girl this was.

Do you believe this *shit*?

So now I'm here.

I'm not loving this "here," I can tell you. For one thing, it seems like some sort of cave, except the top stretches up for goddamn ever, which would be enough to make you wonder how I know it's a cave in the first place. Because if you can't see the top, then how do you know there's a top at all? It only makes sense. A cave, or maybe a cavern, although I'm not sure what the difference is. I think a cavern is bigger and deeper.

And then there's the smell.

There isn't any.

I mean, you'd think there would be, right? Deep underground, with the dirt kind of spongy under my feet. The walls are dripping in a steady *plink, plink* kind of way, the droplets coming from somewhere above and hitting in a steady, rhythmic manner that sounds vaguely like a heart beating. It's like being in the middle of somebody's body, shrunk down like one of those guys from that movie, what's it called, *Fantastic Voyage*.

And now I'm wondering, y'know, how come I can see *anything*? There's no torches along the way, and if it really is open way up above, I'm still not seeing a ton of light just streaming in, with little dust motes or something dancing around and chasing after each other. But I can still see just the same. You know what it's like? It's like those TV shows where they're shooting at night, and they're using that kind of film or maybe it's special lenses, infrared. A word, by the way, that when I read it as a kid, I said *in-FRAYRD*, like it rhymed with "impaired." Then I said it in sixth grade science class, and this snotty teacher, Mrs. Morris, told me it was "infra" and then "red." And I didn't know why the hell they couldn't spell it with a goddamn hyphen or something, and said so, and all the kids laughed but I bet the little bastards didn't know the right word any more than I did.

I don't know why I thought of that just then.

It's like I'm remembering all little bits and pieces of my life, shit I haven't thought about in years and years, and it's all coming back at me like acid reflux.

Anyway, *infra-red* is how the world looks to me right now. That small piece of the world that I can see, at any rate.

In the fucking head he shoots me. Christ.

"Hey!" I shout, and my voice echoes, ricocheting all around me. I can practically see the sound hanging there, whipping past me like a racquetball. I shout "Hey" again and amuse myself for a few minutes by seeing how many times I can say "Hey" and even get it to overlap. An endless stream of "Hey." Good for a few laughs.

A tunnel.

Yeah, there was a tunnel right before this. I remember that. Dunno why. That flash of the bullet (which, by the way, he put in my fucking head between my goddamn eyes, son of a *bitch* when I get my hands on him) and suddenly there was this tunnel. It was long, real long, seemed to go on forever and ever. And at first I was walking in, and then suddenly I was running. Not just regular running. Not that I'm a slouch at running. I was varsity in high school, and man, when I was a kid I could fly.

That's when Cherry first noticed me, and I noticed her.

She was a cheerleader, see. Cherry really was her name, which was bad 'cause when I was first introduced, I kind of laughed because I figured it was a nickname she'd picked up. Because she had that whole sweet-faced innocent virgin thing going for her, y'know? With the blond hair framing it like Doris Day. Well, like most anybody, Cherry didn't cotton to somebody laughing at her name, although I really doubted that I was the first one, so I wasn't sure why she made such a damned fuss about it. Later, when we were older, she admitted it was because she liked me the minute she laid eyes on me, and hated that I was laughing at her for any reason, much less something like her name, which she couldn't do a damned thing about.

At any rate, Cherry quit high school late in her junior year. Word was whispered around campus that it was 'cause she got herself knocked up, but I knew it was because she was bolting New Jersey to go and be a major Hollywood movie star. Me, I stayed in Asbury Park, helping my dad around the hardware store, knowing someday I'd be running the place. Cherry was this high school crush, and not much more.

And ten years later, she came back to Asbury Park. And we got it on again.

I shake off thoughts of Cherry for a minute and walk over to look at the water that's flowing along some feet away from me. Seems to be a stream or river of some kind. But it has the same weird lack of smell like everything else in this place does. Considering how black it is, you'd think it would be really rank. You'd think it'd have a stench that would carry to high heaven. But no. Nothing.

The thickness of it is so strange, I find myself wondering if someone spilled something into it. Tar, maybe, or some sort of chemical dump. I lean in close. I'll be damned if I'm going to stick a finger in it, but at least I can see it more clearly.

There's something swimming in it.

It's some kind of fish life, I think, except I got no idea how anything can possibly be living in there.

Then I realize.

Whatever it is, it's got faces. Human faces.

The creatures are long and slender, almost like tadpoles or like that, but their faces are human faces. Faces etched in misery and sadness, and with their mouths hanging open like that *Scream* picture. Not the movie, the painting. And as I listen very carefully, it's almost like they're whispering to me or calling to me, except I don't know what they want or what the hell I'm supposed to do about them or for them or anything like that. No wonder I didn't recognize them at first for what they were. They're like ripples of the water come to life—or death, or whatever they are.

"Yo. Dude."

I hear the voice but don't turn fast. I take a deep breath, and it feels weird though I'm not sure why, and then I turn. Eddie's standing there.

He's looking kind of sheepish.

He raises a hand, waggles his fingers, and has that same kind of hangdog look he had the night he wrapped my Camaro around a tree.

"Hey," he says.

Naturally I'm all over him.

The dope actually has the nerve to look surprised. He puts up his hands and I think he tries to say "Stop," but it doesn't mean a thing as I slam right into him. We go down and I'm just pounding on him. It's not like those fights you see on TV with karate and kung fu and carefully planned out punches and shit. Instead I got him pinned to the ground, with one knee jammed into his chest, and my fists are just whacking away. He's got his arms up over his head to cover up, and I'm probably not doing him any damage 'cause of that. But that doesn't matter to me. I just keep hitting him and hitting him. And every profanity I ever learned is spilling out of my mouth. I'm not even saying anything you can really make any sense out of. It's just pure, raw anger, and he's taking every punch and not saying a word, just defending himself by making sure my punches don't rearrange his face.

I'm not getting tired. If he's counting on my wearing myself out, he's gonna be disappointed, because I'm not feeling any strain. I could keep it up all night, presuming there's a night and day wherever we are, which I'm beginning to suspect there ain't.

Eventually, though, I do start to slow down, just out of sheer boredom. There's only so long you can whomp on a guy before the charm starts to wear off . . . especially when he's not doing much of anything except covering up and not fighting back. So I stop and say, "Am I hurting you?"

"Not really, no," says Eddie, "but I didn't wanna make you feel bad."

"Make me feel bad? You put a bullet in my fucking brain!"

"I know . . ."

"Don't you think it's a little late to worry about my feelings?" And I punch him again.

"I know! I'm sorry!"

"You're sorry! In my *fucking brain,* man!"

And his face gets all twisted up like he's the one who's in the right here, and he shouts, "Well, it's not like you were *usin'* the damned thing for anything!"

Well, y'know, I've heard of the whole "adding insult to injury" thing. But when a guy has just popped a cap in your brain and then says you weren't using it anyway, that just sets a whole new level to it.

So I draw my fist back to punch him again, but Eddie sits up suddenly and shoves me off. I roll back, skidding down the embankment, the dirt and mud mushing up under me, and suddenly my head and right shoulder are underwater.

And I realize just how much I wasn't feeling anything up until that point, because suddenly I am cold, man, stone cold, and it's worse than any cold I've ever felt in my life because it's like nothing you ever can feel in your life 'cause it's got nothing to do with life at all. And at the same time, it's scalding hot. I don't know how something can be freezing cold and burning hot at the same time, but there it is. And there's this moaning and screaming and shrieking and there's a million million billion regrets coming at me from all directions, all these thoughts, every "woulda coulda shoulda" that ever was or will be, and thoughts of "not yet, please God, not yet, just one more year, one more day, one more minute to breathe and taste and feel," and then I'm out. I'm shivering like a son of a bitch and there's Eddie, hauling me back to shore.

And I'm shaking like a goddamn baby, it's pathetic and I'm totally embarrassed that anyone's seeing me like this, much less a former friend who shot me in the face, but he's the only one there. So I wrap my arms around him like a bat and just hold on and every muscle is trembling. And Eddie, thank God, he don't say a damned thing, because how pathetic would that be? Like he's my goddamn mother or something.

I don't know how much time passes, because this is a place where that kind of shit doesn't mean much of anything, and then I push him away and we sit there. I'm trying to catch my breath and then it slowly starts to come to me that the reason it keeps feeling weird is that I don't actually have any breath to catch. That it's just reflex.

"For what it's worth, I'm sorry," Eddie says to me.

"It's worth dick, is what it's worth," I tell him.

He shrugs, like he feels he's done everything he can do, so he's off the hook.

"That's it? You shrug?" I say.

"I didn't mean to shoot you—"

"*Didn't mean to!*" I don't know whether to laugh or punch him again. "What, it was an accident?"

"Yeah, it was." His long brown hair is hanging around his face; he looks like a basset hound.

"How the hell was it an accident?"

"I thought the gun wasn't loaded."

I stare at him. "You thought—"

"Yeah."

"—the gun wasn't loaded."

"I took out the ammo clip. But I forgot—"

"About the one in the chamber," I say, and slap him upside the head. "You almost blew your goddam foot off in high school because of that, remember? When you were cleaning your dad's S&W? I told you, always remember the one in the chamber."

"So I forgot. So sue me."

"I can't sue you because I'm *fuckin' dead.*"

The words echo and we kind of stare at each other, and I realize it's the first time I've actually said that out loud, or even really thought it. A lot softer so it doesn't echo so much, I repeat, "I'm dead."

"Yeah," he says, even softer.

I stare at him. "So . . . what're you doing here. You're the one who shot me. What, the bullet ricochet or something?"

"No. I just—"

He folds his arms, turns away from me. Now I'm getting pissed off. I'm standing here next to some damned river, dead and all, and Eddie, the guy who put me here, is getting all woogity. "Christ," I say, "you're doing that same thing like when my mother hauled your ass over because you put a baseball through the window. You haven't changed, like, at all. Now what the hell happened?"

"It's your fault," he says, which is exactly what he said during that whole baseball thing, when he was ten and pointing at me and tears were smearing the dirt on his face, which kind of went to prove my point. "You made Cherry cry. You shouldn't have hocked her radio."

"It wasn't *her* radio! It was *my* radio!"

He turns to face me and he's got this pissy indignant look. "She gave it to you! You don't hock the gift your girlfriend gives you, man! It makes her feel like . . . like shit on your shoes!"

"But . . ." I gesture helplessly. "Man, you knew the deal! It was a sure thing!"

"It was the Super Bowl, it's never a sure thing!"

"But I won! My team won! Two grand, man!" And I thump my pocket. I can feel the wad of bills sitting there all nice and comfy. "Two grand from the bookie, right here! I rolled two hundred bucks over into two grand!"

"And was it worth it?"

"Hell yeah, it was worth it!"

"How can it be? You made Cherry cry!"

"Her face was gonna dry off! And why am I defending myself to you, the guy what shot me in the brain!"

"Because you know I'm right!" he stabs a finger at me, thumping me in the chest. I don't feel it. "You treated Cherry like she was nothing, man. You always did."

"That's not true."

"Is so true, man. And don't you lie to me. You can lie to anybody else you want, but not to me."

"Whattayou care?" I ask. "You always said Cherry was a skank anyway."

And he swings on me, if you can believe that. Fortunately Eddie swings like a tortoise. All I do is step back and he almost falls on his face. He catches himself, stands and glares. "I never said that."

"Yeah, you did. Two years ago, at Al's kegger."

"Oh. Yeah. Well . . . I didn't mean it."

"Didn't mean it. Christ, Eddie. What, were you boinkin' her behind my back or something, you're so defensive of—"

He doesn't say nothin'. Again comes that baseball-through-the-window look, and comes the dawn. "Christ, Eddie," I say real softly this time. "You were—"

"Just once," he says. "When you broke up with her that time, six months ago." He shrugs. "It happened. And then we both felt like shit about it, because of you, and then you and she got back together and . . ." He shrugs a second time.

"You screw my girlfriend, you shoot me . . ."

"Not all at the same time," he says defensively, like that makes it better somehow.

I shake my head and sink down to the shore.

"I just . . . I wanted you to be happy," he tells me, kind of kicking the dirt with the toe of his sneaker. "And you walked into the bar, and you were just boasting about the Super Bowl, and the money you'd made, and Cherry was just standing there, and she felt so bad, and you're all Mr. Big Man, gonna show her a good time, and you're not getting past the whole thing about why she's upset, and you're laughing at her, and it just . . . you pissed me off, dude. That's all. You pissed me off, and I'm thinking, Y'know, he made her feel like shit, so I'm gonna make him feel the same way. Scare the crap out of him, literally. Because that's what I do."

"That's what you do?"

"Yeah." He nods. "I keep you honest, man. That's what you need me for."

I snort at that. "Yeah? And what do you need me for?"

"To bum cigarettes off."

"Christ."

I just shake my head, staring at the river, thinking about how little Eddie knows about anything, and I'm thinking about the voices that were in my head when he pulled me out of the river, and then I hear a splashing. Eddie hears it, too. It's coming from farther down the river, around the bend. It's slow and steady, and I realize it sounds like somebody rowing. Some sort of regular, steady splash. Eddie looks at me in that way he always does when he figures I'm gonna pull some answer out of my ass. I shrug.

Then we see it. A big open flatboat, like one of those things in that Italian city that's all water roads. There's some guy standing toward the back of it, and he's pushing the boat along with a long pole. He's got a hood pulled down low, and a large cape or robe or some shit like that.

There's someone leaning forward in the front of the boat, and if I'd been chewing gum, I'd've swallowed it. "Cherry? *Cherry*!"

She nods, sitting even further forward, so much so that I'm worried she's gonna tumble into the drink. "*Oh, thank God! Honey!*" she calls out, and then she fires a dirty look at Eddie, for which I can't entirely say I blame her.

"I was gonna get the radio out of hock!" which is of course the first thing you wanna say in a situation like this if you happen to be, y'know, a total moron, but it's all I could think of.

"I know you were! It's okay!" She's still glaring at Eddie, and if looks could kill and if we weren't already dead . . .

And I go, "Wait . . . Cherry? You're dead, too?"

The boat bumps up against the shore line, but she doesn't get out. Instead she nods. "Yeah. When Eddie shot you, I ran screaming out of the bar just as a police car came pulling up. Rammed right into me. Bounced me off the far wall like an eight ball."

"Who says there's never a cop around when you need one?" says Eddie, and then he kind of shrinks into himself from Cherry's look.

In that super huffy way she can sometimes do because she watches movies featuring British chicks, she says, "I think you're the last one to be making jokes right now, Eddie."

"Sorry," he says. He'd been standing, but now he slumps to the ground and won't even make eye contact with her, which is probably better since all he was gonna do was piss her off even more.

"Cherry, what the hell is this place?" I ask.

"Oh," she says, like she just forgot her lipstick at a diner. "Right. Okay. This is the River Styx," she says, "which runs down to the land of the dead." She points to the boat guy. "And this is Charon."

"Hey," I say.

"Hey," says Charon. He's an old guy and I can see he's got a thick beard with some sort of fungus hanging from it.

"So . . . this is like heaven?" I ask.

"Well . . . kind of," she says. "It's Greek myth, actually. But since the three of us are Greek Orthodox, this is what we're stuck with, since it predates Jesus. Apparently the Greek part takes precedence over everything else."

I laugh at that. "Well, *that's* gonna toast Father Katsulas's buns when he gets here."

"Yeah, well, go figure. C'mon, get in."

"Get in?" I'm looking at the boat and it doesn't seem like the sturdiest thing.

But she thumps the side of it. "Of course! You don't want to just stand here all your li—all your whatever. Charon is going to bring us to Hades, the man on the other side, and the place is named after him. Actually, I hear the place isn't any great shakes, but Charon says you can work your way up to Elysium, which is supposed to be really nice. Like moving from the crappy part of Atlantic City to a boardwalk hotel."

And then Charon holds out his hand and he says, "Payment."

"Oh, right," and Cherry shakes her head. "You have to pay."

"Pay?"

"Yeah. Thank God I had my Visa card, because he doesn't take American Express."

I check my pockets. I don't have my wallet. But I pull out the two grand. Cherry's eyes widen as she sees it. "This cover it?" I ask.

Charon nods.

"C'mon, Eddie. I caught us a ride," I tell him.

But now Charon shakes his head. "He can't come," he says.

"What? Why? Two grand ain't enough for two passengers?" And then I realize. "Oh. It's because he killed me, huh."

"Oh, no," says Charon. "We have lots of killers in Hades. Soldiers, world leaders, policemen, incompetent doctors . . . we're pretty flexible about that. But we're strict on suicides."

"Sui—?"

I stare at Eddie. Again he looks away. "Eddie . . . ?"

He lets out a long sigh, like a death rattle, and says, "I killed my best friend. What did you *think* I was gonna do?"

"Jesus Christ, Eddie, you said it was an accident."

"Yeah. It was. But when I shoved the clip into the gun and shot myself, that wasn't."

I don't know what to say to that.

What would *you* say to that?

Well, Cherry, she knows just what to say. "Leave him, honey," Cherry says to me. "He ruined our lives. It's all that he deserves."

"He ruined our lives because of you, you dizzy bitch," I snap at her.

Her face goes red as her name. "Dizzy bitch? You go to hell!"

"Hello? There already!"

Eddie pushes at my arm. "Dude . . . it's okay. You get in. There's no reason you shouldn't. This is . . . I had it comin', okay?"

"No, you didn't, man. Things just got out of hand, that's all, which, y'know, things sometimes do. But this is . . ." I turn back to the old man at the boat. "How long does he have to stay here?"

"Until the end of time."

"Honey," and Cherry's sounding sweeter this time. "Honey . . . I'm sorry I snapped at you. But Eddie made his own bed, and he has to lie in it now. Now come on," and she holds her hand out to me. She smiles with those luscious lips, and the boat is bumped up right against the sand. One step and I'm in.

I look at Eddie.

I look at Cherry.

I walk over to the boat, the money in my hand. I stare at it for a long moment, and think about the folks who say you can't take it with you.

"Honey," and Cherry's sounding imploring, and Charon's looking impatient. And I realize this is our last chance.

I hand the money to Charon, put a foot against the edge of the boat, and push. The boat slides off into the River Styx, smooth as butter.

"I'll wait for the next one," I say.

Cherry lets out a cry that's half mourning, half really-hacked-off, and she's calling to me even as the boat cruises away. I hear her yelling at Charon, telling him to turn it around, but he says nothing. Her voice echoes a long time after they're out of sight, but eventually it fades.

I hope that spooky boat guy chokes on the two grand.

I trudge back over to Eddie and drop down onto the shore next to him. He stares at me for a long moment, then punches me in the shoulder. Hard. Doesn't hurt.

"Pretty fuckin' stupid, man," he says.

"This from the guy who put a bullet in my brain."

We don't say anything for a while, and then Eddie says, "You got a cigarette?"

I reach into my shirt pocket and pull out a pack. I hand him one, take one for myself. No matches. No problem. I go to the edge of the River Styx, lean over real close with the cig in my mouth. The tip barely touches it and then it ignites. I suck it deep and good, knowing at least I won't have to worry about cancer. Eddie follows suit.

We sit there and puff on the bank of the River Styx for a few minutes or hours or whatever, and then Eddie says, "In case you forgot, you're the one who really did put the ball through your mother's window. I was just covering your ass."

"Yeah, well . . . you shot me in the head."

"Chrrrrriiist," says Eddie. "Are you gonna hold that over me for fuckin' *ever*?"

I take a slow drag and then nod. "Yeah, that's pretty much the plan, Eddie. That's pretty much the plan."

Last Call
EDDIE MULLER

"SO IT WENT good, right? Just like you figured?"

Eddie doesn't glance over when he talks. He just stares straight ahead at the lights on Canal Street and aims the Cadillac toward the tunnel, getting us the hell out of Manhattan and back to Bayonne. He's got that far away look on his busted-up mug, same one he wore in the dressing room before a fight. Makes him look like a moron, as if there's only one tiny thought trapped in there, knocking around like a moth. Thinking has never been Eddie's specialty.

"Yeah, it went fine, Eddie," I tell him. "Piece a cake. With plenty of icing."

The icing, all five grand, is in a valise between my feet. Tight wrapped stacks, crisp and fresh, my ticket out of Jersey and into the life. After sniffing everybody's ass all these years, things are finally breaking right. Can't wait to see Cherry's face when I drop all this cash on her. She'll go nuts.

"Eddie, you were great," I add. Reassuring him, like always. "Thanks for backing me up. And letting us use the car." I always make sure to say *us*, so he'll feel he's part of the plan.

Eddie turns and smiles. Probably 'cause I mentioned the car. Land yacht with a two-tone custom paint job, whitewalls, long as a fucking float in the St. Patty's Day parade—the Caddy means everything to Eddie. Literally. It's all he's got left to show from a once-promising middleweight career. Thanks to the car, people remember him wherever he goes. The Bayonne Bruiser, 18–5–1 on the final ledger. He could handle himself in there fine, till he had to think. Big money wasn't in his cards, you could see that. I could, anyway. That's why I told him to take Carbo's deal, tank the Bellini fight. The boys all got well on that one, and Eddie ended up making more than if he'd won legit. Not that he woulda gone in the bag without my coaxing. Not that I got any fucking credit, or a decent taste of Eddie's payday. Pay*off*, should say, you wanna be straight about it.

I squeeze the valise between my ankles, feeling the firmness of all that bricked-up cash. "Always told you, Eddie—winning and losing, it's a day-to-day thing. Coming out ahead in the long run, that's what matters. And we're on our way."

"Them guineas liked my car," Eddie announces.

Jesus Christ, it's pathetic enough to break your heart. This past year he's gone downhill: gotten sullen, slower, draggin' ass when he used to bounce.

The punches are finally catching up, I guess. He was lucky to survive the pasting that flashy Philly spade laid on him. Once again, who was there to give him the good advice—*Quit*—when the goombahs wanted to rake in a few more bucks off the local hero?

Alright, admit it Rooney Higgins, you're no saint, you're not above using the poor schmuck yourself. You knew that Cadillacing Eddie down Spring Street would divert attention, let you handle your business in private. Everybody wanted to see the Bayonne Bruiser, and the legendary limo Carbo gave him for letting Mario Bellini knock him out. And Eddie, he's so busy getting his back slapped, he don't see the deal go down, or even bother to ask. We'll book two grand, I told him going in. You take five hundred—just for driving, just for being good ol' Eddie, just for being the kind of pal who doesn't ask for a count.

I don't look at it like I'm screwing him. Five fucking years I've scratched to get those greaseballs working with me, bringing them all kinds of sweet deals, offering to handle heavy work, always eating their shit with a smile, letting them treat me like some mutt scrounging at the curb for a scrap. It's different now. Soon as Cherry sees this dough, she'll take back every miserable word she's said about me. She'll forget it all. She'll never run me down again.

'Cause this time I pulled it off. Exactly like I planned. *Better.*

"Let's celebrate, Rooney," says Eddie. "Buy me a drink."

"Nix, genius. I'm carrying a shitload a cash here. Let's get back home. Divvy up."

"Hey, what're you worrying for? You're with me, remember? Just a quick one, 'fore we hit the tunnel."

"Not a good idea. Once we get across. We don't know no bars around here."

"There's a place right ahead they know me. Always on the house."

"Jesus, you been in 'em all, haven't you?"

It's a cheap thing to say but if Eddie's offended, it doesn't show. He gives me more of that thick, lopsided grin.

"One pop," he promises. "That's all. Call Cherry, tell her how great it went."

I know better than to get between Eddie and a drink. Truth is, it wasn't those last two bouts that finished his career. It was the booze, and the glad-handers, and the lure of one bar after another where everybody's excited to see you and they buy you all the drinks you can handle. Eddie thought he could handle them all. And being a square guy, he bought regular rounds for the house. Then the house next door, and the one across the street. Pretty soon he was doing roadwork hungover. When he *did* roadwork. After a while only his elbow was getting a workout. And I had to watch him drink down the dough and piss it all away.

I figure it's already half past midnight when we fit the Caddy into a space in front of a dive called Malachy's. Crummy neighborhood, but at least it's Irish.

"Still got that piece I gave you?" I ask Eddie.

He rubs the bristly red stubble on his head and shrugs, the silly grin creeping back on his face. "Never had it, Roon. I left it home."

"Jesus, Mary, and Joseph—it was for your own protection."

"Didn't feel right, me carrying a gun. I ain't about to kill nobody. 'Sides, everything went down smooth like you said."

Climbing out, Eddie studies the car's half-acre of hood, reflection of the tavern's neon signs squiggling all over the metal. He stops to run the sleeve of his leather jacket along a fender.

"One ah those goons got something on here," he says. "Leaning on my machine like they owned it."

In the wash of neon, Eddie seems pretty beat, not nearly as eager as he usually looks striding into a barroom. He shoots a glance at the valise: "You want me to hold that? For your own protection?"

"I'm a big boy. Let's go. One and done."

It's a fight bar, of course. Pictures of pugs all over the walls. The bartender sees Eddie and lets loose with the familiar shout, "Hey Champ!" The handful of customers roust themselves from the ant races to pump the Champ's mitt. After he won the Jersey state middleweight belt I took to calling Eddie "Champ," but he finally told me to put a sock in it. "You ain't the Champ till you win a *world* title," he scolded me. That was back when Eddie had a future. Nowadays, he eats up being called "Champ" the way a scrawny dog eats up supper from the trash.

Before we settle in, Eddie drags me over toward a pinball machine in the corner. So he can point out his picture, hanging there.

"This was my first public'ty picture, wasn't it? I 'member the guy coming to the gym to take it. You thought he was kinda a fruit, 'member?"

"Yeah, I remember."

Who the hell paid for it, Eddie? *'Member?* Not Egan, your imbecile of a manager. I lent that brainless prick every idea he ever had. Would it have killed you, Eddie, to say *Thanks, Roon*—one fucking time? In all those years?

"What'll it be, gents?" The runt behind the plank flips his bar rag over a shoulder with a puffed-up flourish and throws Eddie a manly shake. Looks like every ruddy-faced paddy towel-swinger I ever seen. Bucket boys turned bartenders. Eddie must know hundreds of these guys, throughout North

Jersey and all five boroughs, ready to pour a free one when he struts through the tavern doors. Connect the dots: free-drink-to-free-drink. Is that all you need, Eddie? Your face on the wall and drinks on the house? When you hit bottom, let's see if any of them come running to pick you up. 'Cause that day's coming on fast, old pal. And Rooney won't be there anymore to wipe your ass. When you're shuffling around in your bathrobe, sparring with shadows, me and Cherry will own ten places classier than this dump—West side, midtown, far the fuck away from here.

"You must be Rooney," says our host, grabbing my hand. "Eddie talks about you all the time. Feel like I already know you."

"Yeah, well . . ."

"Give 'em whatever he wants, Mal. Bourbon for me."

In the mirror behind the bar, I watch Eddie shoot his cuffs and climb onto the stool. I try to find something in his face that reminds me of the guy who crouched in his corner at St. Nick's and the Hippodrome, unafraid of the mean-looking jigs across the ring. But there's nothing left in Eddie that I recognize. Any good is long gone.

You've had the radish, partner. And you're not taking me down with you.

"Gimme a Rheingold," I tell the barkeep. "You got a pay phone?"

"In the back. Can't miss it."

I turn to Eddie: "I'm gonna tap a kidney and give Cherry a call. Let her know everything went okay."

"I can hold that if you want," Eddie offers again, tapping the valise. He's awful interested in the bag all of a sudden, which I don't appreciate.

"No, I got it, Champ," I say low, so the bartender won't hear. "Don't worry yourself. Drink up."

I scoped the clientele soon as we walked in: nobody with the stones to juke me up, even if I wasn't with Eddie. I take the valise with me to the back, slip into the tiny men's room, and lock the door with the slide bolt. Smells of piss and disinfectant fight it out in the cramped space. I'm surprised how my heart starts racing. It's the first time since we got off Spring Street that Eddie hasn't been right next to me. Shit, my whole *life* he's been right next to me, crowding me. Maybe I'm just getting excited about how in a few hours, that hump will be out of my hair for good.

I peel off my coat and shirt and drape them over the toilet. I'm wearing a vest underneath, one Cherry made special. Left the zippers open so I can do this fast. I count out three grand from the valise, stash it evenly in the pockets in the vest's lining, and zip back up. In case Eddie wants to watch me count the take when we get back to my place. Not a chance, but you can't be *too* careful.

Putting the shirt and coat back on, I check myself in the filthy mirror above the sink. There's something different about me all of a sudden, that's obvious. What I can't tell is if it's really there in my face, in my eyes, or if it's only in my head. Tonight—man, tonight was like I always knew it could be—sweet and easy, getting respect like I've always deserved. Finally . . . finally, I've crossed over to someplace new, crossed over as quick and clean and smooth as we slipped under the river.

In the hallway, beneath a string of permanent Christmas lights, I dial up Cherry. When we were first going out, she used to answer the phone with this sexy, husky voice, laying it on extra thick for me. Every goddamn time I saw a pay phone I'd call her, just to hear her say my name. Christ, she was a looker—and those shitheels from the neighborhood couldn't stand seeing her on *my* arm. Even after we were hitched, I never got tired of looking at her. She's got her moods, no question. But when I'd bitch and moan endlessly about never getting a break, she'd whisper to me in the middle of the night *Baby, you're a world-beater* or *Your time will come, Rooney Higgins.* I'll always remember that. She's stuck it out, that woman, through the worst, through all my big schemes and broken promises. Be our fifth anniversary next month. Now we'll do it in style, like I told her. She's been drifting away from me lately, I can tell . . .

But tonight—tonight changes everything.

Looking around the corner I see Eddie and the bartender hunched over the plank, in deep conversation. Well, deep as it can go with Eddie.

Cherry doesn't answer after five rings, which pisses me off. I told her to wait by the phone, that I'd call the first chance I got. Everybody else in the bar has taken off. The clock shows it's almost one. Bar time, but later than I thought. *Shit.* Ten rings now. *Wait by the phone!* Goddamn bitch never listens to what I tell her.

Eddie swivels and hoists his drink, giving me a little toast. There's that stupid smile again, the one I'll never hafta see again after we get back to Bayonne.

Something bumps me hard in the neck and I tur—

I've seen plenty of ugly shit in my day, but I nearly gag when I see Rooney's brains blow out his forehead.

From behind the rail, Mal yelps, "Jesus H. Christ." More annoyed than shocked. Pieces of Rooney's head have splattered high above the bar, on somebody else's pictures.

"I'm gonna be cleaning all fucking night now," Mal gripes, slapping his rag down on the plank. He flips a bunch of switches, killing the overheads, the neon. He leaves on the Christmas lights, so we can see our way around. He collects bar towels.

I hop off the stool and hustle to the back. Stepping over Rooney, I try not to look at his head. But I can't help it. Like a big red sponge with a chunk missing, lying in a puddle of blood. Cherry is standing stone still, little puffs of gunsmoke floating around her in the colored lights. I tug the pistol out of her hand and stuff it in my jacket. When I hold her, she's shaking inside, the way you do before a big fight. Scared, but excited.

"It's okay," I say. "It's over."

"Are you sure he's dead?" she asks in that husky voice of hers.

Mal chuckles as he throws down towels to soak up the mess. He gives Rooney a kick. "Hey, squire—last call. How's 'bout one for the road?" Quickly, he snatches up the satchel before blood gets on it. "I'd say Mr. Rooney Higgins has officially shuffled off this mortal coil."

Mal tosses me the bag.

"There's more on him," Cherry says, gazing down at her late husband. "He's hiding the rest of it in a vest he had me make special."

I hand the bag to Cherry and hunker over Rooney, trying not to toss my cookies as I grab fistfuls of his coat and turn him over. His eyes are open, one bulging out of its socket like it don't fit right no more.

Behind me, Cherry groans. "Oh shit, oh shit, oh shit," she keeps saying.

I tear apart Rooney's shirt and have a helluva time getting the vest undone. Mal does his best to keep the blood dammed up, building a mound of soaked towels all round Rooney's head. I don't want to look at his face, but, as it often is with me, I can't resist. And though I know he ain't hearing me, there's things I need to tell Rooney, in case he hasn't made it to wherever yet.

"Still looking down your nose at me, huh, Roon? Surprised? How long did you think we could all stand it? Smart little man and all his big plans."

I yank money from pockets sewn into the vest, hand it back to Cherry.

"Smart little man who beats on his wife every time his big plans fall through. The smart little man who keeps pissing people off until they want him dead."

My voice comes back to me different, like it's somebody else's.

"That was you, Rooney," I rant on, past the knot in my throat. "So fucking full of yourself you could never see how sick of your act everybody was. So tell me, Roon—who's stupid now? Huh? Who's the stupid one now?"

Something wet drips onto my hands as I'm digging out the last of the cash. I'm crying, for fuck's sake. I swipe at my cheeks real fast, hoping Mal won't see. I sit back on my haunches, holding the wrapped dough loose in my fists. Christmas lights are floating all over the place. Same as the night Bellini needed those extra punches to put me down. I sat there, like I'm sitting now, 'cause I wouldn't go out flat. No fucking way. Not for Carbo, not for Rooney, not for nobody.

Slowly, things stop spinning and the rushing noise in my head starts to fade. It's always like that after you get your bell rung good. But it only takes a minute till you're squared away and ready to go again. This time I hear a buzzing sound, off and on, off and on. I shake my head, but it won't go away.

I realize it's the phone, dangling on the cord a few feet away. Still ringing.

Something about that familiar sound pulls everything out of me, and I mean everything. I try to plant my feet under me, but this empty feeling makes my legs give way. I crash to my knees, in a way I *never* did in the ring. My face falls against Cherry's legs.

"You're not home," I say, over and over. I start laughing, so they won't get the idea I'm all broken up.

Cherry strokes my hair and says, "C'mon, Champ. Get up. It's not over yet."

I've always been a finisher, so I stow my mud quick. While me and Mal get Rooney and all the bloody towels into a tarp, Cherry goes out to clear space in the trunk. When we first worked all this out, the plan was to leave the body here, so it'd look like a robbery or a bar beef gone bad. Nobody but me liked that idea. Cherry said she wouldn't be able to act sad enough when the cops came round, and the mob guys didn't want bad publicity for one of their joints. So they told me 'bout a place in Jersey to dump the body, but that I got to do the dumping myself.

While Cherry's outside, Mal pulls something from under his apron. An envelope.

"Here's the other five. They told me to tell you, 'Thanks for curing the pain in our ass.' There's a bonus grand, too, for giving up Rooney's source."

I stuff the envelope in my jacket, in there with the gun. They're the only things about me right now carrying any weight. Me and Mal bend down, ready to drag the body.

"Let's carry him," Mal says. "I don't wanna hafta scrub the *whole* floor."

It's so quiet I can hear Cherry outside, popping open the Caddy's trunk. As we struggle across the dark barroom, Mal gives me a look I barely make out. "Does she know about this other five grand?"

I don't say nothing, 'cause the money part is none of Mal's business. But, like always, I can't resist.

"I did it for her," is what I say. "She's a good woman. She deserves a break."

"You can use some money yourself, Champ," Mal says. "Don't let her play you for a sap."

Then the door opens and Cherry's waiting there, biting her lip, her curls shining with all the different colors of the Christmas lights. Behind her on the wall, in the shadows, is the portrait of me, an up-and-coming world-beater.

I wish she'd knew me back then. Back when I was something.

*   *   *

I hold the Caddy steady under the limit, heading toward the marshlands. Cherry is next to me, both of us not talking, just staring out at open road and all that night rushing past. Sick of feeling the gun pressed against me, I stash it in the glove box. Since we first got in the car I've been wondering how this was gonna finish, the way we'd say good-bye. I try to think of words that could explain how I feel about her, how I've always felt about her, but that kind of stuff never comes easy to me.

I decide to pull out the envelope and hand it over.

"Put that in with the rest of it," I tell her. "It's another six grand."

Cherry looks at me like she believes in something again. Makes me feel great, I'm not gonna lie. I want her so bad, have for so long, it's some kind of miracle that I've been able to resist. She's the only temptation I *have* resisted. Maybe 'cause I've screwed up everything else in my life, I still need to believe in one perfect thing. Looking at her face in the dashboard light, I know I make Cherry out way more special than she is. But I want her to be untouchable, unbeatable, like she used to be. Like I used to be. I don't want her down in the same shithole with the rest of us.

After all the crap she took off Rooney, she has a right to be untouchable. Even from me.

"That should set you up pretty good," I manage to say. "Far away from here."

All she has to do is look me in the eyes and say "Wanna come along?" and maybe I'll be a man again. Maybe I'll be the man I never was.

But she keeps staring through the windshield, staring hard at some future I won't know nothing about.

That's when I see the flashing lights in the rearview. No siren, just the light, spinning. I pull to the side of the road. Cherry takes a long look through the back window, then at me. She's scared as anybody's ever been.

"Just stay cool," I tell her. "You don't hafta say anything." Exactly what Rooney told me—for the hundredth time—when we turned into Spring Street, hours ago.

The roller sits in the shadows, dust from the shoulder drifting up around it. The roof light keeps whipping round, painting the whole road red. Without looking over, I set my hand on Cherry's leg and give it a squeeze. The wait's worse than anything in any dressing room before any fight, ever. Finally, the trooper climbs out and walks toward us, real slow. I watch him coming in the side mirror, trying to pray but not remembering how.

Cherry remembers, muttering a string of Hail Marys under her breath.

I roll down the window and notice right off that the trooper's sidearm is still strapped in—good sign. He's holding a clipboard and a pen. I look up to his face, and I'll be damned if he's not smiling at me. It's a look I seen hundreds of times, on hundreds of different faces. It's the look they all get right 'fore they say, "Hey Champ, how 'bout an autograph?"

I'm about to laugh, but it never gets out. The gun is inches from my head when Cherry opens fire. Two shots burst the cop's chest, putting him down. My ears scream and my eyes catch fire. She's still pulling the trigger, gone crazy, as I try to gra—

TROOPER SLAIN, BOXER HELD
IN HIGHWAY HOMICIDES

New Jersey Highway Patrolman Joseph Roberts, 42, was killed last night in a bizarre incident on Interstate 95, north of Newark. Roberts was shot twice in the chest, during a routine stop of a vehicle belonging to former middleweight boxer Eddie Higgins.

Higgins, 36, was found by police staggering alongside the thruway, several hundred yards from the scene. Reports indicate that the one-time professional fighter had been blinded, apparently by a gunshot wound.

An empty .38 caliber revolver, discovered several miles away near a highway exit, is believed to be the weapon that killed Officer Roberts and wounded Higgins, investigators said.

Further inspection of the crime scene uncovered a body in the trunk of the abandoned vehicle, a 1957 Cadillac registered to Edward Sean Higgins. The deceased was later identified as James Rooney Higgins, 39, the boxer's older brother. The elder Higgins had suffered a fatal gunshot wound to the head. Authorities have yet to determine if the same gun was used in all the shootings.

According to sources at Newark General Hospital, where Eddie Higgins was rushed in police custody, the boxer confessed to both killings, although he has not been formally charged with either.

"We've only started piecing together what happened out there," said Newark Police Sgt. Clyde Callaway. "We have reason to believe there is another individual connected to this incident, and we are confident that very soon we will have him in custody."

The Other Side
AIMEE LIU

CHERIE HAD JUST finished reading when she felt the man's gaze settle over her. He'd arrived late but elderly elegant. Turned out in creamy white linen, he gleamed among the collectors, who tended to favor denim and shirt-sleeves and heavy brown paper shopping bags. This old man held nothing. He stood behind the last row, backlit by bookstore fluorescence, and chewed his white mustache as he watched with intensity like a prick of conscience. An Armani-clad Santa, Cherie thought (buoyed by the polite applause—including his—that followed her remarks), out to gauge whether she'd been naughty or nice. She could have made it easy for him: not naughty enough.

The notion nearly made her laugh out loud. Her days as a renegade were so far behind her, she could hardly remember where she'd been bad. She'd tried, just this morning, to locate the scenes of what once passed for her youthful misbehavior. There had been many—uptown and downtown bars alike, and Bowery lofts and West End pool halls, and the Other Side, of course—but either her old haunts had vanished into unrecognizable middle age or they'd been reincarnated into other species altogether—a pocket park, say, or a skyscraper shaped like a ski slope. This was her first time back in more than twenty years, and the city had altered even more than she had.

There, the dapper old man was edging away now, had merely been marking time before his dinner date. Cherie Moore's relative naughtiness or nice-ness was her concern, not his. She sat down, began smiling and signing with emphasis, just her name, please, and thanked each collector in turn for priz-ing her work, as if it were some fine literary wine that might actually im-prove with age. These slim little volumes of "larceny and murder in paradise"—her editor's brilliant catchphrase three titles back—had indeed caught and held, corkscrewing her into best-sellerdom. Paradise being the south of France, and larceny and murder being two of the more worthwhile products of Cherie's repressed naughtiness. It was all perfectly frivolous and light, or would be if not for her annual book tours to sell the latest title across the States. Invariably on these tours there turned up among the col-lectors certain other characters, lurking and eyeing and muttering, some-times leaning too close and smelling too bad, once following her to the parking garage before bursting into song: "Hello, Dolly!" It took her weeks to shed the refrain. Cherie used these stalkers in her books, only translating them into madmen of Provence. Bonnard gone berserk, as she thought of them, supplied a certain edginess that had become her trademark. They served as incidental victims. "*Rien*," her heroine, Marie Noir, would say, exiting the morgue.

This penchant for stalkers was why she'd taken note of the man in white, though he clearly was nobody's victim. Nor had he disappeared. As the line shortened, Cherie was surprised—and intrigued—to see that he'd returned, had in fact taken the last position. So upright, polished, and manicured, he looked as if he'd never before set foot in a Barnes & Noble. Rizzoli, possibly, Harrods, of course, but a connoisseur is no mere collector.

And yet when he finally stepped to the front, the inelegance of his words and voice jarred her. "I heard you before I even got to the top of the escalator. You still sound the same."

So did he. The growl lodged in the back of his throat before rolling forth into a mumble. His lips barely moved. She remembered once he confessed to her, as a child he had stuttered and the nuns slapped him raw.

"Frank?" The transformation confounded her, though a closer look told her the only significant change was the color of his hair and suit. He had shrunk a bit, but his broomstick carriage offset that, and his eyes had lost none of their glittery green. The gray mote lurked like a secret, low in the left retina only. You had to know to look for it.

Now that she recognized him, she couldn't imagine how she had not recognized him, except that age was like that.

She stood and stretched across the table, dipping awkwardly to meet him. His beard still scratched as they kissed, and she almost recognized his cologne, only it smelled both too expensive and emphatic for recall. "My God," she said.

He smiled. "Nah. We just look alike."

She shook her head, embarrassed and perplexed by the exasperation that immediately followed. There had always been that disconnect. He owned five-star restaurants overlooking Manhattan but favored anatomical slang like "jugs" and "nuts" and "screw." Though as a good Catholic he never swore, he'd once drawn her head down into his lap to give him a blow job behind the wheel as he drove the Long Island Expressway.

He handed her a book. "Sign it, Cherie? For old times."

She sat down, ignoring his request. Paul Simon piped from the loudspeakers. "Diamonds on the Soles of Her Shoes."

"I was up there this morning." One of those urban transmogrifications. Delilah's Diner from the Other Side.

"We closed," he said. "Finally."

"I guess so." She scowled at him, thinking, irrationally uncomfortable as he lowered one hip onto the table edge, rearranged the drape of his trouser. His clothes never fell to the floor. To make sure, he always undressed himself, complete with hang and fold. He took care of his belongings ahead of passion. Only once, the last time, had the urge overcome him. She'd chopped off her hair, cleared out her apartment, was leaving for Paris the following morning, and stopped to return his key. He'd been napping, came to the door disheveled, and with a single motion yanked her inside. When she left fifteen minutes later, his clothing lay clumped along the hallway like deflated Jim Dine sculptures.

That was the last time she'd seen him until tonight.

"I heard you had a new place," she said. "Several, actually. Successes."

"Like you." He smiled appraisingly behind his beard. Naughty? Or nice?

"Did you take anybody with you?"

"Some."

She fingered her pen. She would have to write something in his book. "For old times . . ." But how had he found her? Of course, there were ads, notices. Was this why she had not been back in twenty years?

"AIDS got Eddie."

She looked up, startled. His eyes were shining.

"That doesn't make sense." Eddie had gotten married just weeks before she left. Back then they were waitresses, busboys, cooks, bartenders—they'd traveled by chartered bus across the river and into the Catskills. A fat woman named Amy hooted "Amys!" and broke poppers under unsuspecting noses. Accordion music played at the wedding as the amyl nitrite blew the backs of their skulls off and Eddie danced with his new five-year-old stepdaughter, his hair a crown of yellow curls, the girl giggling uncontrollably as she tripped over his loafers.

Eddie the Teddy, women at the bar called him. Cherie remembered, "Hanna. Eddie's wife. She sold baby clothes at Saks."

"Wife number two of four," said Frank, who hadn't attended the wedding.

"But everybody loved Eddie."

He shrugged. "And apparently Eddie loved everybody."

"AIDS . . ." She swallowed hard. For months after Ryan broke her hand, the first words out of Eddie's mouth when he saw her were, "How's the paw?" She, too, loved him, but he didn't know. Eddie's loyalty to his best friend, it seemed, surpassed his fidelity to his wives. Never once did he hit on her. He knew the hand was an accident. Ryan couldn't tell his own strength.

The Barnes & Noble customer relations manager, a narrow woman with a lustrous red permanent and a rose tattoo sneaking out from under her sleeve, hovered alongside the signing table. "Everything okay?" she said, eyeing Frank.

Cherie frowned. "Fine."

"You'll sign the stock?" The CRM patted the unsold stacks of books. "I already flapped to the title page for you." She was chewing Dentyne. This smell of America struck Cherie sequentially as foreign, forgotten, familiar. "*The Other Side*," the CRM read off the jacket. "Good title."

"Fine," Cherie said again, "thanks," and waited as the woman edged away.

Frank glanced at the cover image, a drawing after Cézanne, of a sun-drenched river with three figures shadowed beneath a plane tree on the distant bank. He rubbed one forefinger across it as if to change the screen. His Other Side had been a pun. Instead of slaw and hash browns, Frank served velvet beets, water chestnuts, yellow carrots, arugula and balsamic before New York ever heard of Alice Waters. In more than one way, he taught Cherie the value of exotic edibles.

He asked, "Want dinner?"

She felt her cheeks redden. It's funny, she reminded herself. This meeting is absurd. How many times had he taken her out? Fifteen, twenty maybe, all told. His other girls he showed off more. At twenty-two Cherie was already his "older woman," filler only while Bo or Peep or whatever his "real" girl-friend's name had been, spent the summer modeling in Europe. Frank was then thirty-nine. Still, he did trot her around. Le Cirque. The River Café. Nicola's. Manhattan's then temples of trend. "You've got a beautiful body," he said one glittery summer midnight as he drove her back to her sublet downtown. A quarter century had taken care of that body. It would never be the Four Seasons tonight.

"My husband's waiting at the hotel," she lied, adding quickly, "you never married?"

"Nope." His eyes danced as if this were his little joke. "Always the best man, never the groom."

She opened his book to the title page. In the too-white light of this cav-ernous room the black print seemed to drill down through the paper. She stared at the dark recesses of her made-up name as if waiting for something—or someone—to pop out.

"Ryan was killed by a hooker," he said, and the air left her. "I found him. His own apartment. He'd closed up Sunday night, had about two grand on him from the late shift. I came by in the morning to pick it up. The door was unlocked. She stabbed him with his Swiss Army knife."

He patted his beard with fingertips, as if it were pasted felt. *You love this*, she thought.

Her ribs ached. No tears. Ryan had been the Mateus man. She'd fallen for his freckles, the coppery sheen of his hair, his optimism. He filled his days with acting lessons, commercial auditions, photo shoots, spent his nights with Eddie behind the bar. Two boys from Toronto. She met Ryan at a stu-dio in Chelsea when she was giving up. He took her down to his room on Hudson Street with its red bordello curtains and they made love to the

Moody Blues with the radiator clanking. He kept the radio on when he left
the apartment because he worried about break-ins. And to keep his cats
company. Her modeling days were finished. A degree in art history had cost
her the prime of one career and prepared her for no other. She loathed the
pretentiousness of the gallery scene and balked at academia. That left her
broke, in need of a job. Ryan, who hadn't gone to college but had more
plans than she ever would, took her up to the Other Side and introduced her
to Frank, who asked how soon she could start.

"How long ago?" she asked.

He lifted one shoulder. "Three years. The Side's days were already num-
bered. They caught the girl right away. Marked bills. We got scammed in a
money laundering ring in the eighties, I stopped taking chances. Last thing
Ryan did before leaving each night. Wound up nailing his own killer." He
breathed in sharply and straightened his spine. "For two grand!"

The plans had shifted. She sat alone in a car in the dark in Jersey City
while he scored. His radio broke. He borrowed hers. Then that, too, disappeared. He cried when he figured out she was doing more than waiting tables for Frank. He grabbed her hand and broke three bones before realizing
he'd hurt her.

"You're not with him anymore." Frank had called her into the restaurant's cramped back office. He'd seen Ryan's eyes as she walked past the bar.
He wanted to give her fair warning. "You're going out with me. You see
strangers, that's your business, but not my employees and not my friends."

"I'm just the filler while your girlfriend's gone," she reminded him, feeling
the dinge and dust from the stacks of liquor boxes and account books like
plaque between her teeth.

"All the more reason. Take it or leave it." That morning Ryan had slept
until noon, having been high until five. Frank sipped expensive wine. He
wore designer clothes. He didn't do drugs, would never marry, and probably
had a net worth of several million. He would take care of Ryan, give him a
place to work until he self-destructed, but he would never share a woman
with him, no matter how little that woman meant to him, or how much to
Ryan. No risk either way with a hooker. *Rien.*

That Mateus commercial was Ryan's high point. She felt a chill cradle her
heart. Ryan was not the last fragile man she had broken, and she knew she
could not blame that all on Frank.

"I'm sorry."

"Why? Think you could have changed things for him?"

"No. Just the opposite."

Frank's knee creaked as he stretched his leg and slid off the table. The air
stirred, and now she identified the distinct scents of starch and silk and

Bulgari, but as carefully as these had been layered, they could not disguise the underlying rankness of his flesh.

She looked down and inscribed his name and the date, then turned the pen in her hand. She measured the space that remained to be filled.

From Cherie, she wrote finally, *still searching for the other side.*

Claustrophobia
PHILIP REED

HAROLD DODGE WAS standing at the bar nursing a bottle of Tecate when he began to feel like things were about to start falling apart. He often felt like this in Mexico on Sunday afternoon when people came down from San Diego and L.A. and hit the bars in Ensenada. They'd booze it up all weekend and lie around in the sun and by Sunday afternoon the fights started and the car wrecks, too. Bloody head-on collisions where the dead and bleeding were strewn across the hot pavement. And when the ambulances came if you didn't have enough money for a bribe they left you lying there on the asphalt like a hunk of meat. That was the kind of thing that happened in Mexico on Sunday afternoon.

And now Vicki was walking up to Harold, leaning on the bar at La Fonda and looking around for the bartender and saying the meeting was all set up. Everything was going to be fine, she said. But he couldn't help feeling that things weren't fine at all. They were just about to start falling apart.

Harold had been there for practically an hour waiting for her while she ran off to find a pay phone to make some calls because her cell didn't work down here. So he ordered a Tecate with a lime but he really didn't drink it. He had this bad feeling and knew it would only get worse if he drank a lot so he just stood there trying to nurse the damn thing and get rid of this feeling of dread. He was only here because he was trying to help Vicki out. Help her deliver a car—that was what she said last night when she called him at about midnight—she wanted him to help her deliver one of those new Crossfires to some honcho in Ensenada, some gringo dude on a yacht who didn't want to sail back to L.A. and had the dough to drop fifty grand on a new Chrysler to drive back in.

But now Vicki was standing by the bar looking like everything had changed, looking excited, her skin showing red underneath, and her blond hair across her forehead, dark eyebrows and blue eyes. She was breathing hard and her white shirt opened at the throat when she breathed in, and he saw her neck and throat were red, too, the skin on her freckled chest was a blotchy red like he had seen it one other time, a time he thought about a lot. A time just before a very bad time.

Vicki Covo was a truly beautiful woman. A fine woman. Some women were beautiful and others were just attractive, or they looked great one day but not the next. But Vicki was beautiful and she was always beautiful. It seemed like her heart beat faster than any woman you'd ever met. And when she spoke her voice was smoky like she was saying something in the dark, in the bedroom, in between jagged breaths with her eyes closed. It made all men want her. And now she was telling Harold that the meeting was all set—everything was going to be fine.

"It's all set up," she said, looking around for the bartender. But the barkeep was down at the end of the bar and everyone was leaning in yelling at him and waving American money. The music was pounding and everyone was shouting at each other to be heard.

"Everything's going to be fine," Vicki shouted, leaning close to Harold's ear, her breath warm and moist on his face. "We're going to get all this straightened out once and for all."

"You called him?"

"Who?"

"The honcho. The guy on the yacht buying the Chrysler."

"Not that guy. I talked to Fallon."

"Fallon?" He hadn't heard the name for a long time.

"Yeah," she said, reading his face for a reaction. "Remember him?"

"Yeah, of course I remember him," he said, his voice sounding croaky. Harold hadn't used his voice lately and it sounded like it belonged to someone else. He had been inside himself for the past hour nursing a couple of beers and he felt awkward with her and her sudden excitement that he really didn't understand.

When he was alone in a bar he tried not to talk to anyone. If someone started talking to him he didn't say anything, just listened to them go on and on like drunks do in a bar, saying stupid things that made him mad. Stupid opinions about things they didn't know anything about, like cars. A guy might try to tell him some car was good when it really sucked. Harold knew a good car in a second. He could tell before he turned the key. A car had a feel to it and he always picked up the feeling and he was always right about it in the end. So if some asshole in a bar started spouting off about some car being good when it wasn't, he let him know that he was dead wrong. And then the trouble began.

"Want another beer?" Vicki said, bringing him back from his thoughts. "I could use a drink. Oh boy, could I use a drink."

"Why?"

"Because it's hot as hell and I'm thirsty." She laughed and the red in her neck glowed and made him think of that one time in the past.

"No. I mean, why did you say that? That you could really use a drink."

"Because we're close."

"To?"

"To being done.

"Okay," he said. Then, "Done with what? I thought we were delivering a car."

"It's a little bigger than that, Harold," she said, opening her eyes wide, as if he should already know that. "This is bigger than just a damn car. This is a chance to set everything right. Everything going back to Joe and how he— he disappeared. And all the stuff after. All the bad shit. We can finally get rid of it all."

"Okay." Really, he had no idea what the hell she was talking about.

She touched his arm and leaned in a little. "And that's very good news for us."

"In what way?"

"For the dealership. Think gross profit. Where the hell's the bartender? Oh the hell with it. Let's go upstairs and I'll tell you what we need to do."

"What about the Crossfire? That's why we're here, remember? To deliver a car." Her face was still blank. "You called me last night, asked me to chase the documents on this Chrysler so you can deliver a car to some honcho down here."

"Oh, that. The deal fell through. He doesn't want it. Do you want a drink or no?"

"So all this is for nothing?"

"You worried about your cut? Don't worry, I'll spiff you big time after tonight—two grand. That enough? But there's something I've got to tell you."

"What?"

"Let's go upstairs. I need to get changed. I've got a bottle up there. We can talk."

"What do you want to tell me?"

"I need a favor."

"What kind of favor?"

"Upstairs."

He finished his beer in one long swallow. It was warm and tasted too much of lime and he wanted something with more bite. But it still gave him the glow he needed so he slid off the bar stool and followed her as she threaded her way through the pack around the bar, turning her hips in the tight black pants. Tough, fast, smart. She was one nice package. That's why he had said he'd help her. Besides, she was a good friend and Harold felt it was important to help your friends when they needed you. Really, that was what life was all about.

She stopped and he almost bumped into her in the gloom under the low ceiling with the fans turning and the sun still white hot outside and the wind starting to kick up. That was another thing about Mexico on Sunday afternoon. When things started to fall apart it got windy while it was still baking hot. But by then you were drunk and dizzy and the wind stirred everything up inside you. And that was when you realized you weren't in control anymore. It was the heat and the wind and the booze that was making you do these things. And that's when things really went to hell.

"Thanks for coming with me, Harold," she said, squeezing his arm. A guy nearby was watching a fight on the TV above the bar and shouting something to his friend nearby. The guy had on a Hawaiian shirt and his face was red and his forehead and cheeks shone with sweat. Harold could tell by the guy's tone that he didn't know what the hell he was talking about and he wanted to tell the guy to shut the hell up. Just another loud-mouthed gringo drunk.

"It's very sweet of you to help me," she said. She usually didn't say things like *sweet*. But when she did he liked it. Sweet. He laughed. He knew he wasn't sweet.

"No problem," he said. "But now the deal's fallen apart."

"The deal?"

"On the Crossfire."

"Yeah, well." Her eyes slid away and she smiled a little.

Now he knew there was something underneath this. It started with delivering a car to some honcho on a yacht in Ensenada. Now they were meeting with Eddie Fallon.

She started moving again, mounting the stairs up to her room, her thighs pumping, taking her up, up. They were in a dark narrow hallway now and the carpet was worn through in sections. That always depressed him, worn carpet, but here it was just part of the general landscape, part of a Sunday afternoon in Mexico. She stopped in front of her door, digging in her pocket for the key.

"How'd you hook up with Eddie Fallon?"

"When I called the honcho he said he knew Fallon was down here fishing. Fallon sold him a car three years ago—right after Joe disappeared." It was strange the way she always said Joe "disappeared." But he was actually shot through the head, put in a car trunk, and thrown into a ravine.

"So the guy said did I want to be in touch with Fallon. Asked me if I wanted to know where Fallon was? I said I certainly would, particularly if he was down here."

"How's that change anything?"

"Come on, Harold. We're in Mexico." She gave him a wicked smile. "We can do anything we want."

"What do we want to do?"

"We get Fallon away from his lawyer and all, we make our own deal with him. He drops the suit and the dealership is mine, free and clear. What do you think?"

"I like it. Where's the meeting?"

"Motel in Ensenada. You know the river there?"

"Yeah."

"It's just across the river. La Polapa. Follow me in the Crossfire. When we cross that bridge, pull over for like five minutes. I'll set things up. Then come join me."

They were still standing there in the hallway with the music system's bass thumping downstairs under their feet. Harold was breathing hard from the stairs and still trying to put all this together in his mind. He heard shouting from behind a door nearby, a woman's voice swearing at someone. Her voice was enraged and the obscenities hissed like snakes. He paused, waiting for the answer. But there was none. Weird. He turned and Vicki was standing next to her door, holding it open for him with a look on her face. He stepped in.

Inside her room he saw the balcony door was open and the curtain was blowing in and flapping like a flag. Looking outside he saw the flat horizon of the ocean and the surf and the wind tearing the tops off the cresting waves to show white foam. The beach was hard and flat with waves running up a long distance and sliding back. An abandoned car was half buried in the sand and some boys were jumping off the roof. He thought it was a '49 Caddy but he couldn't be sure unless he saw the taillights. That was how you could tell. The taillights changed between '48 and '49.

"There never was a honcho, was there?" he said. "Some honcho that was supposed to buy the Crossfire? There never was such a guy."

She was pouring tequila into one of those plastic motel cups, pouring it over ice, and she didn't stop pouring even when Harold said that.

"Does it matter?"

"I'm just trying to get things straight in my mind. I like to know what's going on and I don't see why you had to get me to come this way."

She turned and handed him the plastic cup. The tequila was to the top and it just looked like a glass of ice water. It was Don Julio, white, in a round bottle. She must have bought it while she was out making calls. He reminded himself not to really drink it, just to get a taste—just enough to get a burn all the way down—and then nurse it. He took a swallow and it had the bite he was looking for earlier. He took another belt. That would be enough. And now he would let the tequila sit there in his gut and do the job while he figured this deal out.

"With you and me, the history we've got, there are a lot of unfinished things," she said, looking out the window and speaking in the smoky voice, the voice that made him think of the bedroom and how she looked with her eyes half closed and a pleasure-pain look on her face. He had to stop these thoughts because he knew what it got him last time—a long stretch of darkness. Two weeks in a small, dark, hot place. He never liked being in small places and now he really hated it. Two weeks locked in a car inside a cargo container in the hold of a slow boat to Asia. He had food and water but still—he almost went nuts. He found that the only way to survive was to hold himself very tightly. Or not at all. That was the only way to survive. He knew that from the last time.

"How do you mean, unfinished things?"

"What happened to Joe. How I got the dealership from Fallon—and how that bastard is suing to get it back. But there were other things, too. A lot of really, really bad things."

"Dash."

She looked around quickly. "Dash was the worst. Thinking it over, I realized he was the worst. It all goes back to him. But anyway . . ."

"So tonight . . . ?"

"Yeah, tonight. I need a favor. Will you help me?"

Harold thought again how important it was to help friends. Even if there was nothing in it for you. He had once seen a saying about the "circle of giving," about how, if you did something for someone, it would eventually come back to you. It seemed so true at the time. He tried to memorize it for repeating later. But the only time he tried he got mixed up and sounded like a goof. So he kept the phrase to himself and just thought about trying to help his friends, like Vicki, when they were in a jam. He hadn't answered yet and she was watching his face.

"Will you help me?" she asked again.

He answered slowly, "Sure."

"Oh good," she looked relieved. "This is going to be tricky."

"Why?"

"We don't want to go too far."

"We're trying to get Fallon to drop the suit."

"Correct."

"How could we go too far? Either he drops it or he doesn't."

"There's something I haven't told you yet."

"Something?" He laughed. "I'd say there's a lot you haven't told me. A whole lot."

She smiled and her eyes slid away. "I ran into someone else we used to know."

"Jeez, you were busy. No wonder you were gone so long." He jiggled the ice in his empty cup.

"Another?"

"No. I'm okay."

"Remember that guy, that really huge guy that—"

Vicki didn't say any more. She didn't have to. She poured him another glass of tequila.

"We never even knew his name," Harold said. "That was an amazing night. Things got a little out of control."

She laughed. "Just a little. Thank God you were there. You bailed me out, big time. And I found out what his name is—Skura. Fabian Skura."

"The hell kind of name is that?"

"The name of a really big guy. A guy who's going to be there tonight."

"Along with Fallon."

"Yeah. But the thing of it is, Fallon doesn't know he's coming."

Harold thought of it and then said, "The guy was huge. So what about him? He's going to help us with Fallon?"

"He's going to help me convince Fallon," she said, and toasted him with her cup.

Harold looked down into the clear liquid as if there was an answer there. The edges were melting off the ice cubes and they were rounding in his cup. He saw this as he noticed that his arm was raising the cup to drink, the ice cubes coming closer and a sharp smell of tequila just before he tasted it. Funny how his arm did things he didn't want it to do.

"Convince him?" he asked, swallowing.

"To drop the suit."

"Okay."

"But one thing has me worried."

"Just one thing?"

"Smart ass." Then serious again: "I'm afraid he'll go too far."

"Who?"

"Fabian—the big guy. He doesn't know his own strength."

"Go too far and . . ."

"Well. We wouldn't want him to do something permanent, would we? That's where you come in. You have to stop him."

"I can't do that."

"Sure you can. Harold, I've seen you, you're good."

He stepped toward the balcony and let the curtains swirl around him, felt the wind drying the sudden sweat on his forehead. Looking out, he saw the kids playing on that old Caddy. They would wait until a big wave came up and then jump into the water with a splash. Kids could make a game out of anything. He always wanted a kid of his own. Sometimes he imagined what it would be like to hold his own kid, hold him in his arms or hold his hand or something. And as he thought of this he felt his eyes get hot. And the regret and longing that was always with him came flooding to the surface. He took another belt of the tequila.

"So that's something else you'll have to help me with. I wanted you to know ahead of time so you can be ready. Will you help me, Harold? Please." She was standing behind him. Close. Very close.

"Vicki, Jesus, I'm not like some bodyguard or something. I'm just— what?—I'm a guy who tries to help people. That's what I am. I try to help my friends so that nothing bad happens to them. But then, lots of times things get screwed up and I'm the one that gets left holding the bag."

"I love the things you say sometimes. Like that. That thing about being left holding the bag. I've never known someone like you. You have no idea how good you are."

"I'm not good at anything except getting things all screwed up. And I want to be done with this sort of thing. I just want to live in a house somewhere, with a family and maybe go off to work and sell cars without cheating people. I'm pretty sure I can do that without screwing it up. So I don't want to do this thing for you, Vicki. I mean, there's got to be some other way."

"Like what, paying my lawyer all my profits we could make from the dealership so I can run a business that belonged to Joe and was left to me when he disappeared? No way. I'm doing this and you're going to help me."

"But what if things get out of control—"

"They won't get out of control. When Fallon sees this guy, this huge guy, he'll sign off."

"Sign off?"

"I had my lawyer draft a release. All we need is Fallon's signature on it and we're done. Out of there. We can go into Ensenada and celebrate. You and me. I know a place that has awesome seafood. You won't believe it. It's up on a cliff with a view of the ocean. Then, afterwards, the best suite at El Presidente. So will you do it? Please?"

Harold turned and happened to look at the tequila bottle. It was half gone. He looked at the cup in his hand. The ice cubes were gone and it was full to the brim again. Weird thing was he didn't feel drunk at all. He felt great. Vicki was in front of him and he knew he could help her. Then, somehow, Vicki and the sight of the kids on the car and his feelings about kids became connected and he had this feeling that he understood why things were the way they were. Why he was the way he was. And he even understood what he should do. He should help Vicki out of this jam. Because, damn it, he was good at what he did.

"Sure. I'll help you out," he said. "No problem. Piece of cake."

She came toward him, arms out, and he set his drink down so he could hug her. Just a friendly hug. She wrapped her arms around him and said,

"Thanks, Harold," into his shoulder as he held her hard. He kept waiting for her to let go but she didn't and he had time to feel her breathing, and her breasts pressing against him and the warmth of her body and the curve of her back and the small of her back under his hand. He became strong against her and was a little embarrassed as he pressed into her but she didn't back off. He still kept waiting for her to let go and then realized it was his own arms that were still holding her there. He told himself to let go. A few moments later he did. She stepped back breathing hard, eyes on fire.

"Afterwards," she said with her hand on his waist. He felt himself under her hand and wished he had lost the extra weight he was carrying. He wanted to feel sleek and muscular under her touch like all the other slick assholes in Southern California. But that just wasn't him. He had a few extra pounds and he knew it. It really wasn't anything to be ashamed of for a guy in his forties. In every other way he was in really good shape. Except for the heart murmur. That was a little iffy. But as soon as he lost the extra twenty pounds or so he'd be in really good shape.

"I'm going to get changed now," she said and backed away. She picked up her bag and went into the bathroom. "I'll leave the door open so we can talk."

Harold followed Vicki with his eyes as she stepped into the bathroom and saw that the mirror above the sink was angled so he could watch her change. If he wanted to. But he felt this wasn't appropriate so he watched her unbuttoning her white shirt, watched a little more, then turned away. Vicki was more like a little sister to him, someone he had to protect. He would go with her tonight and show her who he was. He'd take charge of the situation. He'd show her that she could count on him, that he could swing a deal like this. And then they would get all the bad stuff behind them and then they would go out to dinner at that seafood joint she knew in Ensenada. Then they would go out walking. They could walk down by the marina while the sky was black over the Bahia de Todos Santos. And then . . .

Harold couldn't think about what might happen beyond the seafood dinner because that was a little dangerous. A little dicey. Things could get out of control if they had too much to drink. So he'd probably just drink water with dinner. Maybe have a wine glass in front of him but not drink it. Just sip it a little now and then and drink the water. That's what he would do.

Looking through the curtains he saw the sun was almost down and the wind was still blowing and the kids weren't on the Caddy anymore. He looked around for the kids thinking they'd be walking across the beach and up the rickety wooden stairs that led up the side of the cliff and looking at them he'd remember what it was like to be a kid, and be tired and happy from playing. Tired and happy from playing but hungry, too, and looking forward to going home to dinner. But he looked for the kids and even went out onto the balcony to look for them but they were completely gone. He'd never see them again. And the feelings of regret and longing were with him once more. And so was the emptiness and, suddenly, the impossibility that it would ever change.

"Ready to roll?" She was standing behind him, brushing her hair. Her hair was very thick and when she brushed it off her forehead it would slowly fall back. Looking at her hair he could imagine what it would feel like between his fingers.

"Ready," he said, and was surprised at the sound of his voice. It sounded hard and flat and lifeless.

"You ready to do this thing?"

"I told you I'm ready. What more do you want? You got me down here to deliver a car and now I'm going to do this other thing but, yeah, I'm ready so let's go."

She looked at him, seeing things in him that he didn't know were there. She smiled and turned.

Harold drove carefully because of the tequila but he also drove very well and he decided the tequila had no effect on him at all. He drove perfectly and followed Vicki at a distance in the new Crossfire with the smell of plastic heavy in his nostrils and the damn sticker still in the window. They headed south with the sun setting out over the ocean, making the water look like hammered brass. Later, as the lights of Ensenada appeared in the distance, the bridge was in his high beams and Vicki was signaling for a left into a miserable looking dump called La Polapa with a dirt parking lot and a bunch of shacks scattered up the hill among cacti and boulders and hulks of rusting junked cars.

Harold pulled over just before the bridge and bumped down onto the dirt shoulder. He waited for five minutes, listening to the blood in his ears and the wind outside the silent car. Then he drove back onto the pavement and over the bridge with the white railings and the dried riverbed below. He turned into the motel and his headlights showed Vicki's car parked by one unit, a shack off to the side. Vicki was opening the door to the unit, the only one with a light on in the window. Light was coming through dirty yellow curtains and Harold could see through the open door and inside where a man was in a chair with his arms behind him. When Harold got to the door of the room he saw the man in the chair had a stained pillowcase over his head and his arms were pulled behind him and duct taped.

Harold found that it was a very small room—more like a closet, really—and it reminded him how he hated small spaces. His feet stopped moving him forward before he got there and he had time to see that the pillowcase had dark blotches on it and it was then that he saw the big man standing behind the man in the chair and the big man was grinning at Vicki. On the floor in front of the seated man was a wooden keg with a board over the top of it and a brick on top of the board.

Vicki looked around for Harold and saw him standing outside and waved him in.

"Harold," she said, urgently waving him in. "Jesus, you want someone to see?"

The room wasn't a room at all. It was a friggin' closet. He forced his feet to move forward because Vicki was inside now and he had to go in there and protect her. But Christ, how he hated small places. The only way to do this thing was to hold on to himself very tightly. Or not to hold on to himself at all. He saw the tequila bottle was in Vicki's hand and he knew if he could get to the bottle he could let himself go.

He stepped inside. She gave him the bottle and he drank.

"You got him," Vicki was saying to the big man.

"I got him all right," the big man said. He spoke in a voice like rocks bumping together under the ocean.

Vicki high-fived the big man.

"Any trouble?" she asked.

"Not much. Couple of his friends tried to be heroes." He grinned. "No. No trouble."

Harold saw the man's hands were dripping blood on the floor. His fists were sledgehammers.

Harold was in the small room now and Vicki moved behind him and shut the door. The room suddenly got very hot. It was so small they were practically touching. Harold heard the man in the chair breathing loudly. The sweat started on Harold's back and dripped down his armpits. There was a single bed along one wall with a dirty blanket and the edge of the bare mattress showing. A dresser in the corner was a sick green color with yellow flowers painted around the knobs. A painting was crooked on the wall and a door led into a dark bathroom where Harold could just see the edge of the toilet.

The keg on the floor jumped around and there was a hissing noise from inside like sandpaper on wood. But it was continuous, an angry hissing, and the keg was jumping all over the place like something was inside.

"So what's in there?" Harold pointed at the keg.

"Snakes," the big guy said.

"Snakes?"

"Biggest damn snakes I could find."

"A snake'll lie quiet in a dark place," Harold said, trying not to think too much about what he was saying.

"Yeah, but these snakes got the treatment," the big guy said.

"The treatment?"

"That's what the Mexican mafia calls it."

"Okay," Harold said. He really didn't want to know. But then: "What's the treatment?"

"Inject 'em up with amphetamines. They strike at anything that moves."

Vicki let out a lusty, cruel laugh.

"Tell him," she said to the big guy.

"This guy"—his big hand slapped the seated man on the back of the head—"he hates snakes. Don't ya? I got one in there thick as my arm."

The seated man lurched forward in the chair and almost hit the keg. The big man laughed. "Whoa! Don't turn the snakes loose. They'll git ya."

Vicki pulled a wad from the hip pocket of her jeans. She handed it to the big guy. The money disappeared in the huge fist.

"Thanks, man," she said. "We'll take it from here."

His big face went slack with disappointment. "I can stay."

"We can handle it."

His mean, sad eyes looked Harold over and seemed satisfied that he could do the job. *Christ, what's he see in me?* Harold wondered.

The big guy pulled the door open and left. A few moments later a car started and pulled away.

"Okay," Harold said, holding onto himself. "Let's get this done and get out of here." He turned to Vicki. "Get me the release."

"The what?" she was staring at the seated man.

"The release from your lawyer. Give it to me."

Harold reached for the pillowcase to pull it off. Vicki stepped in and caught his hand.

"What are you doing?"

"We're here to make a deal." Harold shook her hand off.

He looked at Vicki. She said, "Actually, Harold, here's why we're here," and hit the man in the chair. It was a pretty good punch, she turned her hips into it and the contact was solid. It made a sticky, smack sound. Harold heard a grunt and the head inside the pillowcase snapped to the side, hung there, then came back upright, groaning.

"I just wanted to do that," she said, rubbing her knuckles. "I think I'll do it again."

Harold wanted to see her do it again. He wanted to do it, too. But he wasn't quite there. He wasn't ready to forget everything about who he was. Vicki stepped in to punch him again but Harold said "No," and stepped in front of her.

"We're here for a reason," he said to Vicki. "Let's do it and get out of here. I hate this place." When he said that he noticed he was breathing like he had run a race. His heart was jumping out of his rib cage.

"You're right, Harold, we're here for one reason—to get rid of all the bad shit."

"So get him to sign off and we're out of here."

"There's something I haven't told you."

"Oh Jesus," Harold said, beginning to realize where this was going.

"You know how bad things happen and you try to live with them," she said, breathing hard. Her face was tight with a look like sex on it but it was beyond lust. And it was the lust on her face that made him realize where this was really going.

"I don't know about you, Harold, but I'm not good at living with the bad shit. And I can't imagine that you can live with what this bastard did to you."

"Fallon never did anything to me," Harold said.

They were both looking at the man in the chair now, the man who had been silent all this time. And then it struck Harold that the man in the chair was too big for Fallon. Eddie Fallon was a little potbellied guy with a bald head and greasy hair combed over. The guy in the chair was lean and tall and wearing shorts and the hair on his legs was blond.

"Can you live with the bad shit?" she said, nodding at the man in the chair. Then she added, "It's all right here in this room, Harold. Everything that happened to you, to me. All the bad things."

Harold wanted to get the hell out of here. The walls were coming in on him and he felt his shirt pasted to his back. He wanted to reach for the door handle and just leave. Instead he saw his hand reach for the stained pillowcase and jerk it off the man's head. He looked into a pair of eyes he had seen just before the long dark stretch began. Those eyes had buried him, had put him in a car, in a cargo container, in the hold of a ship. Those eyes were the last thing he thought he would ever see. But he discovered that he could survive, by holding onto himself very tightly. And, finally, not at all.

All the bad things came back to this man. To this man named Dash. This man with duct tape over his mouth but contempt in his eyes.

"So this isn't about contracts," Harold said. "It's about payback."

"Yeah," Vicki said, "And you know what they say—payback's a real bitch."

Payback, Harold thought. Am I the kind of guy who goes for payback? I'm not a thug. I'm not a killer. All I am is a guy who tries to help his friends. But here he was with his friend who was asking him to help kill another man. He couldn't do that. He wouldn't go against who he really was.

Vicki said, "Harold, we owe it to ourselves before we can go on to clean it all up. And when Fallon hears what happened to Dash, he'll drop the suit. So we can start fresh. You and me. Don't you see? It has to be this way."

"I don't buy it," he said, panting. "This isn't the way anything good starts."

"Maybe we're not so good, Harold—you and me." She had that sex look on her face again and he knew just what she meant. He wanted her. But not like this. He'd have her after he had stopped everything from falling apart. But the room kept getting smaller. It was the size of a phone booth—a coffin—a straitjacket. He felt someone had pulled a sack over his head. He wanted to step outside for a second. Feel the night wind on his face.

Vicki saw Harold was about to leave. To stop him she said, "I think Dash has a message for you." She reached around and stripped the duct tape off Dash's mouth.

"Hey loser," Dash said in a velvety smooth voice, not at all the voice of a man whose face was dripping blood. "Know what I'm gonna do to you? I'm gonna find you. And I'm gonna put you back in your box where you belong."

The sound of the voice and what it said did something to Harold. It brought back two weeks of panic and torture in that coffin. And it pushed him over the line. A membrane inside him broke and all the hatred and evil spilled out into the room. Harold heard himself say, "There's a difference between you and me, Dash. I got out of the box you put me in. You—you're never leaving."

Harold didn't really mean what he said. It was more as a threat, really, a way to scare the shit out of the guy before he cut the lights and left him there in that room with the snakes in the keg to think about what he had done. But then things got screwed up.

First, he opened the door and shoved Vicki outside. Then he cut off the lights, to scare the guy. Just to scare him. But then, when he went for the door to leave, he must have tripped over that keg and knocked it over. Next thing he knew the angry hissing was much louder and the snakes were streaming out all around him. He jumped free and jumped again for the door. And just before he reached the door the screaming started. He slammed the door shut on the screaming but it didn't do any good. It went on and on until it drowned out the wind and filled the night and even filled all the spaces in his brain and made his head feel like it would explode.

And then, suddenly, it stopped.

Harold turned and saw that Vicki was standing next to the Crossfire watching him.

"It was an accident," he said to her. "I just tripped and then—"

"I know it was." She was very calm. He sensed that she understood exactly what had happened.

"I didn't mean to do it."

"It's okay now." She touched his arm. It was a comforting gesture. "It wasn't your fault."

"Right, it wasn't my fault," he said. Then he added, "It really wasn't any-one's fault."

"No. It wasn't."

Standing there, with a cool wind drying the sweat on his forehead, he was surprised to find how much better he felt. And it was then he realized just how bad things had been. Sometimes, when you go through a bad stretch, you can't admit to yourself how bad it is until it's behind you. But it was finally behind him now. He was a new man and he felt much better. So good, in fact, that he was getting hungry.

He turned to Vicki and said, "So where's this seafood joint you've been telling me about?"

Payday
BARBARA SERANELLA

SIMMS SAT IN the Ford Bronco with the oversized tires and cutaway roof. He had the engine off and his beanie pulled over his ears for warmth. He'd grown a mustache in the last few months and let his hair get long enough to brush the collar of his blue work coat. Cherry said she liked it longer. He told her all the girls said that, which pissed her off. Half jealous and half because she didn't like to be lumped into a group. As payback, she had taken to singing the words "I am the Frito Bandito" when he packed for one of his trips across the river.

No, he thought, Cherry was one woman who would never be easily stereotyped. She was a true original. He loved her. He must. Why else would he put up with her shit?

There had been no movement from the house for at least an hour. His neck ached from watching. The house, a fortress really, was built on a small hill with a view of all approach roads. The sloping yard surrounding the two-story adobe was patrolled by scarred pit bulls. He heard the owners salted the animals' food with cocaine and gunpowder to keep them mean and awake. He thought of the warm bed waiting for him in his other life and wondered what the hell he was doing parked on a dark, dirt-paved road in the middle of the desert, freezing his *cajones* off.

Actually, he knew exactly what he was doing. His only hope was that it would pay off soon. Eddie had been gone too long. As soon as Simms picked him up for tonight's mission, he realized including Eddie had been a mistake. Eddie had lost his nerve. His sweat gave him away, the fear rising from him like a flare on a moonless night. The *pendejo's* last stretch had really gotten to him.

Simms knew Chino prison was no picnic, but c'mon, dude, he'd told him. Get a grip. Be a man.

Eddie said Simms had no idea what he was talking about, as usual. Simms had wanted to bitch-slap him, but he needed his talent so he just grunted and said, "Whatever." Making his tone all dark and mysterious to keep Eddie wondering if he'd overstepped.

Shame, really. The dude used to be fearless. Now he was a liability. If the job hadn't called for two drivers and someone who could handle a big rig, he wouldn't be bothering with the lame punk.

Truth be told, Simms was about done with the life himself. Cherry's news had changed him. He thought she had been bitchy lately, now he understood why. It was the hormones. Man, he hoped she wasn't going to get all fat now. Let herself go. He hated that.

A mongrel darted from the bushes. The sudden movement put Simms's senses on alert. The sounds of the dog bounced through the night and suddenly the world around him came alive. Something winged and angry-sounding buzzed past his ear. He swatted in reflex.

A twig snapped. An owl hooted. Gravel rustled. Simms cocked his head, concentrating on the source of the noises, evaluating the threat of them. It was too cold for snakes.

The next sound to reach him was unmistakable. The slide action of an automatic racking one to the chamber. He reached for his own weapon as he felt the cold metal on his temple.

"*No se pase de listo*," the voice said.

Don't get clever.

"Anything but," Simms replied in Spanish, smiling to show the guy he wanted to keep this friendly. "Freeway Rick sent me." He gestured with his head toward the house on the hill. "Said you needed drivers for the L.A. run."

"Your Spanish is terrible," the gunman said, switching to English.

"I've been away for a while." Simms had a sudden terrible fear that he would never leave this place. This wasn't going down how he rehearsed it. Not even close. Where the fuck was Eddie? Had he bolted? "Get that thing out of my face," he snarled, his anger at his life fueling his words. The raw, continuous litanies of injustices that were his existence. He never could catch a break. One last deal. One final score. He wasn't even doing this for him. It was for Cherry. For the kid. He felt tears in his eyes but refused to blink.

"Do you have an appointment?" the guy asked.

What Simms thought was: *An appointment? Why, you green-card toting motherfucker, I've got an appointment hanging for your brown ass.* Then he remembered that brown ass or not, this guy had the *pistola* and what Simms had was basically his dick in his hands. So what he said was, "I'm not here for my health."

The guy called him something nasty in Spanish and Simms thought it was a lucky thing for the dude that he had managed to get the drop on Simms or he'd be singing soprano right about now. Yeah, the guy didn't know how lucky he was.

"Rick said he'd call," Simms said.

"You got some ID?" the guy asked.

Simms reached for his pocket, but stopped when the guy swung his piece around and pointed it at Simms's nose. Simms's felt his stomach contents liquefy. "Relax," he said. "I'm just going for my papers." He thought about making a joke about not needing no stinking papers, but decided this Mexican national might not get the pop reference. So instead, Simms used two fingers to slowly extract his DMV printout, willing his palms not to sweat. Suddenly two grand didn't seem like enough money, not to be putting up with this kind of drama.

The guy took his paperwork and pocketed it without looking at it. Spic probably couldn't read the *inglés*.

"So now what?" Simms asked.

"Follow me," the guy said. "We gonna make some calls. If you check out, you work."

Simms looked out at the expanse of open desert. A coyote yipped in the distance, sounding like he was in pain. More likely he'd scored a meal, but they always sounded panicked and afraid to Simms, especially when they were killing.

Eddie was still nowhere to be seen. Fuck him, Simms thought. If he wanted in on the deal, he should have stuck around. He must not have wanted his payday that bad. Simms fired up the Bronco and followed the Mexican through the gates up to the big house, being careful not to grind the gears.

Something made sparks at the base of the fence surrounding the house. Simms smelled meat and hair burning, and saw that it was a rabbit still twitching but long dead. He made a note to himself for future reference. The only way in or out was through the gate. Or under, if the rumors about the tunnels were to be believed.

These guys were into some serious James Bond action. They had the bread for it.

Simms and his escort reached the top of the graveled driveway. The house was bigger than he first thought. More of a compound with multiple bungalows. The sounds of metal being drilled and pounded echoed from a long Quonset hut. A plume of sparks danced across a soot-filmed window. The breeze carried a hint of kerosene. Men laughed. TexMex music played from what sounded like small speakers. A radio probably.

One of the dogs came over with his head down. Simms watched the animal warily as he climbed out of the truck. The dog ignored him. Stupid mutt. Didn't know a threat when he met one.

The Mexican had put away his gun and stood waiting for Simms to join him.

"You got a name, amigo?" Simms asked, extending his hand at a forty-five-degree tilt for a bro shake.

"Memo," the guy said, ignoring Simms's offer.

Simms brought his hand to his face and rubbed the thick hair tickling the bottom of his nose as if that had been his intention anyway. Fuck it. He wasn't there to make friends with some underling.

"I'm Tom," Simms said.

Memo's expression seemed to say, "So what?"

But Simms wasn't saying it for Memo's benefit, he was just making sure it sounded natural. The driver's license Simms showed the guy had the name Tom Carter on it. The address was a P.O. Box in Elko, Nevada. Tom had met his demise hauling dynamite to the gold mines in the Four Corners area. Poor old Tom's record was intact, as was his commercial status certifying him to drive the eighteen-wheelers. Even his Teamster dues were paid up.

Two could play this double-oh *siete* shit.

Memo whistled and a young boy of about ten emerged from the shadows. Memo gave the kid Simms's papers. The kid ran toward the main house. Ten minutes later he returned with Simms's documents and a map. "Es okay," he told Memo, handing him the papers.

"Let's see what you got," Simms said.

Memo led him around the side of the Quonset hut, through a door cut into the metal wall. A diesel gas tank lay open at its seams. One of the welders, his visor now pushed on top of his head, was peering inside, taking measurements, and scrawling yellow chalk marks at one-foot intervals.

An eighteen-wheeler cab with an empty flatbed took up the majority of the space. The truck's chassis was brick red. An older Mexican was feeding a long spring with a paperback-sized board attached into the hollow core of one of the lengthwise beams. Simms was reminded of one of those PEZ dispensers, only the "candy" being loaded into the compartment was bricks of dope. The spring inside the hollow I-beam compressed to accommodate the payload and would expand as each bundle was unloaded at its final destination. He definitely wasn't getting paid enough even if he wasn't splitting it two ways.

Eddie was such a loser. Cherry was getting on his nerves, too, come to think of it. Always complaining, riding his ass. She'd better toe the line when he started delivering the goods. He was the one taking the risks.

"You wanna check it out?" Memo asked, pointing to the cab of the truck.

"Absolutely." Simms climbed up the running board and settled in the driver's seat. He put his hand on the shifter and wondered how hard could it be to handle a rig like this. He had miles of open road before the border to get the hang of it.

Outside, the dogs began barking furiously. Memo turned and ran for the door, his gun back in his hand and shouting orders to the Mexicans working on the truck. Whatever he said got them rolling up the equipment. The guy working the spring mechanism disappeared as had the opening in the chassis. These guys were good. Simms had to give them that.

Simms wiped his sweating palms on his pants and waited for Memo to return. This was the part he hated the most. The stuff that went on that he couldn't see. When this was over, he was making some changes in his life. Cherry wouldn't mind. She thought he was crazy for not taking the old man's offer to join the family business.

"You're not the one who would be knee-deep in bullshit all day," he told her.

She begged to differ.

Men were shouting outside. Their voices sounded as hysterical as the dogs. Something was going down. Simms wished he had a gun as he slid over to the window and looked out. His dad's nursery business was looking better all the time.

A single shot rang out. The dogs went silent. Simms pressed himself against the wall and waited a minute. No other gunfire answered. He sneaked a look out the window. The lights in the main house were out. Eddie appeared at the top of the hill, his hands held high in the air. Memo herded him toward the Quonset hut.

Fuck, Simms thought. He stepped away from the window and was standing innocently in the middle of the floor when the two men arrived. His hands were loose, empty, and out of his pockets. The expression on his face as guiltless as he could make it.

"You know this guy?" Memo asked.

Simms looked at Eddie, knowing he was at a crossroads. Eddie could blow everything if he hadn't already.

Memo put the barrel of his gun against Eddie's temple. "He says he's with you."

"Where have you been, asshole?" Simms asked, praying that Eddie had remembered to call him Tom or Carter, anything but—

"I got lost," Eddie said.

"Not another word," Simms said. He turned to Memo. "We gonna do this thing or what?"

Memo grunted. He still hadn't holstered his piece. "You always leave your friends in the desert?"

"Hey, he's a big boy. I'm not his mother. I came here to do some business." Simms felt the muscle under his left eye go into spasm. So close. "Make yourself useful," he told Eddie, pointing to the rig. "Get this shit turned around while I get directions."

"He stays here," Memo said, "until you come back."

"Fine," Simms said. "Let him do something half-assed helpful first." Eddie would have done himself a bigger favor if he'd stayed lost, but that was out of Simms's hands now. Eddie fired up the truck's diesel engine. The welders swung open the hanger doors, and Eddie managed to get the truck out into the graveled yard and pointed toward the driveway. Memo gave Simms a map with a highlighted route to a furniture warehouse in L.A.

"See you in a few days," Simms said, replacing Eddie behind the wheel.

"You're coming back, right, man?" Eddie said in a low voice as they passed.

"Have I ever let you down?" Simms didn't wait for an answer. He adjusted the mirror, revved the engine a few times, pushed the gear lever into what he hoped was first, and said, "Here we go."

Five miles down the road, flashing blue and red lights filled his rearview. Simms pulled over. His eye was still twitching. He shut the engine off, relished for a moment the absence of noise and vibration. The scent of diesel fumes lingered. He knew he'd be smelling it for days.

The cop greeted him with a hearty, "How you doing this evening?"

Simms didn't smile as he climbed out of the cab. The cop followed him to the empty flatbed.

"Where's your cargo?"

Simms pointed to the almost invisible panel. "Under there. Pretty ingenious, really."

"They give you any trouble?"

"You're gonna need a tank to take down the compound. I'll draw you a map."

Another car pulled up. The district chief of operations got out and walked toward Simms and the other cop. "Good work in there tonight, son."

Simms sighed with relief. He'd come to a decision. If this is what he had to do to get overtime, it just wasn't worth it. He was quitting the police department and getting himself a normal job.

Mosquito Incense
CARA BLACK

NO MORE, HE promised himself, as the bullet train edged into Tokyo station. The last time had been the last time. He dumped Eddie's letter into a porcelain toilet hole, flushed it down the white tiles, as loudspeakers blared in Japanese.

He left the station, slipped into Tokyo as easily as a hand into a rubber glove. Seamless. Like sliding into a gigantic steam room. The sliver of pain flared but he willed it away to a dull throb.

August Obon festivals had begun, the season of returning ancestor spirits. Near Kitazawa station, the discount mini-market was jam-packed. Air conditioner blasts hit his face while sweat trickled between his shoulder blades. Housewives, fanning themselves with folded white handkerchiefs, bought prepackaged cellophaned baskets. The woven green plastic was filled with grapes, an orange persimmon floweret, delicate eggplants, and a molded pink sugar confection lying supine on a bed of pine needles.

These offerings would sit in place by photos of the departed on family altars. Few had time to make these from scratch anymore. And it hit him. If he didn't help, Eddie's photo would stand on someone's altar.

Commuters loosened their ties and collars, spilling from the fetid subway station. Going perhaps a nanosecond slower than usual.

"*Irasshaimase!*" welcomed the pharmacy girl, whom he'd spoken with during the years she'd worked there. No smile and she'd gained about twenty pounds.

When he and Eddie first came to Japan they only ate in restaurants displaying plastic food simulations in the window. He would pull the waiter outside and point. Now, by intuition or osmosis, he'd absorbed the style of those restaurants that served the type of food he liked. He'd never mastered a menu.

Up from the station, around the corner, and past the drama school he trudged. Past eighteen-year-olds performing acting exercises in the alley. In twos and threes they breathed out from their stomachs and practiced pointing with index fingers. It felt like he'd never left. The only difference was that every year they were younger.

He rounded the corner. And it was the same.

He always came back to her. In the end it always came to that. Her and her wooden Japanese-style house that was still his. Faded photos from their past strung the walls. The residue of their life together.

His sweat teared his eyes as he paused, pulling out his key. Inside he suffocated in the close atmosphere of the tatami room. He crawled torpidly to the window overlooking the garden. Lush green moss slid over the rocks and dotted the old stone lantern. She was trying to resuscitate a milky white koi with orange gills. But it flopped listlessly, sending wavelets out of an old chipped blue-and-white ceramic urn. He slid the shoji door open quietly and inhaled the rank odor of the almost empty fish pond. She was poking uselessly with an oxygenator wand, sending bubbles over the koi's translucent lips.

Almost in a stupor, he managed to say, "Give up, it's dying."

The wand became still, but diaphanous bubbles popped to the surface. She half turned in the wheelchair. "Is that you?"

Her hair, more gray than black, hung thick to her shoulders. Smooth white skin stretched taut over her cheekbones. A shapeless maroon smock filled the wheelchair where her withered leg dangled uselessly.

"You never come in the summer," she said, her eyes flashing. She knew too well that he couldn't stand the sweltering heat.

"I almost forgot how hot it really gets."

He stretched his linen-trousered legs onto the flat wooden platform and reached for his toes. The throb of a distant bell reverberated in a nearby temple. Dusk settled over the stone-fenced garden.

"To what do I owe the pleasure?" she asked. The emerald he'd bought in Bangkok was still on her little finger. It looked bigger.

"Business. The usual," but his reply came out too quickly. And she noticed.

"Where's your sidekick, Eddie?" she said.

"In trouble, as usual," he said.

He'd been about to ask when she beat him to it: "Akemi's at nature camp in Komoro."

Their daughter.

The twangy buzz of cicadas came from the clumps of dark blue rhododendrons. The insects' drone lulled him and he must have passed out.

He dreamed he stood on the pedestrian walkway over four-lane Yamate-dori. The one that crossed in a diamond shape and stopped in the middle. Where he'd pause to look for Fuji. A long time ago he'd glimpse it on his way home if the smog wasn't heavy before sunset. A miniature white cone on an orange horizon.

Of course, that was fifteen years ago. But he always looked. Just in case. Maybe that was why he always came back to this dream. Just in case he would find Fuji again. And the hum had felt the same in the dream. The hum of people passing, scurrying to overcrowded, hot buses. Bicycle bells tingling and announcing a warning, *abunai*, as they pedaled past.

Damp, muggy, and overcast. A weeping monsoon probably poised over Korea ready to airbrush the landscape. When the inside of his eyes felt as wet and hot as the air outside he breathed in. His hair curled and his skin stayed clammy.

He heard the other silence of Tokyo in August. When the people and trucks still slept late on mornings. To cheat the humidity of their sweat and perspiration.

Suddenly horses galloped past him, running amok into the train station. But when he opened his eyes, only darkness. He'd slept sprawled on the tatami mat, with his shirt sticky and melted to his chest. The staccato clunky sounds from over the stone fence weren't horses but wooden geta sandals clopping down the lane.

He stumbled into the kitchen. She sat enthralled at the kitchen table, watching television. Watching obscenely fat sumo wrestlers with waxy top knots attempting to throw each other to the ground. Her eyes, glued to the TV screen, glittered each time one of them fell heavily into the ritual sand-pit of defeat.

"Hiryu's getting old, probably his last season," she said, not looking up. "There's *mugicha* on the counter."

Humidity hit him like a damp sock and clung.

Rubbing his eyes, he padded groggily and opened the refrigerator door to a blast of cold air. He stood there several minutes enjoying arctic cool before he noticed among the scattered vitamin drinks, bins of carrots and daikon radish, several green bottles of Veuve Clicquot champagne. Frosted green and unopened. He poured himself a tall glass of brown roasted barley tea and sat down next to her at the table.

"Reacquired your taste for champagne?" he asked, now wide awake. "You never used to drink it alone."

She shrugged her shoulders and smiled.

And he knew. She had a lover. A knowing silence fell between them. He noticed a difference within her. A glow radiated out.

He felt jealous and stared at her while the pulse in his neck throbbed. Jet lag, anxiety, possessiveness, or middle age. Choose from the four, but he knew it was probably all of them.

What right did he have to be jealous? After all, he lived in New York. He'd left a year after the accident. They'd been separated for years.

All of a sudden the shrill drilling of the telephone came between them. Her businesslike voice answered.

"*Moshi moshi*, hello."

Her tone changed immediately.

"*Anata*," she breathed.

He could never get over how that Japanese pronoun *anata*, which meant "you," could mean so much. A simple pronoun. But the way a woman said it spoke volumes. He left the table and went to the garden.

A faint breeze floated over the lighted paper lantern. The candlelight inside flickered and spun with the air current. It showed a scene of kimono-clad children catching fireflies. He'd bought it for Akemi at a mountain hot spring resort when she was six. Sulfuric acid fumes had steamed and bubbled up from the rocky earth. Merging with water from icy mountain streams the mineral water hissed and dribbled into the carved boulder pools. They'd stayed at a small Japanese inn full of dark gleaming polished wood. Slept on tatami and wore starched *yukata*, the summer kimono. They'd eaten fresh stream trout, the local delicacy cooked on hot flat stones with tendrils of mountain fern fronds.

The inn's blind shiatsu masseuse, eighty years old but with fingers like a young man, had pounded and scooped away at the knots in his back. A deep, soothing relaxation had settled over him. Vibrating and strong, as if the peace would stay. Some portion of it anyway. Akemi had held her nose and laughingly called it the rotten egg vacation because of the sulfur fumes. It had been their last holiday as a family.

He had to get away from the house.

Pulling on his jacket, he left and walked to Shibuya. The warm soft rain made the air cooler. Bearable. Like a kiss. Damp and wet from an insistent lover. Plastic bags of garbage laid in heaps along the walkway, smelling of last night's fried fish dinner. The narrow lane passed the *koban* police box and widened.

The outfits changed from delivery uniforms to suits with jackets over white short-sleeved shirts and ties. Young women head to toe in lintless black and fashion runway ready to go pose at the pedestrian crossing. Bored and beautiful in the heat. All in black. In this heat.

The children's center was full of retired oldsters with a craft mission. Coiffed and stockinged young mothers, slender and swathed in navy blue, chatted amiably, ignoring their sons in designer shorts and play shirts. The Mou Ton Ton label, a popular one, he noticed.

Eight stories above Shibuya, he slurped cold noodles served on ice. Exactly like the plastic model in the window. Even down to the shaved yellow strands of cooked egg that trail perfectly in sync with the dark green seaweed. The spunky grandmother-type cashier waitress, with brown matte lipstick, jokingly refused to bring the shaved ice dessert until he finished his noodles.

It was like wearing an old sweater, cloyingly familiar and safe. He knew just how it felt because it always felt the same. Always safe, always taken care of. *Owasuremono-no nai yoo-ni*, "Don't forget anything," drones in recorded annoying regularity at every train station. But of course he did. Forget something.

And then he saw her. His quintessential Japanese woman. She hadn't changed in fifteen years. Even in modern-day Tokyo. A bulging infant criss-crossed and strapped to her chest, she was loading shopping into her front bicycle basket and admonishing an older child to climb on the back bike seat before navigating the narrow congested lane. All the while smiling, conducting a polite exchange with her neighbor, and not even breaking a sweat in 90 percent humidity. Concentration, running interference, and doing a balancing act with a cool exterior. She could run parliament and the country better than the current prime minister. But then a lot of people could. Hats off to her, he thought, what she did every day would probably kill a horse.

Noise levels three-pronged deep came from below the ground: the rumbling low click clack of the train wheels, mid-level conductor's voice blaring, and the searing high-pitched *wha-wha* of the signal. Throngs insistently pushing and shoving to board a stifling train while performing acrobatic avoidances of physical contact. Had he done this every day?

He'd numbed out on the intenseness of it all. Had to. There was no other way to live here. But as a stimulus junkie he'd thrived on it, too.

Breathing heavy air that felt the same temperature as his body. No difference. Almost as if his insides would mesh with the air. Past Chinzan-so, the summer firefly fest in the long rolling green-hilled garden. Buzzing cicadas chirring as their newly opened wings hit their legs. Little blinking lights behind the bamboo fences.

"*Hora!*" said a child. She squatted, gently cupping her hands and capturing millimeter-sized black bodies with incandescent birthrights. One night to live and burn bright. One night. Booths of bright red, with swirling blue waves captured by single fluorescent bulbs. Orange goldfish darted nervously in pools, pursued by single-minded three-year-olds with green nets.

His cell phone rang. He looked at the number. Eddie's number, and with a pang of guilt, let it go into voice mail.

The crows of Tokyo emitted shrill caw, caws. Glistening black with beady eyes and cawing until they spy and swoop on bounty left in the garbage.

The shoji door scraped open, she released the brakes on her wheelchair and rolled squeakily down the ramp into the garden. Crickets cheeped from behind the mossy rocks as she carefully lit the green spiral mosquito coil. Halfway between incense and disinfectant, *katori senko*, which translated to "mosquito incense," kept the mosquitoes away.

He grinned at her for the first time, "Aah, the smell of summer in Japan." She nodded, "Want to talk about it?"

Startled, he almost dropped the cigarette he was lighting.

"About why you're here, I mean," she said.

The Mild Seven filter tip trembled in his fingers so he cupped his hands and steadied them on his chin. Click. His Zippo lighter snapped loudly shut. He couldn't tell her just yet.

"Time to tie up that business with Tohoku. It's been years but there's a settlement in the works," he said, feeling the explanation too lame.

"Do you still want a divorce?" she asked.

"Not anymore," he said and looked away.

The rhythm of splatter plop, plop beating on the tin roof of the shed outside the window woke him up. Torrential typhoon downpour cooled the air. Heavy raindrops weighted down the trees and the budding camellias sagged by the mucky fishpond. Dampness clung to the futon covers and the moist corners of the room. Mildew was a fact of life in the rainy season. His pores oozed fine beads of perspiration. Gray blanketed the sky.

He'd felt drugged last night, in a stupor of jet lag and heat reaction. Still in his crumpled sweaty clothes from the plane, he longed for a bath and something clean to wear. Upstairs he still kept clothes in her closet. At least they'd been there last time. He padded up the polished wooden steps next to the mini lift she used to get upstairs. A shaded lamp let out a faint blurry yellow light. She was asleep. Her hair fanned out over the bean-husk pillow and she smiled in her sleep. The years lifted away from his eyes and he saw the real woman. Not the broken one. The one he'd been consumed by. The one he'd moved here for. Not the one he'd abandoned.

She stirred, still smiling. He lay down on his stomach next to the futon and studied her. Her breath rose and fell subtly with little exhalations and a scent of lemon wafted from the sheets. He moved to feel her skin under the cover but his arm hit something hard. A book. Pulling it out he saw it was in French, a mystery thriller. When did she learn French? Intriguing. And still mysterious.

He'd always been afraid that she was smarter than he was. But of course she was. Hadn't Eddie told him that?

He wanted to crawl under the cover, feel her skin all over him, suffocate in that lemony smell of her. Surround her with himself. Take her like he used to, rubbing, urging her insistently until she let go and wrapped her legs around him. And they moved together in their old familiar rhythm. Her eyes opened and she said something. A word in French he couldn't understand. A drunken white moth, heavy with moisture-laden wings, crashed into the window with a small thud.

"What are you doing?" she asked.

He ran his fingers over her right cheekbone

"Checking your geography." He paused. "That's right, turn left at the mole and go past the dimple. The same ravine under the eye socket and feathery lashes." He murmured, "Have to check the hard-to-get-to places," inhaling the warm, musky hair entwined at the back of her neck. Black diaphanous net draped her body in a web under the cover.

"What's this?" he asked in her ear as he reached and stroked her gauze-covered thigh.

"A zen monk's summer kimono," she said languidly. "But they wear another one underneath."

"I like your style better," he said, moving on top of her, breathing her lemon-tinged sweat.

Propping herself up on an elbow she nudged him off. "You don't feel sorry for me anymore, is that it? Or is getting another man's woman more appealing, maybe enticing to you?"

Surprised, he moved and lay back, shifting horizontally beside her.

"Probably. Oh, I don't know," he said honestly, stroking her bony arm while his head rested on the musky scent of her pillow. He stared at her for a moment. "I want you. It's selfish and so am I. But that's not news to you."

He almost told her then. Almost told her about him. About Eddie.

Instead he rolled away and sat up.

"Who is he?"

A shade of amusement passed her eyes. How many times had she asked him the equivalent.

"My doctor, the specialist from Geneva."

That explained the French thriller and the good champagne.

"He's a widower, not that I care. He's here teaching at Waseda Hospital. He talks of marriage but I think affairs are more exciting, don't you? Perhaps I sound cold and manipulating but I'm thinking of Akemi. If we divorce, she'll get less from you. It wouldn't be fair for her."

Now he felt utter shame. Full of disgust for himself that she would think like that.

"Do you really think I'd ever leave Akemi or you in the cold? I couldn't." He hung his head. "I still pay for everything, don't I? A blank check comes every month, doesn't it?"

"Yes, it does. A guilt remittance arrives from a father who isn't a father and a man who stopped being a husband long ago." And she stopped there.

He waited for her to say it, to accuse him. To just say it once. But she'd never done that, never gone that far. He wanted to push her.

"Why don't you say it? Say what you really mean! The ultimate indictment you've been dying to charge me with for years. Go on, say it!" He was shouting.

A single tear escaped and slid down her cheek. He watched the glistening drop until she brushed it away.

"You mean that you ran off the road when you were too drunk to drive . . . my legs paralyzed in the accident? Is that what you want to hear?" she asked softly.

Numbly, he nodded his head. He shouldn't have driven but Eddie insisted. Some scam of Eddie's, always a scam he had to rush to.

"I forgave you a long time ago for that," she said simply. "Maybe you haven't forgiven yourself."

"I always thought—"

"Life is too short to be eaten up with guilt over that. That's a cancer of the soul. But I have another kind of malignancy. It's that I can't quite forgive your running away with Eddie, not dealing with what happened. That's my problem."

Totally amazed, his mouth dropped open. "Is that true? But when I couldn't sleep with you after your legs . . ."

"Your loss, so my French doctor leads me to believe." A shy smile came across her face.

A white-winged moth, superimposed with yellow dots, fluttered from the rafters between them. "What a good omen!" she exclaimed and sat up. "A cyclid is so rare. Born open-eyed, it becomes totally blind and dies in three days. It's said that a cyclid's life cycle is a symbol for a human who's lived fully. They make the most of the time they're allotted. Each female lays several hundred eggs with help from several males." A snort escaped her lips. "Maybe in my next life I'll be reborn as an insect. But sappy as it sounds, life is precious for me now. I want it all."

And then he knew he couldn't tell her. Wouldn't reveal the malignancy eating his body. Wouldn't ruin her new-found grasp of life with his terminal one. And he'd send the check to Eddie. It didn't matter anymore what Eddie did with it.

They sat quietly on the fresh straw tatami. From the garden, the stone lantern cast a greenish glow through the rice-papered window and together they watched the almost blind cyclid hover and flit around them.

Bobby the Prop Buys In
DAVID CORBETT

A QUARTER TO midnight, Bobby Roper sat in the cluttered, nicotine-stained office of the Eucalyptus Room while his boss, Sal Lazzarini, ran a tape on the week's damage. Sundays, Sal closed up at eleven, kicking out the last of the weekend losers. They'd sit there at the sucker tables till daybreak if you let them, pissing away the mortgage, the alimony, the kid's tuition. It hurt, Sal told Bobby, giving them the boot. A card room's bread and butter, types like that, but you had to run the numbers sometime.

Sal squinted in the dusty lamplight at his desk, collar tugged open and shirtsleeves rolled tight up his forearms as he punched the figures into his adding machine. Tallying up the cage drawer shortages from his cashiers, he muttered, "Little skinks are stealing me blind." He winced at the total. "Amounts are fucking ridiculous."

"It's a great deal, gotta admit." Bobby was the only employee left, the others having long ago headed home. He could speak freely. "Short-term loan, till next payday. No interest."

"I ain't a fucking bank."

"So ax somebody. Make an example."

"Where you been? Last month alone, two, okay?" Sal held up his thumb and index finger, drive the point home. "Sent the little thieves packing. Guess who hired them back."

He meant his partner, Phil Vogel. Phil came from money, the family black sheep. Like most guys of that stripe he was scared down deep. He tried to cover up by playing the world-wise big shot, but he knew it was all a lie. And so he drank. The drink, it made him an easy play.

"Show up in a leather skirt and a Wonderbra," Sal said, "tease your hair like cotton candy, Phil can't feel for you fast enough."

"Same deal with the chip girls, be my guess." Bobby knew that total was coming next. Sal growled and shook his head like a drowsy ox then ran the shorts. The chip girls worked the floor and, from time to time, snuck loans from their aprons to gamblers, hoping by shift's end to make it all back with "interest." Sal made a little moaning sigh, licked his pencil tip, then entered the sums in his ledger.

"You try and tell 'em, guy's already on a downslide when he hits you up. Luck don't change in here. It's what the place is for."

He glanced up darkly and winked. Bobby smiled back. There was an odd simpatico between them, not so much boss and employee or even mentor and student as—it scared Bobby sometimes to admit this—father and son. Bobby'd been little more than a smart-ass with a talent for cards when he'd shown up at the Eucalyptus Room. Sal had made a gambler, a man, out of him—not so much because of anything he'd said or done, just by example.

The connection between them seemed all the more curious given how different they were. Bobby had the unwelcome distinction of being the only college graduate in Sal's employ, an all but worthless bachelor's degree from Chico State. It was the kind of thing that got you laughed at around the tables. "Professor," they'd call you, like it was the polite way to call you a fucking fool. Worse, he'd majored in Western civ—the last-chance catch all for aimless party nomads desperate to hustle up a diploma. He could hardly have done worse with a degree in interpretive dance. Which was why his relationship with Sal was so key. Sal suffered no fools. His regard for Bobby meant status. Protection.

Sal finished up with the bum chits and dubious checks Phil had okayed. Tearing off the tape, he tossed it across the desk. "That's twenty-three grand right there." The scroll of white paper fluttered like a tiny kite through Bobby's fingers. "One week, understand? The chits are fucking gone, okay? Never make good on them. And sixty to eighty percent of the checks gonna sail right back NSF or with a stop order." Sal uncapped the fifth of Cutty Sark he kept in his desk and freshened his glass. "That's my partner. Him and that pack of wind merchants he calls friends." He swirled the scotch in the glass, sniffed first, then drank. "Sick of it, Bobby. Only a matter of time before he fucks us all. Which gets us back to me and you." He scratched his stubbled cheek with his knuckles and sat back in his chair, rocking a little, away from the lamplight. "So—got something for me?"

Bobby unbuttoned his sport coat, squirming forward in his seat. He'd been dreading this part. "Sal, you know, that's what I've been meaning—"

"You ain't got it." Cut the nonsense. Like that.

"I've got most."

"Most? What's most? How much we talking about?"

"My player's bank, in the vault there, it's eighteen."

Sal, incredulous, patted his waxy white hair. "*Eighteen?*" He was a beefy man, gone jowly and tub-muscled at fifty, but still imposing, even sitting down. He had a broad pockmarked face that withered up, eyes narrowing to slits, when he inhaled from his cigarette. "You come here to insult me with eighteen?"

"I've got the rest."

"On you?"

"Yeah, well, here's the deal—"

"You gonna tell me eighteen is *it*? Total?"

"The other two's promised to me."

Sal cackled. "Promised. Christ. I love that." He shook his head with disgust. Then it hit him. "*Two*? You think twenty's gonna—"

"Sal, hear me out, okay? You said—"

"Twenty? Never."

"Sal, don't take that tone. It's not right."

"Fuck right. It's fifty a point, always has been. Where you been, the eighties?"

"Sal, there's no need to yell, okay? I'm sitting right here."

"You think I don't know my own damn numbers?"

"Look, let me tell you the deal."

"Midnight's the goddamn deadline, Bobby, I told you. Partnership agreement spells it out. Gotta cut off shares some point. It's the legalities."

"Sal, I realize, yeah, yeah, but listen, okay?" Bobby hated what he had to say next. Not because it wasn't true. It just made him feel weak. "Trink, the asthma, she's got these doctor bills you wouldn't believe."

Sal stiffened, cocking his head. "Shut up."

"Sal?"

"I said shut the fuck up." He squinted, cocking his ear toward the door as he stubbed out his smoke. In a whisper: "You don't hear that?"

Bobby leaned in, whispering back, "Hear what?"

Sal shimmied open the top drawer of his desk, withdrew a nickel-plated snubnose, and checked the cylinder for live rounds. "Stay put." He nodded toward his private door, the one behind his desk, leading from his office into a cluttered little entry then out into the employee parking lot. "Anything goes bad, you run, understand? Don't play hero."

Bobby eyed the gun like it might suddenly fly out of Sal's hand and sail across the room straight at him. "Sal, what's . . . I don't—"

Sal stayed further talk with an upraised palm then struggled from his chair, crouching like a bear as he edged toward the outer hallway. The gun looked toylike in his hand as he pointed it straight ahead of him. He craned his neck to peer through the doorway, down the dark hall to the cage.

Bobby sat mesmerized, watching Sal disappear. Five seconds passed. Ten.

"Hey! Who the hell—"

A gunblast erupted in the hallway, sending a strangely brittle echo along the walls like a hammer striking tin. Bobby dropped from his chair to the floor, covering his ears. "Jesus, God, no . . ." Ashamed at his cowardice, but we are who we are. Straightening up but still on his knees, he called out, "Sal! You okay?"

A stranger inched from the dark hall into the doorway—medium build, medium height, nothing to distinguish him but what he wore: ratty black turtleneck under a limp brown suit, ski mask tugged down onto his head, hiding his face. He had to tip his head back and a little to the side to see out the eyeholes, the mask on so crooked. He held a gun, too. It looked big in his hand, not like Sal's. A faint curl of smoke laced upward from its barrel and Bobby couldn't take his eyes off it.

He lifted his hands. "Please. Listen. I'm just here, you know, I can't . . ." The words trailed away. He had no idea what to beg for, not with so little faith it would matter. And yet as that first wave of terror broke across his brain and then drew back, he suffered an eerie sense of familiarity. The way the man carried himself. His eyes for sure.

Six hours earlier, Bobby'd stood at the stove in his apartment, watching a kettle of water and listening as Trink tore through the bathroom medicine cabinet, the vanity drawers, desperate for an inhaler she hadn't sucked dry.

Begging the water to boil, Bobby called out, "Trink, Trink! What'd you wear last night? Check the pockets!" Easy now, he thought. You freak, she freaks, the whole thing spins outta control. Her raspy breath bit like a saw down her throat and lungs. She would've screamed if she'd had the air. Bottles crashed as she tried to exhale, couldn't. The carbon dioxide was building up, the toxicity in her blood. Couple of minutes she'd black out. Worse if he didn't get her to Emergency in time.

The teakettle whistled and Bobby snatched it from the stove top, burned his hand, dropped the thing. "No. Fuck. No." He grabbed a towel, dodging barefoot the puddle of scalding water as he picked up the kettle and shook it, checking to see how much remained. Spinning back to the sink, he doused the coffee grounds in the drip filter, splashing gritty shmutz everywhere. Just enough for a good half cup. Plenty strong that way, he thought. Think positive.

He stumbled to the bathroom. Trink half sat, half knelt on the tile floor, clutching the edge of the sink with a pale and skeletal hand, chest heaving as she sucked on a small silver canister of Albuterol. She'd used up all her Asthmacort, and her dependency on the Albuterol was the latest turn of bad luck: the mold infiltration in the apartment walls, an endless bout of flu they'd passed back and forth since Halloween, a case of thrush in her mouth from the inhalants. Then, the topper, the elevator gave out. Two months now, the thing was locked between floors. You complained to the landlord, he'd just say, "Blame rent control," and slam down the phone. They lived on the seventh floor. Might as well be the top of Mount Sutro. For all intents and purposes, Trink was a prisoner.

Bobby knelt beside her as she pressed the plunger on her inhaler one more time, sucking deep on the spray. Not much left, he guessed, need to get more tomorrow. Dark patches rimmed her eyes, which were spent and glazed.

"You strong enough to walk to the kitchen, or you want me to bring the coffee in?"

She just shook her head, like she couldn't believe he'd ask such a thing, twitching from the pain in her diaphragm. Her breaths tremored quick and shallow and she rubbed her throat.

"I'll be right back." He retrieved the half cup of coffee from the kitchen sink and carried it back to her like an offering. In a mock accent, vaguely Transylvanian, he said, "Black like night, strong like bull." Trying to joke, turn the mood around.

She'd inherited most of her features from her Slovak dad, her poor constitution and bone white skin from her black Irish mom, as though the gene strands had worked out some kind of truce when she'd been in the womb. Tiny, with birdlike legs and arms, she spread oddly wide at the hips, square in the can, small-breasted, with an upturned nose and a sloping jaw that gave her a strangely vixenish underbite. Her lips were plump, curving wickedly at the edges, and she had the kind of wintry blue eyes that could stop you dead. She had a pixie haircut that traded on how small she was, but that was hardly necessary now. In her cotton briefs and tank top, barefoot, gasping for breath on the cold hard floor, she looked like a dying child. Except for the tattoos.

"Get me the aspirin." She fluttered her hand toward the medicine cabinet. Bobby obliged—it would mean she'd taken every conceivable measure at her disposal to stop the attack—and she popped three tablets with the coffee. Settling back against the wall, legs tucked up under her, she gathered a few even breaths then said, "It's not fair. I eat, like, nothing that's not green. I cut out the sugar. Cut out the salt, the wheat. Well, most of the wheat. No wine, no whiskey, just vodka."

Bobby smiled. Yes, well, ahem, he thought. You still smoke.

"You do what they tell you," she said, "you should catch some slack."

She'd started smoking at age eight. Her brothers were out in the peat mounds that belonged to the greenhouse rimming the schoolyard, all three of them with Danny Mulhern and Petey Costello. Trink—Jennifer Trinka, third grade, Star of the Sea Elementary—snuck up, spotted them passing the Marlboro pack around.

"I'm telling," she hissed, then spun around and fled.

They ran her down, forced her to the ground, and held her there behind the rectory—Catholic priest looks out the window, sees five boys on top of an eight-year-old in her plaid jumper and knee socks, think he's gonna do anything but watch? Her brothers forced her to smoke with them. "Take a drag! On the fag!" A chant, then came the head trip. They said if she told on them, they'd tell on her. Did that every day for a month, till they didn't need to hold her down anymore. Two years passed before she caught on to what a lame threat they'd made, and by then she had a half-pack-a-day habit, ten years old. The asthma kicked in not long after puberty; she had a two-pack

habit by then. She'd been flirting with suffocation ever since, working cocktail, chip girl, rooms hazed with smoke.

With the heel of her hand she wiped at one eye then the other. "Not fucking fair."

"No, it's not." What could he say? She was his girl.

"I don't want to die in this hellhole, Roper. Okay?"

"I'm working on it."

It was why he'd jumped on Sal's offer, decided to buy in to his new secret
partnership. An old pit boss of Bobby's from his Reno days had settled in
Minden, gotten in touch, said he had a housing deal. Come up with thirty
grand, he said, he could work them into a condo meant for the casino staff,
rig the financing through the union. Nothing magnificent, three rooms and
a kitchen, but Bobby had no credit—name a gambler who did—he couldn't
be choosy. And it was high desert. Good for asthmatics.

Bobby'd been doing all right getting the money together till Trink's string
of therapeutic sidetracks and sudden disasters this past year—acupuncture,
allergy tests, a pneumonia booster, four trips to Emergency, where they
amped her up on adrenaline so bad they had to monitor her for heart attack,
after which she felt like the nurses had gone at her with hammers. And given
her asthma, insurance? Forget about it. Every single payout for care or meds
came out of pocket, full price. She couldn't work anymore. With the elevator out, couldn't even leave the apartment. Bobby was on his own, down to
his last eighteen grand, kept in his player's bank at the Eucalyptus Room.
He'd lose that, too, if he didn't do something.

Trink pursed her lips, chest shivering as she exhaled. "Just once in my life,
Roper, I'd love not to have to think about my next breath, you know?"

Bobby had studied enough psych at Chico State to know what was going on.
The imprint, so to speak. He was drawn to women who were helpless victims of their own self-torture. Like his mother.

He'd been an only child, she a single mom, and they'd moved a lot, the
only constant in their surroundings being the mutual loneliness they'd inhabited, and which Bobby'd never quite outgrown. Part of it was the fact he
knew the wound his mother nurtured had been caused by his father.

Bobby'd only known the man through photographs his mother hadn't
hidden well enough. He'd been handsome with an effortless grace about
him, generous with a smile, and never seeming ill at ease in front of the
camera. At least, until Bobby's mother got pregnant. The snapshots ended
then, along with the marriage, and Bobby's father became a rumor told to
him by his mother in bitterness. "A sociopath," she called him. "Born salesman." He'd liked his horses, she said, liked his cards, liked his liquor and
his girls, and he'd disappear for days, weeks sometimes, come back hung-

over and smelling of gin and cigarettes and another woman's sweaty perfume. With tales like that she created a second biography to contradict the one the pictures told. Because Bobby, noticing the facial similarity in those photographs—same deep-set eyes, same Roman nose with laugh wrinkles in the bridge, same willowy frame—and sensing within himself an echo of his father's fascination with chance, knew himself to be his father's son. But looking up, where the old man should have been, an absence loomed.

As for his mother, twenty years after Bobby's father walked out, she finally dragged her middle-aged heart from the shadows and met somebody new. Ralph Stoudemire: He brokered professional liability coverage and taught ballroom dancing, which was how he and Bobby's mom met. The dancing, it was all Bobby's mom could talk about, like she'd been born again with a song in her heart.

"Come down and visit us, Bobby, couldn't you? Your mother's happy for once, good God, do you understand?"

And so Bobby hitched down from Chico for a visit and met them at the Embarcadero Hyatt in San Francisco. Bobby's mom, the chain-smoking high school teacher, wore lipstick and eyeliner and rouge, first time in years, and a cocktail dress, white heels. Ralph wore a blue blazer and brown slacks, reeking of cologne and breath mints. They were like high school kids together, the light in their eyes when they sat together, the giggles, the furtive little pinches. Then the hotel orchestra struck up "Begin the Beguine," Ralph's request. He shot to his feet, pulling her with him, and they were gone. The dark dance floor shimmered from a recent waxing and their reflections flickered beneath them as they swirled and stopped and circled, defying gravity for a little while. Not long enough. Two years later, after Ralph emptied all their accounts then disappeared, Bobby's mom climbed out of the bottle just long enough to say, "That's it. I'm done. Men leave, they take everything, and they don't come back. I'm only so brave, you know?"

And there you had it, Bobby thought. He'd both mimicked and defied the example of the men in his mother's life. Admiring their swagger, their charm, their cutthroat worldliness, but bettering them by being smarter, stronger, loyal. He hadn't left Trink, he'd stayed. He'd taken nothing from her. On the contrary, he'd given all he had. And Bobby knew he owed some of that to Sal. The father he'd been secretly hunting for all his life.

Bobby understood perfectly well that the buy-in for Sal's offer was fifty, but he figured if he could just scratch up an extra two, show up with twenty even, Sal might negotiate. And in three months, the way Sal had pitched the deal, Bobby could turn the twenty into thirty, cash out, send his old pit boss the down, and get Trink where she needed to be, up in the thin cool air, the sunbleached heat, the high desert. But he still needed another two grand. That was where Eddie Mott came in.

Bobby had to cab it to the Richmond District, where Eddie lived, because his own car had died, and he couldn't throw good money after bad right now. As the taxi turned the corner off Clement, he saw garbage heaped along the sidewalks, waiting for pick up. He'd read about it in the paper, some kind of work slowdown ordered from on high at the union, contract renegotiations with the city. Big black plastic bags sagged along the curbs, kids jumping on them like trampolines. From upstairs windows, mothers screamed at them to knock it off, get inside and wash. Some of the bags had ripped open, revealing their disgusting secrets, and from the looks of it, the kids weren't the only culprits. There were rumors union crews were going around doing the damage, get people fed up with the city. But there were always rumors like that, just like there was always garbage.

Eddie's wife, a Korean named Claudia, opened the door, all five feet of her. She wore a washed-out housedress, hair in rollers, gazing up at Bobby through smudged glasses. She had a square face with bushy eyebrows, thin lips, and a flat nose. There was no explaining gamblers and their wives, Bobby realized, but he'd always thought Eddie had stooped particularly low.

"Eddie not here!" Claudia spoke in short bursts of sound, like a swim coach with his whistle. "Mother dead!" Her eyes took on a chuckling glow. She gave Bobby the address then cackled like a magpie and slammed the door.

Eddie's mother's house was clear across town, where the backslope of Bernal Heights rubbed against the Outer Mission. It cost Bobby forty-three bucks with tip to get there by cab, and he figured he'd be wise to hit up Eddie for that as well. He was down to fifty-six dollars pocket money.

The taxi let him out in front of a stucco duplex mottled with bad patch jobs on the outside walls. Mud-colored stains fingered down from the rain gutters and mold speckled the window ledges. Every house on the narrow street looked as bad if not worse, while a brisk wind blew trash down the sidewalks.

Bobby tried the door, discovered it open. "Eddie?"

Passing through the doorway, he entered a museum of motherly kitsch glazed with dust. The place stank of mildew, the windows all closed tight, plus a heavy stench of gas. But there was a foul human smell, too.

Bobby found Eddie in the kitchen, perched like a toad on a tiny wood footstool, staring at a sun-faded flower-print bed sheet covering a lumpy shape. The odors were worse in here. The oven door stood open. Duct tape sealed the windows and still hung tattered along the edges of the doorway.

"Eddie, hey," Bobby whispered, thinking: Good God . . .

Eddie glanced just once at Bobby, nodded, then returned his gaze to the washed out bedsheet.

"I had to move her. They're gonna get pissed, the cops I mean, but fuck them. I had to."

Eddie was possibly the most placid person Bobby knew, but he sensed something dark, something hostile, dragging at his voice like an undertow. Bobby slipped up behind, squeezed Eddie's shoulder. "Christ, Eddie, this is, I don't know, terrible."

Eddie nodded solemnly. He was a hulking, soft, plain man, with a face memorable solely due to his horn-rimmed glasses, behind which his eyes swam lazily in a doleful timidity. His clothes came from Sears—gray, beige, white, more gray—and he had a full head of thick black hair, gray now at the temples, that he finger-combed and washed too seldom. His life consisted of repairing computers in his garage and playing cards.

"People don't die the way you think, Bobby. Smell that?" His nostrils flared and he winced, pushing his glasses up the bridge of his nose. "Not the gas, the other thing. I cleaned up most of it but, you know, the muscles relax. Not right, cops find her like that."

"Respect, Eddie, it's important." Bobby felt desperate for air. "Hey, listen. This probably isn't the best time, but I—"

"Her head in the fucking oven, Bobby. Same oven, all those years, she baked my birthday cake. It's a message. I don't feel despair here, Bobby, I feel anger."

Yeah, but whose, Bobby wondered. "Don't take this on yourself, Edster. Old folks, they get depressed."

"Sixty-two, Bobby. Just sixty-two. That's young."

"Too young, Eddie. You're right, what can I say? Listen—"

"Gotta admit, can't say I cared for her all that much, you know? Used my old man up like a bag of peas. Me, I was just the errand boy. But you know, today of all days, she's my mother, and what ain't right, ain't right."

Bobby was kneading Eddie's shoulders now, working them like a weight room trainer. "Eddie, Eddie, I understand. Totally. The human condition, it's supremely wack. Now, like I said, this ain't the best time I realize—"

A loud knock sounded at the front door. Bobby spotted two cops venturing in through the shadows and dust-moted lamplight in the living room.

"Anybody? Hello?"

Like that, Eddie shot to his feet. "Look who decided to show the fuck up!" He hitched up his belt and lurched into the living room. "I can understand they ain't gonna pick up the goddamn garbage today. You guys with the same union?"

"Sir," the lead cop said, raising his hand. "Back up."

"That all my mother means to you guys? Just another sack of trash?"

No, Bobby thought. This can't happen. Out of the corner of his eye he spotted Eddie's key ring on the kitchen counter as the voices in the living room started to boil. Eddie's headed for lockup, Bobby thought, what good's his car to him. He snatched the keys, shoved them in his pocket, as one of the cops shouted, "I meant what I said. Back the fuck up, fat man, or we do the dance."

The next few hours dragged by like a Swedish movie. The cops wouldn't let Bobby go till they could write out a report and Eddie wouldn't let them so much as start. He just kept cycling through paranoid fits of guilty rage and sad-sack crying jags, at one point mewling in misery on one cop's shoulder, same cop he took a swing at not thirty seconds later. That was when they put the cuffs on, called for backup, and told Bobby to shut the fuck up and sit tight or he'd be joining his friend in stir.

Bobby slinked off to the kitchen table, where he sat and chewed his thumbnail, watching the hands on the clock spin around while more and more cops showed up. Even the Neptune Society got there before Bobby could finally steal one of the cops into a corner and talk him into jotting down enough so he could leave.

"Eddie, Eddie, you be strong!" Bobby waved good-bye through the crowd of uniforms, some of whom were raiding the fridge now. Backing into the living room, he collided with the crematorium's gurney. It scared a little yelp out of him and he spun around, apologizing to the bored tech, who just sat there on the couch, paging through an ancient copy of the *Potrero Bingo Beacon*.

Out on the street, Bobby spotted Eddie's car, one of the new VW Bugs—white, of course, dullest color they had, and automatic, not a stick—blocking a driveway. Check it out, he thought, one of the cops who'd showed up wrote him a ticket. That was cold. He snatched the ticket from under the windshield wiper, tossed it onto the passenger seat once he got behind the wheel, then drove off as fast as he could, planning to tell Eddie later that he'd only borrowed the Bug because Eddie himself insisted, so Bobby could come around the county lockup later, bail him out, drive him home. Eddie'd be too drunk from his own mood swings to remember for sure what did and didn't get said the past few hours.

Bobby gassed the Bug's throaty little turbo up the rim of hills connecting Candlestick Point with the San Bruno range, dropping down again beyond Visitacion Valley and following the Bayshore Freeway south. The Eucalyptus Room sat along the briny mudflats lining the Dumbarton Bridge approach. He pulled into the parking lot just before closing. Okay, he thought, no two grand. But it wasn't like Eddie refused. That's what he'd tell Sal. Just a temporary setback. You know, bad luck.

*   *   *

Two years earlier, Bobby'd come to San Francisco after fleeing his old job at a family-owned casino outside Sparks, Nevada. It was a shame, having to run like that. He'd liked the job, liked the man he worked for. It was a go-for-your-own store, meaning you got to keep your own tokes—tips from winners who had enough class to share the wealth—not pool them at the end of the shift with everyone else. Given the politics of such an arrangement, you were smart to kick back to your pit boss for decent table assignments. That was how Bobby formed his bond with the man who now had a condo waiting in Minden for thirty grand down.

The bad thing that brought it all to an end happened on a weeknight. Bobby was working six to two. Jimmy Taggart, the casino's owner, routinely dragged his swing and graveyard dealers off the floor and into the count room. The grind action late on weeknights was pitiful; no sense just having the workforce standing around. That night it was Bobby's turn.

Just after midnight, two agents from Gaming Control came in for a spot audit during the soft count. They announced they'd salted the box that shift and intended to recover the four thousand dollars in marked bills they'd lost to the house.

If Bobby'd been playing it straight, no worries. But for several weeks he'd been inviting in friends to play his table and then dealt seconds to amp their take—no more than a hundred a night, just enough so they could all go out afterward and put it toward some toot and cocktails. Amusement tax, he called it.

Now he had to sit there while Gaming Control went through every dollar in the count, weeding out their marked bills. For some reason he got the jitters—his hands never settled in his lap, his foot bobbed, a rim of sweat formed along his collar. It was odd. He doubted his scam would get detected in the count. And he'd played poker most of his life, often with the sawed-off roughneck types who inhabited the apartment complexes his mother always chose to live in. He'd learned to hold his own, give away nothing, and those guys were ten times scarier than the agents. But the agents were armed. Bobby hated guns. It was almost a phobia, like some people with spiders or snakes or heights. You could talk a man out of almost anything, you did it right, but a gun, it just does what it was built to do. It tore open flesh. It ripped arteries and muscle apart. It killed. And the room was small. Accidents happen.

By the time he got a grip on himself he noticed Old Man Taggart eyeing him.

Finally the agents gathered their bills, accounting for every one, meaning the cage was clean. They gave the old man a receipt for the four grand so he could trim the amount off the house's gross income come tax time. They

weren't gone thirty seconds before Taggart pulled his chair up close beside
Bobby's.

"There something you'd like to tell me, young fella?"

The old man had those soulful, flinty eyes men get when they've lived in
the desert their whole lives. Before Sal, Old Man Taggart was possibly the
only older man Bobby had ever looked up to. Bobby bluffed his way through
an answer but he knew, if the old man wanted, he could run the tapes right
then and there. Bobby had a deft hand dealing cards, but given time to view
and re-view the tapes, they'd catch him. But none of that happened. The old
man let it go. Bobby knew an act of grace when it landed in his lap. He
walked out the door that night and never went back, telling himself he'd
never do that again. Some men are born to get beat, some you had to honor,
and Bobby'd betrayed his own sense of who was who in that regard and felt
a shame he didn't want to live with.

He had friends in San Francisco and came down for a visit, deciding to
stay when he saw how much money rolled through the card rooms, especially the ones south of the city on the peninsula. He ended up favoring the
Eucalyptus Room, down in East Palo Alto. It had a reputation for hard play
at the 60/120 tables—some quipsters called it the Church of Heist—and
that was fine with Bobby. And there was this chip girl there. Her name was
Jennifer Trinka.

She wore her hair longer then, halfway down her back in long permed
curls. It set off the soft smooth whiteness of her skin and the hard cold blue
of her eyes. Boyish in the chest, she emphasized her legs instead, wearing
kinky heels and shameless skirts. Guys at the tables couldn't love her
enough. Bobby knew he couldn't just make his play from the floor, like every
other mope. He needed status.

He hung around, doing the railbird bit, making idle chat with the help,
and hoping to team up with someone, play partners at a high-spread table.
It was the only way to make real money in a room like that. You had fools
getting hosed at Texas Hold 'Em and Low Ball, forty hands per hour. Meanwhile, across the room, Asians threw insane amounts of money away at Pai
Gow and Pan Nine, thrilling Sal since the house had a stake in every ante
and winning pot.

As Bobby settled in over time, he seemed to get along okay with folks—he
had a talent for that, getting along—but couldn't quite get that second leg
over, especially with Sal. Then one night, he thought he'd finally come
home. Trink sidled up, smiling like she knew something he didn't.

"Mr. Lazzarini would like a word."

He followed her back to the office, memorizing the tiny waist, the rip-
pling black hair, the pendulum action of her strangely boxy tush, marveling
at the strong stockinged legs with the contour of a weeping heart tattoo on

her calf peeking through the mesh. At the office door she turned like a game show hostess and gestured him inside.

"You joining us?" He tried not to sound too hopeful.

She didn't answer, but he noticed that her smile lingered as she walked away.

It was the first time Bobby'd been in the office, first time alone with Sal for that matter. They'd traded nods and smiles on the floor, but never spoken beyond "Hey" and "Have a good night." But Bobby already knew he liked Sal, respected him. He seemed unbothered by doubt. Thought was just a kind of action—you sized up a man asking for credit, you tallied odds—and beyond that reflection was pointless, counterproductive, even dangerous.

The office, small and plain, smelled like an ashtray, hugger-mugger with display cases and file cabinets piled high with tottering stacks of tally sheets, plus two Macao chairs of dusty wicker. Sal sat behind his cluttered desk, rocking in a wheeled swivel chair of pitted gray vinyl. Bobby offered a deferential smile, took a seat in one of the Macao chairs, brushing the cushion off first, and waited to be spoken to.

Sal, a pair of cheaters slung low on his nose, jotted figures in a ledger. "You like it here," he said finally, not looking up. "The card room, I mean."

"Very much."

"See you a lot around the tables, checking things out."

"Yeah." The phrase caught Bobby's ear funny: *checking things out*. He leaned forward, whispering for comic effect, "That's not a problem, right?"

He cracked a grin that Sal, glancing up finally, did not return.

"There's some people out there think you're a cop. Any truth in that?"

Bobby's heart pounded in his chest. His throat closed up. "No way."

"I mean, it's okay if you are." Sal studied him, taking his time. "I don't mind if cops hang out. Kinda hope they do, to be honest. Anything crooked goes down in my store, I wanna know about it."

Horseshit, Bobby thought. There was talk two city council members were silent partners in the club, and that drove the local cops nuts. They saw the Eucalyptus Room as a flash point for trouble. Beyond the hard play and rumors of time advances at the tables, you had chip girls not just sneaking loans but dealing crack out of their aprons, known bookies and fences waltzing around like kings, a couple of Filipino bank robbers who confessed their heists were driven by gambling losses at the Pai Gow tables. Two stolen cars had been found in the parking lot just last week. Some sorry schmuck had been kidnapped after winning ten grand and another'd been robbed and knifed.

"I'm not a cop."

Sal rose to his feet behind his desk and stuck out his meaty hand. His eyes said: *Time will tell.* "That's good to know. Pleasure talking finally."

Back on the floor, Bobby hunted up a house prop named Gap Quattrone. Props were players staked by the house to team up on suckers, hold them at the tables, and keep them losing. Bobby'd sat there one night watching Gap and his partner take a car salesman for twenty-two grand over fifteen straight hours of play. The code they used was primitive, knee knocks and ear pulls so obvious they could've been Little League coaches signaling from the dugout. Bobby found Gap—the name was short for Gaspar—standing at a sink in the Men's, combing his wavy blond hair.

"Join me outside for a smoke?"

It was a clear spring night, the racket from Highway 101 unusually loud, like always after a rain, drowning out the crickets. The Dumbarton flickered with lights from the last of the rush hour commute. Bobby caught a sharp soapy whiff of eucalyptus from the nearby trees. Thus the club's name, he supposed.

He lit a smoke for himself, held the match out for Gap, too, and tried to think of how to begin. Gap cupped his hands to the flame, looking almost perfect in its flickering light, his eyes hollowed out, his cheekbones shadowed.

Gap could have been a Hollywood actor—not a star, but one of those faces you always recognize but can seldom put a name to. The guy, you'd say. Which guy? You know, *the guy*. Bent car salesman whose wife walks out first scene in the movie. The psycho killer's neighbor. First chump in the prison break the alligators drag under. Gap looked good, not great, but he did things, even little things—a wink for a chip girl, a drag from his cigarette— like he knew you were watching. And you were.

Finally, sensing the moment was right, Bobby said, "Look, I know you're playing partners. The guys you team with are a joke. And your code's so gross my grandmother's canasta group could nail you. People think I'm a cop. Well, tell you what. I'll teach you a code nobody will catch, and if I'm a cop that's entrapment, so I've just given you an ironclad defense. What do you say?"

Things improved after that. Gap picked up fast on Bobby's routine— fanning his cards left or right depending on whether he intended to stay in or fold, using stage business with his chips or his cigarettes or his coffee cup to signal ace, king, queen, jack, and how many of each, changing the code around several times a night. They practiced together till their hand movements possessed the required subtlety and they could read the other man's message without needing to look straight on.

On Gap's good word Sal finally changed his take on Bobby, staking him with house money then taking half of what he and Gap won on any night. Business was good. The Nevada houses were closing their poker operations due to the competition from the California card rooms—the casinos never much liked the poker crowd anyway, they generated little side action and tended to prey on the tourists—which meant plenty of money drifting in to the Eucalyptus Room, some players smarter than others, but few of them smart enough. Even the ones who caught on backed down once they realized doing anything meant dealing with Sal.

Meanwhile, with Bobby squarely in Sal's good graces, Trink finally took him seriously. In a span of six weeks they went from after-shift breakfasts— she sent her scrambled eggs back to the kitchen time and time again, till they came back rubbery, like gum erasers—to living together. He'd never done that before. Never bought jewelry for a woman before, either, or sat on the toilet and watched as she lathered and shaved her legs in the tub. Never shared a beer for Saturday breakfast or had a woman tell him, as he lay with her in bed, "You can do anything you want. Just give me some warning if you're gonna hit me, okay?"

But Bobby wasn't a hitter. It was all he could do to oblige her request that he hold her down during sex. One more legacy of the schoolyard bullying she took from her brothers when she was eight: She liked to struggle with him on top of her. Almost as much as she liked to smoke.

One night Sal came up, gestured Bobby and Gap away from their game. Once he had them off the floor, he said, "Come with me, okay? I need somebody to see this."

They drove to a nearby watering hole called the Eight Ball—low ceiling, concrete floor, fake wood paneling grimed with smoke and spillage. It was a jump joint, like most bars in East Palo Alto. Phil Vogel sat alone on his stool, sagging like his spine had turned to putty, and staring into his glass, around which crumpled bills, too many, sat in plain view, inviting trouble. The bartender, who'd called Sal at the club, nodded as though to say, Get him out of here.

The toughs in the room, some of whom wore prison tats or gang colors, sipped bottled malt liquor or cognac and Coke as they prowled around the pool table or sulked and chewed on straws at the tables near the back. Waiting for a chance. They stared at Bobby and Gap and even Sal like their coming here was nothing but an excuse to do it now, more the merrier.

Sal came up, leaned close to his partner. "Time to knock off, Phil. Let's go, while the going's good."

Phil mumbled something, shot a screw-you look at Sal in the mirror, not straight on, then gestured to the bartender for another.

Sal glanced up at the bartender and shook his head.

"You think I'm joking? Come on. We'll drive you back to the club."

Sal slipped his hand under his partner's arm but the sad fat drunk broke free, stumbling off his stool in a wild-limbed stagger, then spinning around. He fumbled in his pocket for something. "Where would you be, huh? Without me. Where? Just another goddamn . . ." He pulled from his pocket what he wanted, finally—a girlish .22, wiggling it in the air. He looked like he wanted to cry, which was what Bobby felt like doing, too, once he saw the gun sailing around like that. He doesn't even have to want to do it, Bobby thought. Accidents happen.

Sal didn't so much as glance at the weapon, just stared into his partner's rheumy eyes. "You sad old faggot." He turned to the bartender. "Call the cops on this piece of crap." Then, turning to Gap and Bobby: "Let's get back to work."

Bobby stood frozen in place, still staring at the gun. Gap took notice and whispered, "Come on," shaking Bobby's sleeve. "Never let jigs see you're scared."

The bartender called out, "I ain't callin' no cops on his ass. Don't need that kind of trouble. You haul his sorry drunk butt on outta here."

But Sal just kept walking, into the night. Bobby couldn't follow him fast enough, and Gap took up the rear, making sure Phil didn't shoot and nobody else came after them.

In the car, once they were on their way, Sal said quietly to Bobby, "What happened back there? Don't think I didn't notice."

Bobby sank in his seat. He hated failing Sal. "Never been much of a fighter."

"Not what I meant." With his thumb Sal plunged in the dash lighter for the cigarette now bobbing between his lips. "I saw how scared you were. But you didn't embarrass yourself. Or me. I appreciate that."

Back at the club, Sal told Bobby and Gap to follow him into the office. "Close the door." He poured each of them a few fingers of Cutty, took a long sip of his own. "Draws a gun, the fat cunt. I'd call that a final goddamn straw, how about you?" Before either of them could answer, he added, "Either of you guys like to buy in to a new room?"

"Gap, Gap, put it down, okay? No need."

Bobby stared up from where he knelt on the floor of Sal's office, hands held out to either side. The man in the ski mask and baggy brown suit stood motionless in the doorway, gun trained straight at Bobby's mouth.

"Think I wouldn't know your eyes? And the shoes, Gap. I mean, I'm sorry, but hey."

The man stood there, blinking, as the gun barrel sank in almost imperceptible degrees. With his free hand, he reached up, pulled the ski mask off. Strands of his curly blond hair hovered from the static. Eyes whirling in pained thought, he seemed wildly confused. He didn't look so much like a Hollywood type right then.

"You know what he was gonna do, right?"

"Gap, what? Sal, he was—"

"No, Bobby. Listen to me. Place in Burlingame he talked about? He's got no lease. Management company's never heard of him."

"But the points, Gap, I know guys, ten, maybe a dozen, they put—"

"Shut up! Listen to me. It's bullshit. There are no points. He was just gonna close up tonight, run with the cash."

Bobby got up from the floor, using Sal's desk to pull himself onto his feet. His head spun. "Sal wouldn't do that."

"You simple? It was done."

"I don't know, Gap. Jesus." Bobby nodded to the gun. "You mind putting that thing away?"

Gap let the pistol hang beside his leg, but didn't slip it in his pocket. "What was I supposed to do, Bobby? He had a gun, too."

Like everybody, Bobby thought, except me. "We should check, see how bad he is."

He moved toward the door. Gap cut him off.

"I'm gonna get inside the safe."

Bobby just stared. "Gap, it's Sal out there."

"I know who the fuck it is. He's a goddamn thief." Sweat broke out on Gap's face, it beaded on his cheeks, his brow, his neck. He raised the gun again, shouting now, "Okay, you got your chance. You want to whine and whimper, go on home. I'm getting in that safe."

Gap waited, trying to nudge Bobby out by waving the nose of the gun, but Bobby couldn't move. Giving up, Gap dropped down behind Sal's desk, knelt before the vault, and reached for the combination dial. Bobby considered going out, checking on Sal, but as Gap worked the tumblers it dawned on him. *Since when has he been planning this? More to the point, why'd he never tell me?*

"I got eighteen thousand in there, Gap. My money, okay?" He eased in short, small steps around the corner of the desk. "I mean, I can't afford to lose my bank. It's all I've got. Trink, she's real sick, I can't—"

Gap said nothing, just kept spinning the dial back and forth. Bobby, watching, got it then. *Gap had no clue what the combination was.*

"Gap, what's going on here? What's this about?"

He stood too close to ask a question like that. Sure enough, Gap spun around in a rattled fury. The gun came with him. Bobby spooked, trying to swat the barrel away but his hand sailed high. Gap took it for a blow and on instinct fired. The bullet ripped upward into Bobby's arm. Maybe a second passed, maybe a thousandth of second, but Bobby stared at the small black hole torn into the fabric of his jacket, a little above the elbow. He felt the first pop of blood. And then, at last, the pain. His whole arm erupted like it had been set on fire. He cringed, winced, danced this way and that, biting his lip with all his might to keep from screaming.

"What the hell you do that for?" Both of them, same words, same time, shouted over one another.

The next thing Bobby knew he was running, out the back door Sal had told him to take in the first place. He couldn't tell if Gap was right behind, didn't dare look. He threw the lock on the door, pushed with his shoulder, and tumbled out into the parking lot.

The leaves of the eucalyptus trees shivered in an eastward wind, driven by an incoming storm. Bobby's cheeks grew wet from tears as he ran to Eddie's Bug, fumbled left-handed into his right pocket, digging for the keys. Gap would be there any second to finish him off and Bobby wondered at what was taking him but then he was behind the wheel, cranking the ignition and lodging the tranny left-handed, fishtailing away toward the freeway.

His vision blurred as he sped north. Not just the tears. The blood loss, he was going into shock, feeling the cold possess his hands, his feet. Bullet must've hit an artery, he thought. Get to a hospital, but Gap would come hunting for him, finish things. Sooner or later, probably sooner, he'd show up at the apartment. Trink was there alone.

He had to fight to keep from weaving lane to lane as he passed Candlestick Point, accelerated to clear the hill then descended past Bay View, Portola, Silver Terrace. You should call 911, he thought, tell them about Sal. But he didn't dare stop and with his arm hurt so bad he couldn't dig into his pocket for his cell phone and try to drive at the same time. "I'm sorry, Sal," he whispered as the pain spread from his arm into his shoulder, his chest, his throat. He wet himself, feeling scared like he'd never felt scared before and thinking of Eddie's mother, wondering which had come first, death or the letting go.

He didn't even remember the rest of the drive or where he parked, just found himself trying to climb the seven impossible flights of stairs to the apartment. Dragging himself up along the handrail, his mind in a fog, he paused for breath at each landing with his bloody arm hanging there, no longer a limb or even his own flesh, just a locus for the pain. He stank and had to fight from hurling but he made it to the sixth floor, stiffened his resolve, and reached the next landing, halfway up.

Wait now, he thought. Maybe she's already used up the last of the Albuterol. Remember, stress is a trigger. Imagine how you look. You just tumble in like this, she'll have an attack. Too many problems at once. Too many patients. Think it through.

He knelt, hoping for just a moment to clear his head. Twisting himself into a seated position, he stared upward, panting, dry-mouthed, drenched in sweat with blood caked down his sleeve, fingers sticky with it. Beneath the gore, the skin had turned a yellowish gray. Phantom shadows darted along the edges of his field of vision and to escape them he closed his eyes.

From above, he heard a door lock click. Eyes blinking open, he saw Trink staring down at him, still dressed in her underwear but she'd pulled on one of Bobby's buttondown shirts as a wrap. A lit cigarette dangled between her fingers. Sneaking a midnight smoke while she waited for him to come home. Bad timing, Bobby thought.

"Roper?"

Before he could get a word out he saw a shadow cross her eyes and her chest started heaving. Her mouth shot open but no sound came. She dropped the cigarette and reached out blindly for the railing, finding it finally, gripping it with both hands, standing as long as she could but then her knees gave way with an awkward rubbery trembling. The whole time her eyes stayed fixed on his, staring down at him like he'd turned into something terrible. An omen. A ghost.

"Baby, you gotta try," he said, loud as he could without drawing out the neighbors, his voice hoarse, throat parched. "You gotta get up, Trink. You gotta turn around now, go back in, get your inhaler. Or if that's all used up, make coffee. Right? A couple aspirin, strong black coffee. You know what to do. Listen. We gotta get out of here. You gotta get me to a hospital, okay? Your turn to take care of me, how about that? Get up now. Come on, Trink. Try."

As he sat there watching, her eyes turned vacant, her chest collapsed against her rib cage, and she dropped sideways onto the landing, not all at once but in jerky helpless staggers, her breathing a worthless hiss as her skin turned a marbled blue. Bobby couldn't get to her, couldn't move—bad idea, he realized now, too late, sitting down, as much blood as you've lost. In his impotence he felt everything give—his vision grayed, his muscles went slack, his pores opened up, and a bitter-smelling sweat beaded on his skin as he whispered, "Trink, please, I am so sorry." She lay on her side, eyes rolled back, mouth slack. *I'd love not to have to think about my next breath*. He closed his eyes as a sickening dizziness swept through him, like he was spinning across a dance floor, his reflection flickering beneath him.

Gap pulled the car up as close as he dared. Patrol cars sat everywhere, their strobes flaring blue and red light across the crowd that had formed outside the apartment building. "Jesus H. Christ." He turned on the wipers, to clear the windshield of spattered rain. "This is too nuts, we gotta book. Now."

Sal, sitting beside him, said nothing, just looked out at the crowd with a mix of despairing fury and guilty disbelief. "I'm gonna go see." He reached for the door handle but Gap reached across, grabbed his sleeve.

"You nuts? We can't—"

"Let the fuck go of my arm."

Gap didn't need to be told twice, not with that tone. His grip loosened. Sal opened the door and stepped out as Gap called after him. "I'm not waiting around forever. I see anything go bad, you get into it with a cop—"

Sal cut him off with a disgusted little laugh. "You'll what—tell your mother?"

Sal kept hidden the fact that Gap was his stepson. It was nobody's business, and you give people something to get all busy and twisted up about, they'll do just that. Besides, Sal and Vivian hadn't spoken in years, and what connection he had with her son he'd forged on his own—most of it, strangely, after the divorce. Sal had that kind of effect on younger men, especially ones whose fathers had bailed. They liked getting near him, prove themselves.

"I need to know where things sit," Sal said, almost apologetically. He closed the car door behind him and sauntered through the light rain toward the edge of the crowd. There were too many patrol cars in the street to mean anything but a dead body. He didn't spot the morgue wagon till after. How did such an easy little plan go so bad, he wondered. Gather the cash, fake a stickup, flash a gun, watch Bobby run scared—that night at the Eight Ball, he turned bone white, nearly crapped his pants—what could be simpler? They had the other marks roped in already, three hundred grand, the only one left was Bobby and he was last because Gap and Sal had fought about it. Sal said he was thinking of the girl, the skinny one used to work at the club, she was sick, but it wasn't that. It was too easy, taking Bobby's money. Sal had no problem milking suckers, it was why they existed, to get used. Maybe it was the way Bobby looked at him—not scared, almost hopeful, like Sal was some kind of promise. But Gap had pushed, they'd need every dime in Belize. The casinos were opening there, so went the rumor, moving south from Cancun. Get positioned now, it'll be like Cuba before Castro, Gap said. And Bobby won't suffer too long or hard, don't waste tears on him. He was young enough, smart enough, to start over, which wasn't true for Sal—a fact that rang true all the more as he felt the painful deadweight of his limbs, standing there in the rain, watching the coroner's staff wheel out a gurney with a body bag on it. Sal couldn't take his eyes away till it finally disappeared into the wagon.

"What happened?" Sal asked the women nearest him. They were in their late twenties, early thirties, law student types or librarians maybe, homely but smart looking and dressed in drab robes, sweats, bedroom slippers. All three studied him a moment. Sal wondered what he must look like. His waxy hair sagged down onto his ears with the rain.

"This couple on the seventh floor," one said finally. She had buck teeth, freckles, and short, sand-colored hair. "They're both dead."

Two, Sal thought. It meant the girl, Trink, too. Good God.

"One of them shot," a second one said, pushing up her glasses on her nose with one hand, the other hand holding her tartan robe closed tight at her throat.

"You guys live here?" It came out strangely needy, but they seemed to want to talk about it.

"Yeah," one answered. All three nodded.

Roommates, Sal figured. "What are you all doing out here, in the rain?"

"We wanted to see what was happening, but they wouldn't let us stand in the stairwell." It was the third one who spoke this time. She was the only one you might call pretty. Tall, thin, with straight brown hair, an upturned nose. "So we came out here. Now they won't let us back in."

Sal nodded, as though to say he understood. "You know them? The two who died, I mean."

"Not much, a little." It was the one with the glasses again, still clutching her robe in her fist. She started describing them, Bobby and Trink, not kindly, a singsong litany of brief, edgy, unwelcome encounters—in the lobby, the laundry room, on the stairs—like in some odd, misbegotten way they deserved to die. Even as Sal told himself he should go—he'd learned all he could without risking a question or two coming his direction, and there was nothing this woman had to say he needed to hear—he couldn't tear himself away. Glancing back at the car he saw Gap gesturing: Hurry up. Come on. Let's go. But the woman's voice, the continuous stream of her pitiless words, seemed oddly reassuring. Sal turned back toward the sound and started nodding along, wanting nothing so much as for her to keep talking.

In the Midnight Hour
PAUL CHARLES

THE DOOR SLAMMED shut behind him.

It wasn't exactly that the slamming created a particularly loud bang. It was more that it was a bang of great finality. A very definite closure as it were.

"Rory," the slammer of the door hissed, sneering through the corner of his mouth, "so what have you been up to this time? For goodness' sake man, don't you realize the Sabbath is only a matter of a few minutes old."

"Ah, now, Inspector Starrett," Rory Sullivan began, his confidence draining the more Starrett's bloodshot eyes bore down on him, "I ah, I . . . well, I suppose I'm what you'd call a victim of circumstance."

"A victim of circumstance is it?" Starrett laughed, displaying two rows of snow-white molars, which created a very nonpatriotic combination of colors with his eyes and jumper. "I'd say it was more a case of light fingers not being capable of heavy work."

"Ah," Sullivan began, openly dejected.

"You know what, Rory, do you know what's really troubling me?"

"What's that, Inspector?"

"I'll tell you, Rory. Even after all these years in the Gardai I'm still bewildered why some people choose the crooked path, the path of deceit, rather than the God-fearing, work-for-a-living type. I mean, take you for instance. It isn't as though we can blame your family. Rory tell me this, why you do it? I really want to know, I need to understand this."

Rory Sullivan clicked his teeth. He was twenty-eight years old, the middle of three brothers. His major problem, as far as he was concerned, was that he was born and raised in Ramelton—a village in Donegal, Ireland's most picturesque county—and not in Santa Fe, New Mexico, in the United States of America.

To Rory Sullivan even the line that summed up the States, "The land of the free and the home of the brave," was seductive, and compelling. He had been hooked on Americana from the age of eleven.

Like a lot of youths growing up in Ireland in the late sixties, Rory was fascinated by the whole American culture. He immersed himself completely and utterly in all things American: movies; television shows; Voice of America radio; comics; magazines; vinyl records; Superman; the Lone Ranger and Tonto; *Wagon Train*; Cadillac cars; Harley-Davidson motorbikes; the Beach Boys; the Drifters; cigarette lighters; and bowie knives.

He even had a pristine one-dollar bill, carefully folded away in an envelope, which he kept under his mattress. From when he was old enough to count, he automatically converted the local currency directly into dollars—it varied from three to four American dollars to the Irish pound, but the fluctuation always ensured that Rory was ahead in his math class, particularly when it came to long division.

As a teenager he modeled himself on the new wave of American actors, changing his short back and sides hairstyle with curls on top for a Tony Curtis ducktail. Unfortunately the end result, for Rory, was more Karl Malden than James Dean.

Rory completed his American look with an extra-white T-shirt (his mother didn't mind spending the extra few pence on Persil, "the results are obvious," she'd say to anyone who'd listen), gray-black Levi's jeans, a cheap leather jacket—black with white piping—and permanently off-white (more Daz than Persil) tennis shoes although few if any who wore them ever got to see a tennis court, let alone play on one.

He was always careful not to smile when he was cutting his James Dean pose. Only his green eyes and apple-red flushed checks betrayed the fact that he was Irish and a wannabe American.

"Well?" Starrett asked after thirty-three uninterrupted clicks of the wall clock.

"Listen, what can I tell you," Rory said expansively, "really, what can I tell you? I see myself more as a William H. Bonney character than a real criminal. Like Billy, I've never knowingly taken from someone who couldn't afford it. I've never touched the poor."

"And you've always proved to be very ingenious in your raids," Starrett sighed, "but my point would be that if you used even a small fraction of that guile and cunning on something more worthwhile and honest we'd all be a lot better off."

"Yeah," Rory conceded, then following a few more ticks of the second hand of the clock, "but if I went straight how long would it take me to save enough money to fly Cherry and myself to New Mexico?"

"What? So that you can follow every other Irish emigrant and spend the rest of your life being homesick for dear old mother Ireland? You know, you really should wake up and smell the Montbretia and all the other flowers that grace this spectular countryside of ours."

"Ah, not Cherry and me, Inspector. In our case the other man's grass is definitely greener."

"Not in New Mexico it's not, sure it's too darned hot there for anything but the flies."

Rory just smiled.

"And tell me," Starrett continued, sure to wipe away Rory's smile, "while we're talking about Cherry, would that be the same Cheryl Mary Teresa Kavanagh who has just sworn a statement charging you with stealing property belonging to her?"

Starrett sighed and picked up the file he'd brought into the badly lit questioning room, which was situated in the basement of Ramelton's Garda station. He opened the file wide in front of him as if he knew he was going to need to view all of the information contained therein.

"That wasn't theft, Inspector. Sure didn't I get the very same radio for her as a present? I just needed to borrow it to raise twenty dollars to bankroll my next job."

Starrett needed the file sooner than he thought:

"By any chance would that be the same radio, a Roberts U.S. Valve Special, serial number 23091949, which we found in the back of Edmund Davies's car half an hour ago?"

"Yes . . ." Rory replied with an implied, So?

"And would that be the same Roberts radio that was originally stolen from Bryson's Electricians in Letterkenny three months ago and mentioned here in their insurance manifest?" Starrett tapped a piece of paper in the file several times with his index finger. The finger was permanently semi-bent as a result of an accident and was always very disconcerting when used to emphasize something. The detective was fifty-four but his finger looked like the finger of a ninety-year-old man. It always looked like it might just break off from the rest of his hand.

"Ah," Rory replied, this time with nothing implied.

"You see, Rory, as I was saying, if you'd just put as much of your energy into going straight as you do into being a highwayman, there would have been a good chance you might have reached your beloved America in the next five or six years, whereas now it's looking like you might be going down for at least that amount of time."

"Ah but . . ." Rory cut in, "I can't be put down for—"

"Armed robbery is a serious offense, Rory."

"Armed robbery!" Rory screamed in a pitch-perfect Little Richard refrain. "I've never done an armed robbery in my life."

"Yes," Starrett said, and again consulted his file, an unnecessary but highly effective gesture, "and a Mrs. Mina Bates has also filed a complaint against you. Apparently you threatened her with a knife in the early hours of this morning."

"Oh, it wasn't anything like that at all," Rory replied, noticeably relieved.

"Okay, Rory, could you tell me exactly what it was like then?" Starrett inquired, for the record, leaning back in his metallic chair and putting his fine-black-shoed feet up on the desk, stretching his arms and clasping his hands behind of, and in support of, his head.

"Okay, you see Cherry, well she said—"

"Rory," Starrett began, closing his eyes, "we'll all be finished here a whole lot sooner if you start at the beginning."

"Okay," Rory replied and leaned in over the desk earnestly. He was so close to Starrett he could smell the mixture of leather and polish from his shoes. If he'd leaned in a little closer he'd have noticed that they were so well polished he would have been able to see his own refection in the toe caps. "Cherry said that was it, we were finished if I didn't come up with the money to buy our tickets to America, like I promised her I would. She gave me one last chance. Now, as luck would have it, it just so happened that I did have a job in mind, over the previous couple of months in fact, and I just needed a small job to bankroll it."

"Bankroll it, Rory? What's that all about?"

"Well, I needed a getaway car—"

"Edmund Davies?" Starrett said without opening his eyes.

"Well, you caught Eddie and me together so you know he was involved. Anyway, Eddie wouldn't agree to doing the job with me unless I paid him for the use of his car up front."

"Ah Jez, Rory, you don't mean to tell me that your accomplice wanted his money in advance?"

"Well, only the car payment part, he needed that in advance, to get the car ready he said, and then I was going to give him a cut as well."

"Ah, Rory, son, you've surely been watching the wrong movies. Come on, will you, I'm missing my sleep, let's get back to your story."

"Okay, so I borrowed Cherry's radio to bankroll the job, but I couldn't get anyone to buy it. Eddie wasn't much help either and he downright refused to accept it as payment for his car for the job. Anyway, as you know, I've done Widow Bates's rectory before and she's always good for a bit of cash."

"Yeah," Starrett sighed, opening his eyes and looking in the file again. "I believe you got fifty quid last time."

"More like about one hundred dollars. I never take more than a hundred dollars from private citizens. Anyway, I break in Saturday morning, in the early hours, to pick up the cash. She always hides it in the same place: in the biscuit tin, which is in the cupboard above the sink in the kitchen. It's always packed with crisp notes, but, like I told you, I never take more than a ton. So I'm in the kitchen, it's five o'clock in the morning, and I'm feeling a bit peckish. Cherry, God bless her soul, never has any food in our house, so I think, what's the harm of helping myself to some of Widow Bates's food? I mean she's a widow, her cupboards are always packed to bursting, how much food does one woman need?"

"Come now, Rory, it's her money, she can spend it on what she wants."

"Right, sorry, of course, so anyway, I stick the old rasher-wagon on the gas ring. I'm assuming Widow Bates won't be up for three more hours and because our Cherry is always trying to catch up on her beauty sleep, I've learned to cook quietly—"

"It wasn't the noise of your cooking that woke up Mina, it was the smell of the bacon frying in the pan. That's what was your undoing, Rory," Starrett offered, unable to resist a smile.

"Yeah, so she sneaked down into the kitchen and caught me . . . but to claim it was armed robbery, well, that's just a downright lie."

"She claims you waved a knife at her as she walked into her own kitchen," Starrett said.

"Not guilty, your honor," Rory said, becoming animated and leaning up from resting on his elbow on the table. "She walks in. I've got the bread knife in my hand preparing bread for toast. I pointed the knife to the bread and asked her if she wanted some. Of course I was referring to the bread and not the knife."

"I sure hope that the judge also believes you."

"Phew . . ." Rory tutted, ". . . with my luck?"

"What exactly did Mrs. Bates say to you as you pointed to the bread?"

"Well, she said, 'As you've already got the pan fired up, Mr. Sullivan, the least you can do is stick in a few slices of bacon and a couple of eggs for me.' "

"And so you, the thief, and Widow Bates, the victim, sat down to break bread and to enjoy breakfast together?"

"Pretty much."

"Un-fecking-believable, Rory." Starrett laughed. "Hardly Al Capone, mate."

"Al Capone wasn't the toughest of the American gangsters you know," Rory said with a bit of a whine. "That honor goes to a Donegal man, Vincent Coll. Have you ever heard about him, Inspector? He didn't suffer fools gladly."

"Oh I've heard all about Mad Dog, Rory," Starrett said smiling. "Talking about famous people, what was it the *Donegal Chronicle* chap wrote about you after your last job?"

"Ah, he said, 'I've seen the future of organized crime in Ireland and it's Rory Sullivan,' " Rory said, recalling the quote. To give him his proper due he didn't recite the quote with any degree of pride.

"Well, all I can say, Rory, is that I hope he's right, so that the Gardai of Donegal can sleep easier at night. Talking about sleep let's get to the last chapter in your recent escapade, the bank robbery, tell me about that?"

When the Garda patrol car picked Rory up, caught in the act as it were, they left him in the back of the car while they viewed the scene of the crime, the Bank of Erin. The bank building directly overlooked the River Leannan.

The two officers discovered nothing, absolutely zero. There were no broken windows, no rammed doors, no sign of explosives, no signs of tunneling on the inside.

Starrett had to admit that tunneling had been his first thought. How else had Rory Sullivan managed to get in and out of the Bank of Erin without leaving any obvious telltale signs? The River Leannan bridge literally ran at right angles up to the front oak door of the bank, which of course meant, to Starrett's way of thinking, that the final arch of the bridge, closest to the bank building, acted as a natural tunnel, which had, as one side, the foundations to the 130-year-old ivy-covered, Georgian, two-story building. Starrett had always considered this to be a vulnerable point in the bank's structure. The bank's manager, the affable Max McDowd, would always cut him off with, "I'll tell you what, Inspectar," the "tar" being the local lazy slant on the word, spoken especially lazy following a few pints, "if someone wants to try and get in that way, I'll not only provide them with the dynamite, but I'll let them take what they find in the vaults."

Starrett could never work out if McDowd meant that the bank was impenetrable or that he'd already emptied the vaults himself. Before the conversation went any further, McDowd would add something like: "Never fear man. I tell you what, let's stop wasting our time on my bank's security and pay a visit to the Bridge Bar for some liquid refreshment and craic."

Starrett wasn't convinced about the strength of the bank but on the other hand he was rather partial to a pint or three of the Bridge Bar's finest black and cream. So, for now, nothing more would be mentioned about it.

That was, of course, until Sullivan's daring and intriguing raid.

Sullivan *had* been caught red-handed but *off* the premises. Starrett even visited the scene of the crime himself, and his investigation, including a welly-assisted visit under the bridge, produced absolutely nothing, not even a dickey bird in fact.

Starrett examined the area immediately around the locks of the door for telltale scrapings of someone trying to pick the locks. Stranger things had happened, particularly involving Rory Sullivan. But the grand door's two Chubb locks and single triple-roll-bar lock were as good as new. Starrett wasn't too preoccupied about the lack of evidence. He knew full well that once Sullivan felt his back against the wall he would be happy to sing sweetly so everyone could stand back and enjoy his handiwork.

Ever since he had started his illicit career, he'd been gaining a bit of a reputation for finding extraordinary means with which to perpetrate his crimes. He'd spend hours working out elaborate ways for his foolproof, he hoped, escapades. Mostly though he'd stumble and fall at the last fence. Just like the time Sullivan carried out the robbery of Bryson's Electricians. He hid away in the lavatory toward the end of shopping hours and then when the shop closed down, he nipped into the stockroom and helped himself before returning to the sanctuary of the toilet. His only problem on that occasion was that Bryson's had one of the most luxurious and comfortable men's rooms in Letterkenny so he fell into a deep contented sleep only to be discovered by one of the staff members the following morning. He had the last laugh though. They repossessed their visible goods and let him off with a flea in his ear, but they didn't bother to search deep enough into his shoulder bag, where, if they had been more diligent, they'd have found, safely tucked beneath the flask of coffee and his stash of lifesaving Cadbury's milk chocolate bars and banana sandwiches, several other small items *and* the aforementioned Roberts Radio; the same Roberts Radio that ended up with Cherry, Ramelton's only Doris Day look-alike.

"Look, Rory," Starrett sighed, betraying his impatience, not to mention the thought of his half-finished pint of Guinness still standing on the bar in his corner of the Bridge Bar, "thanks to Cherry, we've got you on the radio, and thanks to Widow Bates we've got you on breaking and entering at the rectory. Listen, I might even be persuaded to see if Mina could suffer a slight attack of amnesia over the knife incident. But there's more. We've got Edmund Davies two doors down and he's singing like a bird about the Bank of Erin job, so why don't you just come clean about it?"

Rory Sullivan rose from his chair and put his hands in his back pockets, Bette Davis style, and walked around the room. Starrett ignored him, for fear of disturbing Rory's thought process.

"Can I plead the fifth, Inspector?" Rory enquired.

"Rory, old son, wrong fecking movie, we're talking more *Lavender Hill Mob* here."

Forty-five ticks of the second hand later (Starrett counted each and every one of them), Rory said, "It's all about doing your recce, isn't it, Inspector?"

"I'll take your word for it, Rory, but what I want to know is, how you got in and out of the bank without causing any disturbance?" Starrett asked, now genuinely in awe.

"Easy, com' 'ere I'll tell you. Your regular drinking buddy, McDowd, never drinks with you on a Saturday night does he?"

"Actually, that's right, how did you know that?"

"Recce, Inspector, reconnaissance, that's what successful crime is all about," Rory boasted, clearly confident as he sat down at the table again. "And I'll tell you why he never drinks with you on a Saturday night . . ."

"Go on, I'm listening."

"Well, isn't Saturday night the night all married men go out for a drink."

"Yeah, and?"

"And what happens when married men go out drinking on a Saturday night?"

"I don't know Rory, you tell me," Starrett said, and then posted a late, "they get drunk?"

"Sometimes, but not all of the times," Rory said, singsong style. "But what they do all of the time is that they leave their married wives at home by themselves, don't they?"

This woke up Starrett with a jolt. "You mean McDowd has been . . ."

"Well, I believe the way he'd put it would be 'distributing a bit of joy around the village.' "

"Be jeepers," Starrett said, grinning from ear to ear. "And with whom?"

"Well, when you don't drink with your regular drinking buddy on a Saturday night, who do you usually end up drinking with on an average of fifty Saturday nights of the year?"

"Shit, Gary Brittan, you don't mean McDowd and Patsy Brittan. Fecking hell, Gary'll kill him. Kill him dead. The silly . . ."

Starrett's mind raced forward through several scenarios, all of them ending with him undertaking massive paperwork. Most of the little scenes he visualized involved the spilling of blood, and one unsettling little scenario even had some of his own blood splattered around several walls.

Somehow he found his way back to the original track. "But I still don't understand how you . . ."

"Okay, I'll spell it out for you. The Brittans never, ever, lock their back door do they? Gary's always boasting that no one is ever going to break into his house and heaven help the first one who does. Well, McDowd didn't exactly have to break into the house. Patsy welcomed him with open arms. He always leaves his jacket hanging on the inside of the back door. He dallies for a few minutes in the scullery with Patsy, they enjoy a drink or two, and then they go off to find somewhere to recline I imagine. I simply slipped into the scullery, borrowed his keys, scooted down the road, and opened the bank door. It's a noisy old door so I used the midnight chimes of the church clock to drown out the loud creaking, and then I nipped inside and helped myself."

"Ah Rory, how'd you ever think you'd get away with it?"

"Well, I would have gotten away with it; the only thing I didn't calculate was how heavy the jar of money was. I nearly had a hernia trying to carry it to Eddie's car."

"Why did you go for the old jar anyway?"

"Well, I'd worked out how to get into the bank sure enough, but I didn't have time to figure out how to get into the vaults. Anyway, I didn't really need to. There's the big jar of money by the door, it's called the Staff's Pension Plan pot or something, and sure don't some ejits still go and put some of their hard-earned cash in the big bruiser. Some people just need to give a

public display of their generous nature and so they'll throw money at anyone who's collecting. Including the not so charitable bank staff. Then one
day I happened to overhear one of the bank tellers say to a colleague that
there must be over two grand in the jar. And that was more than I needed to
set me and Cherry up in America."

"Ah Rory, you've gone and gotten yourself into a fine mess."

"Aye, well, you caught me fair and square and you'll tell the judge I came
clean with you, won't you?" Rory said and then stopped.

Starrett figured that he'd something else to say so he just continued to
look at the criminal, nodding his head back and forth trying to encourage
the final words out of him.

Eventually Rory Sullivan spoke. "Hey," he said fighting back emotion, "I
suppose you better tell Cherry not to bother waiting around for me."

But that wasn't that.

Inspector Starrett proved that the midnight hour is not as much the end of
one day as it is the beginning of the next. Some could call his action good-
natured; others would describe it as taking action to avoid a civil riot about
the streets of Ramelton.

Starrett proceeded to take a statement from Rory Sullivan. Yes, you could
say that he even coaxed Sullivan to using particular words for the statement.

There were none more surprised than Rory when twenty minutes later he
signed a statement saying in effect that he, Rory Sullivan, was on his way
home from the Bridge Bar when he saw something suspicious occurring
around the door of the Bank of Erin. He spotted someone coming out
carrying something that appeared very heavy and he shouted across to the
stranger. The stranger bolted, dropping the jar and a set of keys to the
ground. Surprisingly the glass didn't shatter into a million smithereens.
Rory went over, took the keys, and with great difficulty, lifted the jar. He was
in the process of returning the jar to the bank when the squad car came
upon him. Clearly the strain of lifting the weight confused his bearings, so
that it appeared he was actually moving away from the bank rather than toward it at the time he was apprehended. Obviously the Gardai officers *mis-
takenly* thought Rory was the culprit. But, the statement claimed, he just
hadn't had time to return the jar to the bank and lock the door.

Inspector Starrett not only stated, for the record, that he unconditionally
accepted Rory's statement, but he also cajoled the Bank of Erin and Mc-
Dowd, the bank manager, into giving Rory a reward of two grand for saving
the bank further loss. Starrett didn't recognize the dollar currency, so he ensured Sullivan was paid his bounty in Irish pounds. Which was how, four
weeks later, Rory Sullivan and Cheryl Mary Teresa Kavanagh were sitting

onboard a Pan Am flight from Shannon Airport to New York City with four thousand dollars to spare.

On Starrett's recommendation, they immediately continued to New Jersey and met up with a colleague of his who made sure Sullivan enrolled to become a New Jersey state trooper. Two years passed and Rory graduated with honors. Many years and scars later, he joined the exclusive Colonel's Row when he became their superintendent, proving for once and for all that he could use his brain to ensure his fame and fortune on the *right* side of the law.

To this day he still has his first American dollar. It's now framed and has pride of place among the awards, diplomas, and celebrity photographs busily littered on the wall behind his desk.

Oh yeah, Starrett was happy as well. With Rory out of the way he found he'd a lot more time on his hands to hang out at his favorite retreat, the Bridge Bar.

Lovers in the Cold
WALLACE STROBY

THE FIRST FLAKES of snow were starting to fall, the wind blowing them against the hotel room window, when Jimmy Aloha showed them the gun.

Eddie watched Billy take it, turn it over in his hand, weighing it. The gun was blue steel with a short barrel, checkered wooden grips.

"Thirty-eight special," Jimmy Aloha said. "Just like we talked about. Five-shot. Snub-nosed. Cops here in the city use them as backup guns, 'cause they're easy to conceal. Here."

He reached out and Billy handed the gun back. Eddie felt himself take a step away, almost involuntarily. Jimmy Aloha squinted at him through the smoke from the cigarette that hung between his lips. He popped open the cylinder, rotated it to show the chambers empty, thunked it closed. He lifted the tail of his Hawaiian shirt—middle of December and he was wearing a Hawaiian shirt—and tucked the gun into the small of his back.

"Look," he said. He took the cigarette from his mouth, turned so they could see that the fall of the shirt hid the gun completely. He faced them again, reached up and under, and brought the gun out easily, smoothly. "What I tell you?"

He reversed the gun, held it out butt-first. Billy took it, snugged it into the right-hand pocket of his leather jacket, turned to look at himself in the mirror above the narrow bed. It fit without showing.

"How much?" he said.

"Like I said. Two hundred."

Wind rattled the window, snow swirling against the glass. Outside, streetlights began to go on.

Billy took the gun out, hefted it. Jimmy Aloha watched him through cigarette smoke.

"Shells are extra," he said.

"Just the gun for now."

"Whatever."

Billy pushed the gun back in his pocket. From the other he took a wad of folded cash. Eddie knew where it had come from. Billy handed it over and Jimmy Aloha took it, unfolded it, counted the bills, nodded. The money went into the pocket of his Hawaiian shirt.

"You want anything else," he said to Billy, "you know where to come."

"Yeah, thanks."

Billy zipped up his jacket pocket, the gun still inside. He put out his hand. Jimmy Aloha looked at it, then at Eddie. Billy let his hand drop.

"Where you two from? Staten Island?"

Eddie shook his head.

"Jersey."

"Jersey. I should have known."

"What's that mean?" Billy said.

"Nothing, kid. Nothing at all."

They were driving down Tenth Avenue, Eddie at the wheel of his cousin Mikey's Ford Torino, watching for signs for the tunnel. Snow flitted in the headlights.

"It's not too late," Eddie said.

"What do you mean?"

"To forget this whole thing."

Billy looked out the window, didn't answer.

"We can go back up there," Eddie said. "Ask for the money back."

"You kidding? He'd laugh at us. Besides, he's probably not even there anymore. That kind of place rents by the hour."

"Just an idea. How'd you meet that guy anyway?"

"Rafer knows him."

"I should have figured."

Eddie turned left onto Fortieth Street and they joined the queue of taillights crawling into the tunnel. Above them, a floodlit billboard advertised *Pippin* on Broadway. The commercials for it were all over TV. It occurred to him he'd lived his entire life an hour south of the city and never been to a Broadway play.

"What did you tell Cherry?" Eddie said.

"About what?"

"All this. What's going on."

"Nothing. What, do you think I'm crazy?"

"She's worried about you."

"She told you that?"

"Not in those exact words maybe."

They crept along. Billy shook his head slowly, looked back out the window.

"She's always worried about me. She's told me a hundred fucking times. But sometimes she just doesn't . . . oh, forget it, man. It doesn't make any difference anyway."

The snow was sticking to the windshield now and Eddie turned on the wipers. They thumped back and forth, the only sound in the car. He wanted to be home, out of this traffic, out of this city. He heard a siren, looked in the rearview, saw a police car fly by on Tenth Avenue, lights flashing. He thought about getting pulled over on the turnpike on the way home, about the gun in Billy's jacket. And him driving his cousin's car. If the cops searched them, they'd all be fucked.

Horns beeped. The cars in front of them crawled forward, brake lights flashing. Above the arch of the tunnel entrance, Christmas lights in the shape of sleigh bells and holly leaves. The smell of exhaust filled the car.

"Even if I told her . . ." Billy said and trailed off.

Eddie looked at him.

"What?"

"Even if I told her. She wouldn't understand . . ."

And then he was looking out the window again, lost.

As he made his way up the stairs he could hear their voices through the apartment door. Billy's, loud, then Cherry's, then silence. A door slammed somewhere inside.

He stood on the landing, took a deep breath. The stairwell smelled of cooking, mildew, the wallpaper here peeling and water stained. A cold draft blew up from the ground floor, where the front door was propped open by a cinder block, summer and winter alike. He knocked, waited. Knocked again.

Billy opened the door a crack, saw him.

"Hey. Come on in."

The door opened wider and Eddie stepped through. He could smell her perfume. To the right, off the living room, was a short hallway that led to the bedroom. The door was closed.

Billy shut the door behind him. He wore a sleeveless T-shirt, jeans, was barefoot.

"Everything okay?" Eddie said.

"Yeah. For now. Come on in the kitchen."

Eddie followed him in. The radiator against the far wall clanged, the heat in here oppressive. He unzipped his jacket while Billy took two cans of Schaefer from the refrigerator, handed him one.

"Fucking heat," Billy said. "Thermostat's shot. Landlord keeps saying he's going to replace it, but never does, the prick."

Billy leaned back against the counter, opened his beer. Eddie popped his, siphoned off foam.

Billy nodded toward the hallway.

"She's pissed at me," he said.

Eddie said nothing, drank beer.

"I don't know what to do," Billy said. "We just go round and round."

Eddie looked at the hallway, the closed door.

"So tell me," Billy said. "Is it going to be a problem, the car?"

"That's what I needed to talk to you about." He put his beer on the counter.

"Come on, man. Don't fucking let me down now, please."

"It doesn't feel right."

"*Feel* right? We're way beyond that, man. If you don't do it, I'll have to find someone who will."

"Who? Rafer? Like that guy hasn't gotten you in enough trouble already?"

"I'll find someone. This is too good to let pass."

"I don't know, man."

"Listen," Billy said. "We talked about this. It's all set up. I heard from the guy and he's ready to go. We can't back out now. I'm already two months behind in rent. Another month and we're going to be out on the street. And that's the least of what I owe. At this rate, there's no way I'm ever going to get ahead."

"There's other ways. There has to be."

"On what I make? And you think I want to work at a body shop for the rest of my life? I've got primer in my fucking bloodstream, man. I cough it up sometimes. It's in my lungs."

Eddie picked up his beer again, looked off into the living room. There was a blacklight Jimi Hendrix poster tacked on the wall above the couch, its edges frayed. Billy had taken it with him every place he'd lived, from the time his parents had kicked him out of the house until now. When he and Eddie had shared the apartment in Belmar, it had gone up in the place of honor above the TV. Eddie knew Cherry hated it, knew Billy would never take it down.

"I didn't say I'm backing out."

"You're sounding like it."

"You think I'd let you go alone?"

There was a noise from the hallway and they both turned to see the bedroom door open. Cherry came out. Eddie could see she'd been crying, her eyes puffy and red. She wore a flannel shirt, patched jeans, her long dark hair tied back. She walked barefoot into the living room, got her cigarettes off the coffee table. She shook one out, looked at him.

"Hey," she said.

"Hey, Cherry."

Billy took a lighter out of his jeans pocket, held it out. She came forward, took it, got the cigarette going, handed the lighter back. Billy slid over to make room for her against the counter and she leaned beside him. He put an arm across her shoulders. Eddie looked away.

Billy pulled her tighter and she shifted as if uncomfortable in his grip.

"It's been a while since we've seen you," she said. "How's your mother?"

"She's fine. She's good." He felt her watching him, wanted to be out of there. Billy handed her his beer and she took it, sipped. Eddie met her eyes, the redness there she hadn't tried to hide.

"I've gotta go," he said. He put his half-finished beer by the sink. "I've got to take my brother to band practice at St. Rose."

"Tell your mother I said hello."

"I will."

"I'll walk you out," Billy said.

Eddie zipped his jacket, walked by Cherry without looking at her, smelled the faint musk of her perfume.

Out on the landing, Billy leaned back against the closed door.

"So," he said. "I need to know. You okay?"

Eddie looked at him.

"With what?"

"With this. This thing."

"I told you I'd watch your back. You think I'd punk out on you?"

"No, I never thought that. I guess I just wanted to hear you say it."

"Go back inside, man. You'll freeze your ass off out here."

Billy watched him.

"You won't regret this, you know," he said. "When it's all over. You'll see. Cherry, too. Things will be different."

"Yeah, I guess they will."

"The way I look at it, if we don't do it, someone else will. Sometimes you just have to grab those opportunities, you know? Because they might not come around again."

"I gotta go."

"Take it easy driving, man. I need you."

"I know," Eddie said, and started down the stairs.

He waited in the phone booth, bundled against the cold, watching waves roll in hard on the empty beach. Gusts of wind blew trash along the boardwalk. A sheet of newspaper slapped against the glass, clung there for a moment, blew away. The phone rang.

"Yeah?" The receiver cold against his face.

"What is it, Eddie? What's going on?"

"What do you mean?"

"He won't tell me, but I know something's up. The way he's acting. And you coming here last night . . ."

He looked out at the ocean, grayness that stretched forever.

"I have a right to know," she said. "He keeps things from me all the time. I'm used to it. But this is different, Eddie. I expect that from him, not from you."

"What's he told you?"

"Not a lot. But he has a gun."

"I know."

"He kept it hidden at first. Then one night, he took it out and showed it to me. Too proud of it not to, I guess. Showing it off. I don't like it in the apartment, I don't want it around."

"He doesn't have any bullets for it."

"That supposed to make me feel better?"

"I just wanted you to know."

"He tell you about the radio? And the other things he's taken, sold?"

"Some of it, yeah."

"What's happening, Eddie? What's gotten into him?"

"I'm not sure."

"Do you think he knows about . . . ?"

Silence on the line. Both of them considering it. He thought about Billy on the landing, wanting to make sure he was in, wanting to hear him say it.

"No," he said. "I don't think he knows."

"Thank God for that, I guess."

"But I've been thinking a lot lately . . ."

A pause, then: "Don't do this to me, Eddie. Don't say it. I don't want to hear it."

"I was just thinking . . . maybe we should take a break for awhile."

"Don't give me that bullshit, Eddie. Not after all this. Not after all I've gone through."

"I'm just saying."

"You feel bad for him, is that it?"

"I don't know. Maybe."

"You think I don't?"

He left that there.

"He promised me things, Eddie. He promised himself things, too. And it's like he's forgotten all of it. We were going to get out of here, go down to Florida. He knew someone that had a job for him. We could start over, forget all the things that happened before. And he didn't do it. He knew I wanted to, but he didn't do it. It's like he says what he thinks I want to hear, but then it never happens. It's like he thinks saying it is enough."

Wind whined around the booth.

"It's been four years, Eddie. I know him. He isn't going to change. But I've changed."

"Cherry . . ."

"I've given a lot, Eddie. I've put aside everything I ever wanted, to be with him. And now I've got nothing. No love, no future, no hope. And I'm too young for that."

"Things will work out."

"Will they? We could leave, Eddie. We could leave tomorrow. I could borrow the money for the plane tickets. My cousin in Jacksonville will put us up. We could get a job easy, both of us. It would be a new life."

"I can't leave him. Not like this. Not now."

"You're feeling guilty, after all this time? Is that it?"

"Maybe. But it's something else, too. Something that's got nothing to do with you."

"Then maybe what he needs is a wake-up call, get himself back on track. But I can't do anything else for him, I know that. I've tried. And all he's done is drag me further into his bullshit. I don't blame him. It's the way he is. But it's time to cut our losses, all of us."

"I don't know if I see it that way yet."

"I'm going to leave, Eddie. Regardless. I can't stay here anymore. I wake up in the mornings sometimes and I can't breathe. It's like there's a weight on my chest. I'm going, one way or another. With you or alone. But I want it to be with you."

He didn't answer.

"And I guess I need to know if you want that, too."

He closed his eyes, heard the blood in his ears. Wondered how his life had gotten so fucked.

"Yes," he said.

"What?"

"It's what I want, too."

Silence on the line again.

"I can wait, Eddie. I've waited a long time. I've waited for Billy. I can wait for you. But I can't wait forever."

"I know. I don't expect you to."

"We should leave. It's the right thing to do. And if we don't do it now, we may never get the courage to do it again."

"It's not that simple."

"You're wrong," she said. "It's just that simple. I don't want to hurt Billy. But I can't help him anymore either. I realize that now. And you know something, Eddie?"

"What?"

"Neither can you."

"It's tomorrow," Billy said.

Eddie looked at him. The sky was a bright blue, the ground covered with snow, the sun flashing hard off it.

"What's tomorrow?"

They were walking along the bottom of Cemetery Hill. To their left, traffic droned by on Route 36. Up on the slope to their right, a half dozen kids with sleds took turns riding down the narrow patch of bare hill, laughing, tumbling into the snow, getting up again. Dragging their sleds back up to the top.

"That thing," Billy said. "It's all set."

They crossed over into the cemetery. Billy brushed snow off a headstone, sat down.

"I talked to the guy again last night. He's on tomorrow, he made sure of it. But they have a security camera in there. We'll need to make it look real."

"Camera?"

"Yeah, like TV, you know? Closed circuit. Some stores have them now. They record everything that goes on inside. The old man who owns the place, he won't be there. Just our guy."

"You trust him?"

"As far as it goes, yeah. Why not? He gets his share, twenty-five percent off the top. We split the rest, fifty-fifty."

"Then why do you need the gun?"

"For the camera. And in case there's anyone else in the store. There might be someone in the back I don't see, or someone could come in, who knows? Somebody might get stupid, try something. Better to have the gun, make them think twice. What's some guy gonna do, gun in his face?"

"No security guards?"

Billy shook his head.

"That's why it works. In and out. Two, three minutes at most. Guy says five, six grand there at least. Some in the register, the rest in a strongbox underneath."

"Why so much?"

"It's an electronics store. Sunday afternoon before Christmas. People buying gifts all weekend, but they can't get to the bank to deposit until Monday. Guy says the owner comes in Sunday night at closing, brings the money home with him, puts it under his mattress or something, takes it to the bank the next day."

Eddie watched a pair of kids riding tandem on a single sled, saw them fly off as the sled overturned, heard their laughter.

"Why's he doing it? This guy?"

Billy shrugged.

"Hates his boss, I guess. And that's the funny part. It's his father."

"What?"

"Greek guy. Has every dime he ever made. Forces his son to work there but treats him like shit. Kid's tired of it, wants something of his own."

"Won't the father suspect him?"

"That's what the camera's for. The gun, too. He can tell the story afterward and most of it will be true."

"He hates his old man that much?"

"Can you blame him?"

Eddie walked off a few feet, boots crunching in the snow.

"Second thoughts?" Billy said. "If so, I understand. I can get someone else. It's not too late."

"You don't trust me?"

"That's not what I mean, man. And you know it."

Eddie walked back toward him.

"What time?" he said.

"Seven. They close at eight. Christmas shopping hours. It'll be dark then, but a lot of people still on the street—nothing but stores up and down that block. I'm in and out, then back in the car. No one will even know what happened until we're out of there. He's going to give us as much time as he can before he hits the alarm."

"We should go by first, a couple times. Have a look."

"We will. That's the way I figured it. We get up there and something doesn't look right, we turn around and go home. If I walk in the store and something's wrong, I turn around, walk out. We go home."

"Just like that?"

"Just like that."

The store was on Lexington Avenue, between Thirty-ninth and Fortieth. They cruised slowly, letting the traffic flow around them, Eddie feeling exposed, as if everyone on the street and in each passing car knew what they were there for.

"That's it," Billy said.

Pandera's Stereo Center was sandwiched between a boot store and a camera shop. There was a narrow doorway and a single display window filled with equipment. Handwritten cards were taped to the units with prices Xed out, new ones written in with red ink and exclamation marks. A speaker above the door was playing a Christmas carol Eddie couldn't identify.

He slowed the Torino to a crawl. A lot of people on the street here, walking fast, some carrying shopping bags. The sky was gray, the day still holding on. Flecks of snow dotted the windshield.

"Keep going," Billy said. "We'll swing around again, see if we can spot the guy."

A horn blew loud behind them and Eddie jumped, hit the gas, braked quickly again as an elderly woman stepped out from between two parked cars in front of them. The Torino juddered to a halt a foot from her, Billy putting a hand on the dashboard to brace himself. The woman looked at them, spit, her phlegm spattering the left front fender, crossed the street.

"Jesus Christ," Billy said. "That was close."

The horn again and Eddie saw the delivery van in his rearview. He pulled back into the flow of traffic and the van double-parked in front of the camera store.

They went up a block, waited at the light. More flurries now. Even with the windows closed they could hear competing Christmas music from a half dozen storefronts.

"Busy, this street," Eddie said. "A lot of people. More than I thought."

"That's good for us. The more, the better. More people, more cars. I vanish the second I leave the store."

The light changed and they turned right onto Thirty-eighth Street. A cab blew through the light, nearly hit them, the driver swinging around at the last second. Eddie spun the wheel to the right, braked hard.

"Easy," Billy said.

"I'm trying, it's just . . ." A bus pulled away from the curb in front of them, belching clouds of dark exhaust. He got behind it. "It's this fucking city, man." Thinking then that would have been the answer. Wishing the cab had hit them. A fender bender, police, a report. The whole thing off.

Billy was craning his neck, looking back the way they'd come.

"One more time round," he said. "Then we go somewhere, park, watch the time."

The bus picked up speed. They went up a block, made a right, headed back uptown.

"How do we know it's still on?" Eddie said.

"I talked to the guy today, before we left. Called him from a pay phone in Avon."

"What did he say?"

"The old man's out on the island. Some wedding. Might not make it back into the city at all tonight. We're good to go."

Another right, down a block, and then back onto Lexington.

"After this, I don't think we should drive past anymore," Eddie said. "Somebody might notice us."

"All these cars going around the block? Looking for a parking space, dropping people off? No one's going to pay any attention to us. Day like this, in this city, we're invisible."

The store was ahead on their right, the delivery van gone. A dark-haired guy in his late twenties stood in the doorway, smoking a cigarette.

"That's him," Billy said.

A cab stopped in front of them and Eddie had to brake, waited while it let people out. He saw the guy in the doorway puff quickly on the cigarette, glance up and down the street. He dropped the butt, twisted it out with a heel, went back inside.

The cab pulled away and Eddie slipped into traffic behind it.

"Go down to Twenty-third," Billy said. "Turn right. We'll head across town. Find a place to park for a while."

Eddie counted streets, made the turn, drove west. After a few blocks they were in a warehouse area, the traffic sparser. Water ahead, the Hudson. On the other side, hills and trees and highway. Jersey.

"Here's fine. Pull over."

They parked on a side street, beside a building that had once been a bus terminal, the walls covered with graffiti.

Eddie turned the engine off, put his hands on top of the wheel. His palms were slick, his breathing fast.

"You okay?" Billy said.

"Yeah." He wiped a hand on his jeans. Snow was spotting the windshield now, sticking.

"Turn the radio on," Billy said. "Let's get some music."

"You kidding?"

"Might as well. We're just going to sit here."

Eddie switched the ignition to accessory. Billy reached over, turned the radio on, adjusted the tuner, WABC and Johnny Donovan coming in strong and clear. Billy sat back as the next song started. He listened to it, frowned.

"We had joy, we had fun . . ."

"Jesus Christ," he said. "Are they ever going to stop playing this fucking thing?" He turned the radio off. "Summer's over. Enough with this shit."

"End of the year," Eddie said. "They're doing their Top 100 countdown."

"Make me happy to never hear that fucking song again."

Billy looked out the window, watching the snow, the car ticking and cooling around them. They waited.

The snow was heavier, the roadway slick, when they turned onto Lexington the final time. Billy had the gun in his lap.

"Here," he said. "Here. Don't go past it."

Eddie braked smoothly, nothing in front of them. Billy reached across with his left hand, popped the lock stem, pulled the door handle, and then was out of the car, cold air rushing in before the door swung closed. Eddie watched him ease between parked cars, narrowly avoiding a couple on the sidewalk. The gun was down at his side, almost hidden against his leg. He put his left arm out, pushed the door to the store open. It closed behind him.

The windshield wipers clacked, pushed snow away. A car beeped behind him, then swung around, passed. His foot on the brake, the car in drive, he watched the door. He could recognize the music coming from the speaker now—"God Rest Ye Merry Gentlemen."

The shots were loud, close together. Eddie jumped. The car seemed to move around him. People on the sidewalk looked at the store, kept walking.

Another shot and then the door flew open and Billy came out, walking carefully. He held a metal strongbox to his chest with his left arm. His right hand was empty.

He saw the Torino, started for it. He was between the parked cars when a man with slicked-back gray hair and a mustache came out of the store, a gun in his right hand, aiming.

The gun rose and fell. People on the sidewalk screamed. Billy jerked the passenger door open, swung in, fell across the seat. Another shot, high, somewhere above them, and then Eddie hit the gas, pulled away from the curb, the momentum slamming the door shut. The strongbox hit the floor.

He blasted through the amber light, swung around a bread truck, accelerated, weaved between two cabs, hit the next intersection and turned right without using the brake. Tires squealed near them, a horn blared. Traffic cones ahead, an open manhole. He swerved around them, pulled back into his lane, hung the next left, and then they were alone on a one-way street, faceless concrete garages on both sides of them.

Billy sat up. Eddie looked at him, not taking his foot off the gas.

"What happened?"

Another right. Coming up on Ninth now. He couldn't miss the turn, wouldn't know how to get back to the tunnel otherwise. He made the left, alternating brake and gas, saw the sign up ahead. He swung the Torino down the access street and there was the tunnel ahead of them, no line, Christmas lights glowing above the entrance.

Gas, brake, gas, and into the tunnel, the *whoomph* of the tile walls closing in. Sickly yellow light filled the car.

Billy was unzipping his jacket slowly, pulling the folds apart. Eddie looked over, saw his jeans were soaked with blood, his gray T-shirt black and wet with it.

"The old man . . ." Billy said, winced. He put his left hand on the dashboard to steady himself. When he took it away there were four bloody fingerprints on the vinyl.

"I dropped the gun," he said. "I left it there. I dropped it and I couldn't pick it up."

Out of the tunnel and into the night. A sign welcomed them to New Jersey. Eddie dragged the wheel to the right, crossed two lanes of traffic, saw the sign that said HOBOKEN, went up a curving ramp and under a railroad bridge, and then was on a residential street, cars parked on both sides, houses, trees.

He slowed. Two blocks and he turned left. A park ahead. He slid to a stop against the curb, shut the engine and the lights.

Billy was looking out the window. Eddie saw his breathing was shallow, his face pale in the glow of a single streetlight. Eddie rolled the window down, listened for sirens. Nothing.

Billy sat back, turned to him.

"They're going to be looking for you," he said, and then he didn't say anything more.

Eddie looked into his eyes for a long time, sitting there, the night quiet around them, snow falling softly on the car.

It took him almost three hours to get back to Bradley Beach. He'd wandered until he saw a bus, ridden it to Newark. There he caught the Penn Central train south, walked the mile from the station in the snow. He'd left the strongbox in the Torino, pushed the bills into his jacket pockets without looking at them.

Now, walking the last block to the apartment house, he took them out. Counted as he walked. Mostly twenties, a handful of fifties, two hundreds.

He could hear the ocean now, at the end of the street. Blackness out there, snow dancing in the boardwalk lights.

He'd counted twice by the time he reached the building. Four thousand even.

It was enough.

He stopped in the street, the snow blowing around him, folded the money, put it back in his pocket.

He didn't know what he would say, how he would tell her. Wondered if she was up there in one of those lighted windows right now, looking down at him.

The front door was propped open, the foyer dimly lit. He stood there for a while, in the wind and the snow. Then he went up the stairs and knocked on the door.

Trumpet Blues
ANTHONY RUDEL

THOUGH FADED, THE brass still shone, occasionally reflecting the light from the overheated spot with its stuck-on, blue-gel cover glinting off the tarnished trumpet. Smoke, rising continuously from the steam tables filled with trays of yesterday's food and from the hundreds of spent cigarettes, swirled around, obscuring the view, but not the sound. The trumpet cut through the indoor fog, reaching him at the back table he liked most, the table he sat at every night drinking cheap bottled beer and watching. From there, all in one glance, he could see the musicians on the makeshift stage and the customers around the bar and at the scattered tables.

The music was an accompaniment, a side dish served for free with pitchers of lukewarm beer and bowls of stale popcorn. Three guys with big sideburns were clumped together, one seated at the painted, upright piano, one plucking the strings of his scratched double bass, and the trumpeter. They wore poorly matched outfits of faded jeans, worn boots, and loose-fitting drab T-shirts. But their music was tight, a mellow blues that filled the bar on that hot June night.

The sweltering sidewalks of Broadway—the lights weren't bright on this part of the Great White Way—lay just beyond the wide-open double doors of the West End Bar and Grill. The oak bar with its brass rail lined one wall of the main room, and the steam tables were lined up down the middle near the booths. There was another room, or area in the back. That's where he sat, near the jazz, up close to the sound. The trumpet was playing a solo, a few phrases that took the piano's last triad and turned it inside out, exposing its simple skeletal structure when she walked in. She had that fresh collegiate look, and through the smoky darkness he could see the shape of her legs as she slid into a booth and sat on the cracked red leather bench. The trumpet's theme rose and fell, seductively intertwined with the steady piano chords and the plucked repeated pulse of the bass. All that mattered was the trumpet; the rest was just filling.

She ordered a beer and leaned back letting her blond hair fall unevenly over the back of the seat.

"Thanks," she sang, at least it looked like she sang because he couldn't hear her from where he sat. The bottle's rim was between her lips as the trumpeter blew another high note.

Jim swigged the dregs of his fifth Miller; the warm suds swished in his mouth. He picked up his green jacket, swung it over his shoulder trying to look casual, and walked through the youngish crowd, the music becoming more background as he moved away from the trio.

"Big booth for one girl," he said, his voice raspy from too many hours of smoke. "You waiting for someone?"

She squinted and turned her head away from the light behind him. "Maybe, maybe not."

He was too tired to be irritated, so he turned to go back to his table, to the comfort of his music.

"You take rejection well."

She did sing. Her voice seductively meshed with the trumpet's soulful theme that soared from one end of the bar to the other, a few simple notes that pulled them together. "Sit down."

It was an order and he obeyed. There was nothing to say and they listened in tandem as the trio started another tune.

"You like jazz?"

"I don't come here for the food." She smiled and slid closer, moving her slender butt over the duct tape that kept the remains of the stuffing inside the seat. She had a demonic look in her eyes that at once scared him and drew him to her. The theme grew hotter and the trumpeter's sweat glistened on his dark forehead. Other conversations and the noise from the bar faded into the woodwork along with the smoke.

"He plays well. I like the sound."

She nodded in time to the free-flowing rhythm as she finished her beer. Night was becoming late night.

"Last call," the bartender shouted to the half dozen hangers on.

The pianist started another melody, an undefined idea waiting to be developed by his partners. Jim's arm rested comfortably over her shoulder. Her hair smelled of Herbal Essence sullied by cigarettes and overheated bar food. He was lost in the melody, lost in the scents, and lost in her freshness. The trumpet blew the final notes of the night, although the phrase never really ended, just faded away. They walked out onto Broadway, still hot and steamy.

"You live around here?"

"No," Jim answered. "I'll catch a ride, I guess."

"You wanna stay with me?"

"You live nearby?"

"Around the corner."

"Sure."

He took her hand. It seemed like the thing to do even though he could feel the sweat on his palm. Two cabs screeched to stop for a fare and the IRT rumbled beneath their feet. Her place was on the third floor, a bedroom, living room, and kitchen. The door swung closed behind them with a resounding thud. She flipped on an overhead light.

"Put some music on. The stereo's in there. I'll be right back." She disappeared into the bathroom.

Jim flipped through the LPs, noting the artwork on the covers, the songs, the singles, and the album sides. He wanted to find something like that trumpet sound, something to keep the mood that had brought them here. She owned no jazz, just rock. He pushed the power button on the Kenwood receiver, placed a random stack of disks onto the raised spindle, and hit the start switch on the Gerrard turntable. The hidden motor whirred to a start and the first black vinyl platter dropped onto the rubber mat, hesitating for a second, before spinning at $33\frac{1}{3}$ RPM. The tonearm moved into position over the outer rim, then lowered slowly onto the disk.

The propulsive first notes of "Whipping Post" filtered through the bookshelf speakers, the Allman Brothers blending blues with rock, a shotgun wedding.

She came up behind him and wrapped her arms around his waist, swaying to the inexorable beat. "Come here." She pulled him to the couch. Her lips were on his and he could feel her body against the denim of his clothes. They stayed that way for one side of the album, a fan blowing hot air all around them. As the second disk fell into place, she pulled away, reached into the pocket of her khaki shorts, and pulled out a baggie half-full of white powder. Carefully she poured some out onto the glass-top coffee table. From her other pocket she pulled a twenty-dollar bill and rolled it into a tiny straw. Cream's sweet sounds, "White Room" played as she held the straw in place over the line of powder and sucked it into her tiny nostril. Eyes dreamily closed, she offered the expensive straw to Jim.

"Not for me."

"You're no fun."

She stood up and walked into the bedroom. Jim followed, lay down on the bed, and watched her strip in time to Clapton's guitar rhythms floating in from the next room. The disk ended and a third vinyl fell to the platter. Springsteen's "Born to Run" rocked the hot apartment as Jim played on her body. Their lovemaking was rapid, awkward, two entities unblended and unfamiliar, unmusical. Hot, sweaty, and spent, they lay side by side. She ran her fingers along the tracks on his arm.

"Where'd you get these?"

"Vietnam."

She said nothing. Bruce's smoky voice sang of Eddie and catching a ride. They dozed off.

The familiar piano riff accompanied the lonely blues trumpet locked in his mind for most of that summer. Despite the constant heat, she stayed cool, distant yet physically close. She was in control of everything and he was relieved to be controlled. Their moods, like parallel fifths, went together in a comfortable haze. Week after week, they remained inside, lost amid the music, lying on the bed, the bedspread permanently on the floor, while the sweet smells of Riverside Park wafted through the open windows.

"When were you in Vietnam?"

"Late sixties."

"College?"

"I quit."

"Now?"

"Nothing. You?"

"Graduated last year."

"Job?"

"More school."

"Who pays for all this?"

"Guilty parents." She kissed him, her naked form playing over his body, then ran her tongue up the tracks in his forearm until it nestled in the nape of his neck. "You still use?"

He shook his head.

"Can you get me some?"

He pulled away. A trumpeter playing in the park wailed an ugly theme, his music carried by the warm breezes. "Why?"

"I've never tried it."

"Don't."

The look he feared, her gaze lit up like it was that first night when she took him from the safety of the West End, came into her blue Connecticut eyes. She tossed her hair back over her soft, narrow shoulders and sat astride him, rubbing his chest with her warm hands. "Just once," she purred. Total control and totally controlled is how they stayed until the music from the stereo stopped, the last disk dropped, spun, and played.

"I'll need money."

She kissed him, then stood up and walked over to her desk. "How much?"

"Couple a hundred."

She opened her Gucci wallet, pulled out three fifties, and tossed them onto the bed. Jim dressed and stuffed the bills into his jeans' pocket. He wore his dark glasses and fatigue jacket, the breast pocket labeled with the stenciled word MURPHY.

"Where're you going?"

"Jersey."

"How do I know you'll come back?"

"Fuck you."

WNEW was playing Billy Joel's "Captain Jack," the irony obvious to Jim as he careened through the Lincoln Tunnel under the river. The music's anthemic organ blended with the car horns that echoed on the tunnel's tiles, like a hundred cacophonous trumpets playing out of tune, eating into Jim's brain, forcing him to think of memories of horrors he'd buried long ago. The heat in Hoboken seemed more intense than in Manhattan and the sweat poured through his shirt. He cruised the streets, avoiding the spray of open fire hydrants, turning down back alleys, behind warehouses where deals were done.

Jim probably never heard the gunshots. His radio was turned way up. When the cops found him, he was slumped over the steering wheel, his forehead resting on the horn, which cut through the humid late day air like a solo trumpet, stuck tortuously with no variation on one note.

The cops found her address, no name, on a slip of paper in his shirt pocket. She wore a simple Chanel dress, pumps, and dark glasses to the graveside funeral. It was in Queens, near the airport. Jim's parents and a younger sister sat on folding chairs near the hole in the ground. They didn't cry. She did. She couldn't help herself, especially when they handed his mother the folded American flag while the lone trumpeter with the shiny trumpet sparkling in the midday summer sun played taps.

Coda: Drink to Long Life
JESSICA KAYE

IT WAS A cold night in autumn, the chill requiring a little something to warm one's insides, but the last of my good stuff reposed in a cellar some distance from where I was seated, somewhat impatiently, in the drawing room of an acquaintance. There was a reason that kept me seated, of course. I was to interview the home's owner, a French expatriate, who wished to have his memoirs recorded for the sake of posterity. I, an under-employed writer, was able, if not happy, to comply with his wishes.

The elderly man entered the room at last, acknowledging me with a nod of his head but not extending his hand. I greeted him politely, brandished my pen and writing paper, and settled in for an evening of work.

It turned out to be not entirely disagreeable. The nobleman had some wonderful stories to tell of his early life on the continent and the events which had conspired to transport him eastward. He had been in this town for many years now and although his English was quite good, his accent was still heavy and it took a discerning ear to completely follow his reminiscences.

I do have a knack for finding the interesting points in a story and making them stand out and I had no doubt that this engagement would prove satis-fying to the client.

The question I pondered as we concluded our long night was just how much of what was imparted to me was true, with its elements of swash-buckling, numerous lurid love affairs with royal ladies, and a disturbing tale of revenge for a thousand injuries inflicted by a mortal enemy. It was my agreed undertaking to return within a fortnight with a sufficient sample of the memoir, by which the Frenchman could adjudge me adequate for the task or, in the alternative, find me wanting.

On the appointed date, sheaf in hand, I knocked upon the door and again was ushered into the drawing room, again required to wait, slightly less im-patiently, as I had taken care to fortify my spirits prior to embarking on my evening's journey.

Presently, the old man arrived, and this time greeted me with arm ex-tended, but it was not for a handshake. Rather, it was to relieve me of the papers I held. He offered no refreshment but merely nodded at me, said, "Until next time, then," and, with that, I was dismissed until two weeks hence, during which period he was to read that which I'd written.

My third visit to the gentleman's home came nigh. Would I obtain the commission for his complete memoir, or be required to be satisfied with the retainer paid to me upon my first visit?

As usual, I was punctual, but, also as usual, I was left to await my client's arrival. Thankfully, I'm adept at sitting quietly for great lengths of time, as being found fidgeting would have been most unseemly. After a time, he appeared and greeted me, clasping my hand in his for the first time.

"How very perfectly you've captured my voice," he said. "Every nuance of the tale I've told you, every relevant detail, you've denoted, to my deep satisfaction." With that he reached into his desk drawer, extracting an envelope. I had no doubt that the agreed-upon sum was enclosed therein, two thousand American dollars, enough to bind my services for the coming year and secure the completion of his memoir, following many long evenings such as the one we first shared.

"Eddie," he said, using the comradely nickname which few employ when addressing me. "Surely we must celebrate the commencement of our working relationship. Please ask the valet to fetch my liveryman and have him bring the carriage around. We shall travel across the stream to my private wine cellar. From there we shall select the finest amontillado ever to reach these shores."

My eyes must have widened, as the tale of the cask of amontillado had been the tale of revenge which I'd used as the memoir sample provided to the European. I had not been certain I had believed his tale, and yet nor was I certain I had the heart to accompany him to a wine cellar similar to that of which he'd spoken so chillingly.

A tribute to Edgar Allan Poe

Acknowledgments

Many thanks are owed to our agent, Jay Mandel of William Morris Agency; to our publisher at Bloomsbury USA, Karen Rinaldi, to our editors, Colin Dickerman and Gillian Blake, to Greg Villepique, and with special thanks to Marisa Pagano; to each of the writers who submitted stories to us; and, of course, to the Boss, Bruce Springsteen, for his generosity in allowing creative minds to borrow his work as inspiration for their own.

A Note on the Contributors

Cara Black lives in San Francisco with her husband, a bookseller, and their teenage son. An Anthony and Macavity Award nominee, she's a San Francisco Library Laureate and a member of the Mystery Writers of America and the Marais Historic Society in Paris.

C. J. Box is the author of the award-winning Joe Pickett series of novels, including *Open Season, Savage Run, Winterkill, Trophy Hunt*, and *Out of Range*. He's the winner of the Anthony Award, Prix Calibre 38 Award (France), the Macavity Award, the Gumshoe Award, the Barry Award, and an Edgar Award and *Los Angeles Times* Book Prize finalist. His novels have been cited by the *New York Times* (2001 Notable Book), Book Sense 76, *People* magazine, *Booklist*, and many other publications. C. J. Box lives with his family outside Cheyenne, Wyoming.

Richard J. Brewer is an author and book reviewer, as well as an actor and voice-over talent for films, television, and audiobooks. He currently lives in Los Angeles.

Paul Charles is the author of the acclaimed Detective Inspector Christy Kennedy mystery novels. He lives in London, England, where he divides his time between writing and the music business.

David Corbett is the author of *The Devil's Redhead*, an Anthony and Barry nominee for Best First Novel, and *Done for a Dime*, a *New York Times* Notable Book for 2003 and Macavity nominee for best novel. He lives in northern California.

Peter David has had over fifty novels published, including numerous appearances on the *New York Times* bestseller list, and his novels include *Sir Apropos of Nothing, Knight Life, Howling Mad*, and the *Psi-Man* adventure series. He is the cocreator and author of the bestselling *Star Trek: New Frontier* series for Pocket Books, and has also written such Trek novels as *Q-Squared* and *Imzadi*. Peter's comic book résumé includes an award-winning twelve-year run on *The Incredible Hulk*, and he has also worked on such varied and popular titles as *Supergirl, Fallen Angel, Young Justice, Soulsearchers and Company, Aquaman, Spider-Man, Spider-Man 2099*,

X-Factor, Star Trek, Wolverine, The Phantom, Sachs & Violens, and many others. His opinion column *But I Digress* has been running in the industry trade newspaper *The Comic Buyer's Guide* for over a decade. He is the cocreator, with Bill Mumy, of the Cable Ace Award–nominated science fiction series *Space Cases,* which ran for two seasons on Nickelodeon. He has written several scripts for the Hugo Award–winning TV series *Babylon 5* and the sequel series, *Crusade.* Peter David lives in New York.

Eric Garcia is the author of the novels *Cassandra French's Finishing School for Boys, Matchstick Men,* and three mysteries: *Anonymous Rex, Casual Rex,* and *Hot and Sweaty Rex.* He lives in Los Angeles with his wife and young daughter.

Steve Hamilton graduated from the University of Michigan, where he won the prestigious Hopwood Award for fiction. His first novel, *A Cold Day in Paradise,* won the Private Eye Writer's of America / St. Martin's Press Award for Best First Mystery by an Unpublished Writer. Once published, it won the 1999 Edgar and Shamus Awards for Best First Novel, and was short-listed for the Anthony and Barry Awards. His second Alex McKnight novel, *Winter of the Wolf Moon,* was named one of the year's Notable Books by the *New York Times Book Review* and received a starred review from *Publishers Weekly,* as did his third and fourth novels, *The Hunting Wind* and *North of Nowhere.* Hamilton lives in upstate New York with his wife, Julia, and their two children.

Pam Houston is the author of two collections of award-winning short stories, *Cowboys Are My Weakness* and *Waltzing the Cat.* Her stories have been selected for volumes of *Best American Short Stories, The O. Henry Awards,* and *The Pushcart Prize,* and her story "The Best Girlfriend You Never Had" appeared in *Best American Short Stories of the Century.* Her first novel, *Sight Hound,* was published in January 2005. A collection of autobiographical essays about travel and home, *A Little More About Me,* was published in 1999. In 2002 her first stage play, *Tracking the Pleiades,* was produced in Colorado. Houston has edited a collection of fiction, nonfiction, and poetry called *Women on Hunting* and written the text for a book of photographs called *Men Before Ten A.M.* Houston is the director of creative writing at the University of California, Davis. When she is not in Davis, she lives in Colorado.

Gregg Hurwitz is the critically acclaimed, bestselling author of *The Tower, Minutes to Burn, Do No Harm, The Kill Clause,* and *The Program.* He lives in Los Angeles, where he is currently writing the next Tim Rackley novel and the screen adaptation of *The Kill Clause* for Paramount Pictures. For more information please visit www.gregghurwitz.net.

Jessica Kaye is a publishing law attorney, an occasional writer, and the founder and former publisher of the Publishing Mills, an award-winning audiobook company, as well as a lifelong fan of great music and great writing.

William Kent Krueger writes the Cork O'Connor mystery series set in the great Northwoods of Minnesota. His work has received numerous awards, including the Anthony, the Barry, and the Minnesota Book Award. He lives with his family in St. Paul.

Aimee Liu is the author of more than ten books of fiction and nonfiction. Her novels include *Cloud Mountain*, based on the story of her grandparents' interracial marriage at the turn of the century; *Face*, about a family's struggle for identity in New York's Chinatown; and *Flash House*, a novel of Cold War intrigue and suspense set in India and Central Asia. Her fiction has been translated into twelve languages. Aimee Liu lives with her family in Los Angeles.

Eddie Muller's books, fiction and nonfiction, have earned him the nickname the Czar of Noir. He's both a two-time Edgar Award nominee and a two-time Anthony Award nominee. His debut novel, *The Distance*, won the Private Eye Writers of America's Shamus Award as Best First Novel of 2002. He lives in the San Francisco Bay Area.

Philip Reed is the author of two thrillers about the car business, *Bird Dog* (nominated for the Edgar and Anthony Awards) and *Low Rider*. His newest novel, *The Marquis de Fraud*, is set in the world of thoroughbred horse racing. Phil was hired by Edmunds.com to work as an undercover car salesman to better understand the automotive retailing business. The result was the novella "Confessions of a Car Salesman," which became an Internet sensation. In 2004 his sports memoir of Mike Austin, *In Search of the Greatest Golf Swing*, was published by Carroll and Graf. Phil is consumer advice editor for Santa Monica, California–based Edmunds.com, Inc., where he test-drives cars and writes a monthly column.

Michael John Richardson is a screenwriter and playwright with a love for short stories and mysteries. He and his wife live in Los Angeles.

Anthony Rudel is the author of the novel *Imagining Don Giovanni*, *Classical Music Top 40*, and *Tales from the Opera*. He is a contributor to

Opera News magazine and is a consultant for radio stations and record labels. He lives in Chappaqua, New York, with his wife and two daughters.

Barbara Seranella is the nationally best-selling author of crime novels featuring Munch Mancini. A television series based on the character of Munch Mancini is in development for NBC. St. Martin's Press will be publishing the eighth novel in the series, *An Unacceptable Death*. Seranella divides her time between her homes in Laguna Beach and La Quinta, California, where she lives with her husband, Ron, and their dogs.

Randy Michael Signor's short fiction has been published in numerous literary magazines. He first saw Bruce Springsteen and the E Street Band perform in 1980. He is also a painter and has shown his work in Los Angeles, Chicago, and Seattle, where he presently lives with his wife, Jane Levine.

Martin J. Smith is the author of three suspense novels, the Anthony Award–nominated *Time Release, Shadow Image*, and the Edgar Award–nominated *Straw Men*. He also is a senior editor of the *Los Angeles Times Magazine*. He lives in Los Angeles.

Wallace Stroby is a lifelong resident of the Jersey Shore and the author of the novels *The Barbed-Wire Kiss* and *The Heartbreak Lounge*.